How to Survive Your Murder

DANIELLE VALENTINE

RAZORBILL

RAZORBILL

An imprint of Penguin Random House LLC, New York

First published in the United States of America by Razorbill,
an imprint of Penguin Random House LLC, 2022
First paperback edition published 2023

Visit us online at PenguinRandomHouse.com.

THE LIBRARY OF CONGRESS HAS CATALOGED THE HARDCOVER EDITION AS FOLLOWS:
Names: Valentine, Danielle, author.
Title: How to survive your murder / Danielle Valentine.
Description: New York : Razorbill, 2022. | Audience: Ages 12 and up.
Summary: Alice is sent back to the night of her sister's murder and has until
midnight to figure out who the killer is or risk losing her sister forever.
Identifiers: LCCN 2022011443 | ISBN 9780593352014 (hardcover) |
ISBN 9780593527511 (trade paperback) | ISBN 9780593352021 (ebook)
Subjects: CYAC: Murder—Fiction. | Sisters—Fiction. | Horror films—Fiction. |
Time travel—Fiction. | LCGFT: Novels. | Thrillers (Fiction)
Classification: LCC PZ7.1.V3365 Ho 2022 | DDC [Fic]—dc23
LC record available at https://lccn.loc.gov/2022011443

ISBN 9780593619582

Printed in the United States of America

1st Printing

LSCH

Design by Rebecca Aidlin
Text set in Arno Pro

For Harriet

HALLOWEEN NIGHT, LAST YEAR

Mark Evans was practically cradling the chain saw. You'd think it was his baby. "I don't know, Chloe; that doesn't seem safe."

"It won't even have a chain," Chloe pointed out. "A chain saw can't hurt anyone if there's no chain."

"It's still heavy. And loud. And what about all that . . . what's it called? Exhaust? You can inhale it and stuff."

Chloe closed her eyes for a moment, frustration building inside her. Mark was the biggest guy on the track team. Maybe even the biggest guy in their year. Since when was he *such* a wuss?

To be fair, she hadn't chosen him because he was brave or whatever. She'd chosen him because of his shoulders. Mark had the greatest shoulders at Omaha East, all broad and muscular. She figured they'd look seriously sick holding a chain saw, like the guy in that freaky chain saw movie, Jason, or whatever his name was.

"Can't we just, like, play a recording of chain saw noises?" Mark asked. "Or I could make the noise with my mouth, like this." He demonstrated how he might make chain saw noises by blowing air through his lips and kind of clicking his tongue.

Chloe was at a loss for words. What were you supposed to say when a guy made chain saw noises at you?

Chloe had known, from the moment she convinced her parents

to let her rent out Lacy Farms for her Halloween party, that she wanted scary chain saw guys chasing people through the corn maze. Otherwise it was just a pathetic party in a cornfield. Why could no one else see her vision?

"Mark," Chloe said very carefully. "Listen to me. You're going to turn the chain saw on, and you're going to chase people through the maze, and you're going to be fucking *scary* while you do it, or else I'll have to tell everyone about that thing you do when you kiss."

Mark had swirled his tongue around in her mouth when they made out at Kylie Mack's birthday last year, like his tongue was a weird, wet helicopter propeller. It was seriously disgusting.

Mark paled, then swallowed. "Yeah, okay."

Thank God, Chloe thought as headlights swept through the corn, alerting her to the arrival of her first guests. She loved this part, the beginning-of-the-party part. Absolutely anything could happen now. She checked her phone screen just in time to watch the numbers switch from 6:59 to 7:00.

Showtime.

The genius of her party was this: people had to go through the scary corn maze and get chased by chain saw dudes before they were rewarded with booze and music at the center of the field. Chloe was pretty proud of it. She knew everything was set up, but she still double-checked that the camping lanterns were all lit, that the keg was ready, that the band was getting its gear together. She greeted her first guests, did a shot, and then did a bonus shot (what the hell, it was *her* party), and that's when she overheard someone talking about how the corn maze wasn't even scary, because Mark Evans hadn't turned his chain saw on; he was just making the chain saw noise by blowing air through his lips.

She felt her jaw clench.

You've got to be kidding me.

The sun had fully set by this point, and the only light came from the camping lanterns circling the edges of the clearing behind her, gaslit flames flickering like fireflies. Chloe beelined for the maze but hesitated when she reached the entrance. It was darker than she'd expected it to be, a lot darker than it'd been when she was talking to Mark twenty minutes ago. The entrance was a gaping black mouth. She imagined it snapping closed around her the moment she stepped inside.

She swallowed. "Mark?" she whisper-shouted, taking a single step forward. Fallen cornstalks cracked beneath her feet, and it struck her that the sound was brittle, like bones breaking. She felt a flicker of fear and quickly pushed the thought away. It was the exact same maze she'd been through a million times in the daylight. There was no reason to get all freaked out. She said, louder now, "Mark, get out here."

No answer.

He was going to make her come find him, wasn't he? Well, fine, if he wanted to do it that way. She turned a corner, and then another, and then—

There. A figure in the shadows, holding a chain saw.

Chloe exhaled. "I thought we'd agreed you were going to turn the chain saw *on*," she said, searching for Mark's giant arms in the shadows. "If you just make the noises with your mouth, it's seriously—"

The moon slid out from behind a cloud, its soft silver light glinting off the chain saw's chain. Chloe stopped talking.

Wait. The chain.

It was old and a little rusty-looking, and even from a few feet away, Chloe could see the jagged metal teeth, so sharp.

That chain definitely wasn't supposed to be there.

Chloe blinked, twice, trying to make sense of what she was see-ing. "What are you—"

The chain saw revved to life, those jagged teeth spinning into a metallic blur. Chloe parted her lips, but she couldn't scream. Her voice had shriveled up somewhere inside her throat. Her mouth flapped open and closed, wordless, her hands flying up instinctively to protect her face.

The scream wouldn't have helped her, anyway. It was much, much too late for that. The chain saw flew closer, whirring and grinding, the sound it made an electric howl—

Until it hit bone.

THREE HOURS EARLIER

My friends Millie Kido and Xavier "X" O'Hare were staring at me, mouths agape. I never thought I'd have a reason to use the word *agape*, but it was the only one that fully captured their shock and horror. Not only were their mouths hanging open, but Millie was blinking fast behind her fake glasses, and X's dark eyebrows had practically disappeared beneath the rim of his red beanie.

It was a little over-the-top, actually. You'd think I'd suggested we spend our evening digging up corpses instead of talking about someone who had.

"Guys, come on, you know I'm right about this," I tried. "Ed Gein inspired *Psycho, The Texas Chainsaw Massacre*, and even *The Silence of the Lambs*. He's iconic."

"I think you mean that he's a horrendous monster," X said. "That's what you meant to say, right, Alice? *Horrendous. Monster.*"

He was scratching the back of his neck now, but maybe that was because the shearling in his jacket was bothering him. For as long as I've known him, X's been pretty consistent in his look: jeans, fitted Henley, boots. Recently, though, he's gotten a little bolder with his fashion choices. Today, that meant the beanie pulled over his black curls and a jean jacket lined with tan-colored fleece so perfectly one shade lighter than his dark brown skin that he must've planned it that way. There had to be a guy he wasn't telling us about.

"Beyoncé is iconic," Millie added. "Malala is iconic. Ed Gein is just another disturbing white dude."

I mean, she wasn't wrong. At Gein's farmhouse, authorities had found four noses, masks made of human skin, a decapitated head, a lampshade made of skin and bowls made of skulls, lips used as a pull on a window shade, and a belt made from nipples.

It's not like I wanted to start a fan club.

"If we're going to do another true-crime podcast, why don't we use it to highlight stories no one's heard of?" Millie was saying. Unlike X, she was already in her Halloween costume: Velma, from *Scooby-Doo*, who she'd loved ever since she saw the old live-action remakes where Velma was portrayed by Hayley Kiyoko, who's biracial like her. "Like, maybe we could do our first episode on Sam Little? He's the most prolific serial killer in American history, but a lot of his victims were Black women and prostitutes, so he's not even half as well-known as Ed Gein."

"I like that," X said, pointing at her. "We could use Sam Little as a gateway to talk about the everyday horror of anti-Black violence and racism. Like, how missing Black and brown girls don't get the same media attention as missing white girls, and we could tie the Black Lives Matter movement to the rise of Black horror films like *Candyman, Us*..."

"Maybe point out the moment at the end of *Get Out*, when Daniel Kaluuya's character sees the police lights?" I added.

"Yeah!" X seemed excited for a second, but then, frowning, he added, "Jordan Peele's films aren't technically slashers, though."

We fell silent again. The theme of our podcast was supposed to be the intersection of true crime and horror movies. Preferably slashers, which were our favorites. Millie, X, and I thought we could discuss it in a way that felt intentional and meta, a comment on our culture's fixation on the deaths of teen girls and complete dismissal of the deaths of BIPOC that also managed to be . . . fun? Could you use the word *fun* when talking about murder?

Anyway. That had been the plan. But we were finding the intersection of the two topics a little tricky. At the end of the day, horror movies were supposed to be entertaining. No matter how real something might feel when it was happening in a movie, we still had the luxury of closing our eyes, turning away. Real life, not so much.

Millie opened her mouth and then closed it again. She was blinking a lot again, but I think it was because the lenses in her fake glasses were a little smudged. X, who wore real wire-frame glasses every day, seemed to take offense to the fake ones and said, "Millie, if they're hurting your eyes, just take them off."

"Then no one will know who I'm supposed to be."

"You're dressed head-to-toe in orange. They'll know."

We were in the school's podcasting studio. The words *podcasting studio* probably made you think we were fancy, like maybe we were at one of those rich-kid schools where every student gets an iPad instead of textbooks and the cafeteria sells brand-name junk food—but Omaha East wasn't like that. The podcasting studio was just a room in the basement with carpet stapled to the walls as soundproofing and a couple extra power strips where you could plug in phones and mics. It was pretty crappy.

My phone started playing the *Halloween* theme, which meant I had a text. I glanced at the screen.

are y'all done with your creepy murder club yet??

It was from Eli, my best friend since kindergarten. Most people didn't really get my friendship with Eli, considering a) he was the only person in my life who wasn't a complete true-crime/slasher-film fanatic, and b) 99 percent of our interactions happened in the form of text messages.

All I can say about that is the world is divided between the people who defended you against that asshat Kyle Stahlicker when he said your hair made you look like a deranged clown in the third grade and the people who didn't. The people in the first group are your ride or die. Eli wasn't just my best friend; he was my brother.

5 more minutes, I wrote back.

His response came approximately .025 seconds after I hit send: whatever, I'm out. GBBO isn't gonna watch itself.

GBBO = *The Great British Bake Off*. Eli refused to use the Americanized name out of loyalty to Mary Berry. I shoved my phone back in my pocket.

"I couldn't even finish *Texas Chainsaw*," Millie was saying.

"It was pretty disgusting," X added, but he sounded more impressed than disgusted. He was writing his own slasher, one starring a few Black people, and we all thought he was going to do for slashers what Jordan Peele had done for Black horror at large. One of the reasons he wanted to start this podcast was to start making inroads with Black horror fans so that when he came out with his first film, he had a ready-made audience. X was brilliant like that.

"The thing with the girl on the meat hook . . ." Millie shuddered.

"Totally gross," X agreed, smiling now. "Totally."

"It's too bad Sally Hardesty was such a crap Final Girl," I added, and Millie shuddered again, probably still thinking about the meat hook. Unlike X and me, she wasn't a horror-movie superfan. She tolerated them, and she really liked some of the quieter, more suspenseful Japanese horror films, like *Dark Water*, but all in all, horror wasn't her genre. She was here because of the criminal-justice angle. *Serial* had been her gateway drug into the world of true crime, and from there it was an easy path to *My Favorite Murder* and *I'll Be Gone in the Dark*. But it wasn't the stories about death and murder that got her interested; it was the injustice. Millie wanted to save the world, one wrongfully incarcerated person at a time.

I had this theory that you could understand people better by figuring out the movie genre everyone would star in. Take Millie, for instance. When she wasn't dressed as Velma, she was mostly in overalls (the legs rolled up, like, five times, on account of how short she was) and her favorite purple Doc Martens, her wavy, dark brown hair pulled back in a bun or a braid, the epitome of effortless cool. She'd be amazing in a '90s-era Julia Roberts–esque thriller where she worked tirelessly to uncover some insane conspiracy. If I ever found myself entangled in a secret government plot, Millie would be my first call.

"Did you know Chloe Bree's doing a *Texas Chainsaw*–themed party this year?" X asked.

"Is she?" I said, uninterested. X, Millie, and I weren't exactly "party" people. We spent every Halloween watching horror movies and devouring the amazingness that was pumpkin-spice ice cream with broken-up Halloween candy on top. I mean, we were spending our Friday afternoon in the school basement; do I really need to elaborate on how we weren't exactly the cool kids?

"She rented out the corn maze at Lacy Farms," Millie added. "Our whole grade's going to be there."

She was looking at me like she expected me to say something. In fact, she and X were both looking at me.

"What?" I asked, frowning. They stared a little more intently, and I felt a sinking in my gut as understanding hit. "Guys, *no*."

"Think of it as a social experiment, like when Jane Goodall went to live with the apes," said X, flashing me one of his famous, impossibly wide smiles. In addition to a smile that took up most of his face, X had dark eyes and a jawline made for television. The most important thing you needed to understand about him was that everyone liked him. He could talk to *literally* anyone. If his life were a movie, it would be one where people traveled the world eating all the best food and soaking up the local culture. He had the kind of infectious enthusiasm that made you think, *Why not eat a cricket covered in chocolate? Could be tasty!* It was almost a shame that he wanted to work behind the camera instead of hosting his own documentary series.

"X," I said, trying to keep calm. "I get your point, but these are high school boys, not apes. And I thought we were going to watch *Black Christmas*? Millie hasn't seen that one yet." Eli had even said he'd show up after we were done, probably with some amazing baked good he learned to make while watching *GBBO*. It was the perfect night.

"You know, I think I'll live," Millie said. She glanced at X pointedly.

"And Halloween's on a Friday this year, so there's always tomorrow," he hurried to add. "We can watch *Black Christmas* then."

Millie said, "I really think our horror-movie night works better on the day *after* Halloween, anyway."

"All Saints' Day," said X. "That's still spooky."

I frowned again. It was becoming increasingly clear that the two of them had rehearsed this conversation ahead of time. Without me. They'd known I wouldn't be on board, so they'd practiced what to say to convince me. Which meant I wasn't going to win this one.

"But . . ." I started, then trailed off. I didn't have a particularly good argument here. Who didn't want to go to a party?

Me, that's who. I didn't want to go. I hated parties, and the dark. And corn mazes. And Halloween, for that matter. I preferred my horror confined to my laptop's thirteen-inch screen, where I could pause, rewind, and fast-forward to my heart's content. Where I always knew what was coming next. Movies, even horrible ones, were safe. High school parties, not so much.

I stared back at my friends, working my lip between my teeth as I tried to figure out what to say. Could I claim to be sick? Allergic to corn? Was that a thing?

If this were a horror movie, now would be the perfect time for our first jump scare. I'm not talking about an end-of-the-movie, Jason-grabbing-Alice-from-the-canoe-type jump scare, but an early Act One, Billy-leaping-in-through-Sidney's-window-type scare. The way I saw it, early Act One scares like that had two purposes: First, they set the tone, reminding the audience that they were indeed watching a scary movie long before the plot had a chance to even *get* scary.

And second, they prevented characters from having to answer questions they really didn't want to answer.

Like this one.

I smiled thinly at Millie and X, waiting for a jump scare to save me from this conversation.

Wind pressed against the basement windows. Somewhere in the school above us, someone began to laugh.

Didn't look like I was going to be so lucky.

"Guys," I started, thinking, *Sick*; I was going to have to go with sick. I gave a little fake cough. "You know, I think I—"

"Helloooo?" boomed a voice from the hall. "Anyone down here?"

Millie, X, and I all flinched as my big sister, Claire, leaned into the podcast room.

Here's everything you need to know about Claire: her makeup was perfect, even though she'd just lived through an entire day of school, and she was the only teen girl I knew who could pull off red hair and still look like straight fire.

The hair was dyed, FYI. Claire was naturally dirty blond, like me. We both had the same small frames and oversize features, but on Claire, the anime-character eyes were balanced by Cupid's bow lips and a shockingly wide smile.

I, on the other hand, had inherited my dad's strong Italian nose and my mother's Resting Bitch Face. Whereas Claire got Dad's good, glowy Italian skin that made her look like she was constantly on day two of a perfect beach tan, I inherited mom's Irish paleness that meant I had to slather on sunscreen whenever I even *thought* about the sun. The big eyes just made me look surprised, like the whole world was a little too much for me. Which was fair.

My movie theory sort of fell apart with Claire. She wasn't defined by a single genre like the rest of us were. She was the girl people made movies *for*. She was Emma Stone, Jennifer Lawrence, Saoirse Ronan. Pure Oscar bait. Sofia Coppola was probably writing a screenplay for her right now.

"Alley Cat," she said, aiming her truly ridiculously large eyes at me. "You ready to go?"

"Yes, definitely." I stood up quickly and started shoving things into my bag before Millie and X could get back to the party convo. Saved by Claire. Wouldn't be the first time. "I guess I'll see you guys later."

"At the party?" Millie said.

"Meet at seven?" added X.

"We'll see." I kept my head down so the hair hanging loose from my high ponytail would cover my lying face. "I'll... think about it." I'd already ordered *Black Christmas* on streaming, and I had only forty-eight hours to watch it. I know that sounds like a lot of time, but you really need to watch a movie like that twice if you want to catch all the behind-the-scenes stuff, like the fact that some of the snow was fake and a bunch of crew members made cameos. "I'll text you."

I threw my backpack over my shoulder and stepped out into the hall, but Claire grabbed my arm, holding me back.

"Wait, you're thinking about skipping the party?" she said, giving me her patented Claire Look. Picture Amy Adams's sad eyes and Anne Hathaway's trembling lower lip.

You're disappointing me, the Look said. If only the Academy could see her now.

"Claire," I muttered under my breath. There was a reason I was so obsessed with horror movies: It wasn't just the jump scares and the fake blood. In horror movies, the girl everyone overlooked, the smart, mousy, virginal girl who had no business in the starring role—let's face it, the girl like *me*—got to be the Final Girl. The star.

(And yeah, I know Neve Campbell and Jennifer Love Hewitt played Final Girls, and they're both gorgeous, but come on, this is just a theory; it doesn't account for the fact that Hollywood wouldn't even think of casting a woman who actually looked like a real person. Try to work with me.)

No other genre would cast the girl who liked science and reading in the leading role. Real life didn't, either. In real life, girls like me stood on the sidelines and didn't place in competitions and stayed home on Friday nights.

I knew my role, and I was okay with it. Why wasn't anyone else?

I stared at my big sister, pleading, needing her to understand that I really didn't want to do this. Claire frowned, then nodded. Our sisterly bond was working in my favor for once. She felt my inner turmoil. I was sure of it. *Relief.* I exhaled.

"Alice doesn't have to think about anything," Claire said, turning back to my friends. "She's definitely going to this party. We'll see you there at seven."

"You really shouldn't have said I would go tonight," I told Claire.

"Your friends love you and want to party with you; I don't understand the problem." Claire gave me a side-eye. "Are you wussing out on me, Alley Cat?"

"*I'm* the wuss? You couldn't even make it through the last half of *Hush*." *Hush*, a 2016 slasher about a deaf writer being stalked by a murderous psychopath in the woods. I'd seen it five times.

"Because *Hush* was boring, not because it was scary. Why would you live in the woods, completely alone, if you were deaf? It doesn't make any sense."

"Wow, victim blaming much?"

"More like writer blaming."

I blinked at her. "You did *not* just insult Mike Flanagan in my—"

"*Hush* is a movie, Alice," Claire said, interrupting me. "This is real life." She started walking backward so I could see her dramatic eye roll. Everything Claire did was dramatic, but the eye roll was truly a work of art.

We'd just exited the high school, and I was trailing down the front steps behind her like a puppy, like always. It was a disgustingly beautiful day for October. Crisp autumn air. Golden light. It was like Halloween in a movie. Perfect weather for the vintage leather jacket I'd found at Scout thrift store last weekend. There was even a slight breeze, just strong enough to rustle our hair.

"The party's a costume thing, right?" I glanced at Claire. "I don't have anything to wear."

Claire pursed her lips, taking a second to look me over. In addition to the jacket, my current look involved '90s-style vamp lipstick, a white spaghetti strap tank, layered necklaces, and the high ponytail.

"This isn't a costume?" Claire asked, genuinely confused. "I thought you were dressing like that *Dawson's Creek* character from that one movie?"

"Katie Holmes, *Disturbing Behavior*," I clarified. "But it's not really a costume; it's more of an . . . homage." *Disturbing Behavior* was terrible, but I loved it because Katie Holmes seriously stepped out of her preppy tomboy type to play this edgy alternative chick. It was a major fashion moment back in the '90s. Google it.

When I found the leather jacket—identical to the one Katie wore in the movie—the rest of the outfit just sort of came together.

"Homage, costume, whatever." Claire flapped a hand. "You look hot. You should roll with it."

I bit back a grin. Compliments from Claire always meant more than compliments from other people.

We were crossing the street now, heading toward the Mercer College campus instead of the senior parking lot, where Claire's Jetta was parked.

"Are we going to Dad's gym?" I asked. Meaning the Mercer College gym, where our dad coached collegiate volleyball and softball. Claire and I had been hanging out there since we were tiny children with pigtails and scabs on our knees.

Well, *I* had scabs on my knees. Claire would never do something as prosaic as fall.

"Light's better in the locker room than at home," Claire explained. "They have those light bulbs that go all the way around the mirror like in old-timey makeup rooms. And Kiehl's products in the showers."

I nodded, barely listening. I was already sliding the elastic from my ponytail as casually as I could. "Does my hair look crazy?"

Claire shook her head. "No, it's really good right now. The great Katie Holmes herself would be jealous."

"Well, now we both know you're lying."

The gym was nearly empty. The buzzing fluorescent lights looked dull and artificial after all that glorious October sun, and a stale smell of sweat hung so heavily in the air it was practically visible, mixing with the sharp sting of cleaning products. The temperature inside the gym was always ten degrees past comfortable and strangely humid. I could practically feel my shirt wrinkling as I scanned the room.

Erin Cleary was in the back, huffing away on an elliptical machine. Erin was a senior at Omaha East, but all our school's varsity athletes worked out at the college gym. Erin was a star volleyball player, so she basically lived here, as far as I could tell. It wasn't much of a surprise to find her here on a Friday, on Halloween.

I heard a crash of weights on the other side of the room and glanced toward the sound, staring for just long enough to catch sight of wavy brown hair and boy muscles turned all glowy from a thin sheen of sweat. And then, like someone who'd stared into an eclipse and was now worried she was going to go blind, I looked away again, cheeks blazing.

Claire grabbed my arm. "It's Wesley James Hanson the Third."

Oh yes. I was aware.

Wesley James Hanson III had moved here from Boston and started showing up at the gym around the beginning of the summer, giving me just around five months to . . . notice him. He went by Wes. Claire and I both knew he went by Wes, but neither of us could bring ourselves to refer to him as anything other than Wesley James Hanson III. He was worthy of all seven syllables.

He was a freshman in college this year, which meant it wasn't entirely outside the realm of possibility that he could be interested in a high school girl. I'd done the math at least once a week.

All summer.

"He's going to see you staring," I muttered to Claire. I put a hand on her back and tried to maneuver her in the direction of the locker room. I'd spent a not-insignificant amount of time over the past five months trying to keep my sister away from Wes.

"I'm fascinated by him," Claire said. Still staring, by the way. Claire wasn't the kind of girl who'd be bothered if the godlike college freshman caught her staring at him. "I heard that, back in Boston, he was having an affair with a forty-year-old divorcée *and* her daughter, and that his dad had to pay off the ex-husband-slash-father to hush everything up."

I chewed my lip, adding this rumor to my collection. Claire wasn't the only one fascinated by the mystery that was Wesley James Hanson III. Just yesterday Eli told me he'd overheard someone saying that Wes got kicked out of whatever fancy East Coast boarding school he used to go to for running a fight club out of the common room in the dorms. Millie said she'd heard he was in the Irish mob. X told me he was gearing up to try out for the Olympic rowing team.

There was no way to verify any of the rumors. Wes wasn't on social media. The one and only time I tried to look him up online, I found an entry for a James Wesley Hanson who died in Georgia in 1940 and nothing else.

The mystery made him even more fascinating. He was like no one I'd ever met before. He completely and totally defied the teen-movie-character tropes the rest of us all fit into so neatly. He was well-off, but not into money. An athlete, but not a meathead (to use a term from some of my favorite old movies). Gorgeous, but also . . . sort of *dorky*. But in a hot way.

I let my eyes settle on him for a moment, watching him lift weights on the other side of the room. From the knees up, he was your standard rich jock: gray Nike gym shorts, white Nike T-shirt, bulging muscles. But I noticed he'd paired his tennis shoes with old-man argyle socks pulled up over his calves.

He was always doing stuff like that. Painting his toenails black. Adding a pearl necklace to an otherwise very standard T-shirt and jeans. Tiny details here and there, just enough to make it clear that he didn't care about gender norms, that he wouldn't be boxed in by expectations. God, it was hot.

"I bet he only watches obscure German art films," Claire said, still staring. "Or maybe he does that thing where he pairs *The Wizard of Oz* with *The Dark Side of the Moon* so that the song lyrics match up perfectly."

"Totally," I agreed, even though I knew for a fact that Wes liked horror movies, like me. Last month, I was waiting to give Dad a ride home, and I was watching *Creep* on my laptop. (Underrated 2014 film starring Mark Duplass as this dude who wants to make a movie for his unborn child. Found footage; amazing.) I was almost to the end, and I was getting excited because it was my absolute favorite horror-movie ending of all time, and who should stop by to watch the last two minutes over my shoulder but Wesley James Hanson III.

"You seen the sequel?" he asked when it was over.

"No," I said, which was weird because I'd seen the sequel like two dozen times, but to be perfectly honest, my brain wasn't so much working as it was saying the words *hot guy* over and over and over again, so really I was feeling pretty proud of myself for getting a word out at all.

"The sequel's rad," he said. (*Rad!* my brain screamed.) "You should really check it out."

I thought I'd noticed his eyes lingering on my legs, but he quickly moved them up to my face when he saw me watching. I didn't mind. I'd felt good about my look that day. I'm not some sort of weirdo who always dresses like a movie character, but '90s horror movies got me really into '90s fashion, and I was wearing this great miniskirt with chunky black combat boots and suspenders, sort of reminiscent of a young Winona Ryder. Claire had told me my legs were goals in that skirt, and if Claire said it, then it was true.

"Nice . . . suspenders," Wes had said.

"Nice shorts," I told him. He'd been wearing these insanely short running shorts that day. Really, they were obscene. Only Wesley James Hanson III could make shorts like that look sexy.

I couldn't believe I'd been bold enough to comment on them.

But Wes had stared back at me like he wanted to say something else, and there was this supercharged moment where we both waited for the other one to speak first. Neither of us did. I couldn't tell if Wes was trying to play it cool or if he was actually a little shy.

After a long moment, he'd rubbed the back of his neck and said, "See you around, Alice."

My heart almost stopped right there. Wesley James Hanson III knew my name. Which meant he'd *asked around* about me.

Was it the suspenders? The fact that I wasn't sporty like all the athletes at the gym, that I stood out? I had no idea. But when Wes walked away, he left this amazing smell behind him, this kind of musk, mixed with dry grass and suede, like how I imagined a sweaty cowboy must smell. I wanted to make a candle out of it.

After that, it was like we were both acutely aware of each other whenever we were in the gym at the same time. I'd notice his eyes move my way, and I'd feel a little skin prickle whenever he got close. We talked sometimes. If he saw me watching a movie, he'd stop to watch part of it over my shoulder, and then he'd recommend a movie, and then I'd recommend a movie back. I'd started wearing my suspenders-and-miniskirt combo kind of a lot, and I'd noticed that he'd started wearing his short shorts kind of a lot, and oh my God, was this *flirting*? Were we flirting?

Whatever we were doing had begun in September and progressed through October. I hadn't even told Claire about it. I didn't want to jinx anything.

"Alice? You coming?" Claire was halfway to the locker room, but she'd stopped to wait for me.

I blinked, tearing my eyes away from Wes. "Uh . . . actually, I sort of need to talk to Dad. Meet you outside of his office?"

Claire nodded, digging around in her purse for something. "Let me borrow that lipstick you're wearing?"

"No way."

"Please? I love it on you." She pouted. "I want to try it."

"Is there a word that's stronger than *no*? I want to adequately convey the level of no I feel in my heart." If I let Claire borrow my lipstick, it would suddenly become *her* lipstick, and then everyone would tell her how amazing it looked on her, and then it would become her signature color, and I wouldn't ever be able to wear it again. The exact same thing had happened with this pair of platform loafers I found at Scout at the end of last year. Loafers that Claire was currently wearing. I wasn't taking any chances.

Luckily, she let it go. "Fine. Meet you outside Dad's office."

She disappeared inside the locker room. Instead of heading straight for Dad's office, I turned around, allowing myself one last backward glance . . .

Wesley James Hanson III was staring at me. He caught me looking at him, and a smile slowly grew on his lips.

God, he had good lips. Staring at them, I wondered what it would feel like to kiss them, if they'd be rough or soft, what they'd taste like. It had been too long since I'd kissed anyone. The last time had been X at Chloe's birthday party freshman year. X had told me he was gay about two seconds after the kiss ended, but even before that, it had felt like kissing my own brother.

But kissing Wes . . .

A shiver went through my whole body. When I finally turned back around, my legs were trembling.

My dad's office was the size of a closet, with no windows and an oversize desk taking up one entire wall. Above the desk were a truly shocking number of inspirational posters. Seriously, however many posters you're picturing right now, double that.

Chloe Bree stepped out before I could open the door.

"Allison, *hi*," she said, pushing her long white-blond hair over one shoulder. Chloe has known me since elementary school and has been getting private softball coaching from my dad for over a year, and she still didn't know that my name was *Alice*, not *Allison*.

She'd be perfect in a mob movie where all the women had fake fingernails and bleached-blond hair and were addicted to cocaine.

"Hey, Chloe," I said.

Chloe looked like she was about to say something else when Owen Maddox, this college freshman who worked at the gym as a janitor on nights and weekends, rounded the corner, sweeping. He had long dark hair that fell over his face in a greasy curtain and acne scars.

"Owen, *hi*," Chloe said, her voice a touch fake-sounding. "I'm going to see you both at my party tonight, right?" she asked.

Owen sometimes bought beer for high school students, which meant he showed up at high school parties, but he always hung out in the corners, not really saying anything to anyone. Millie called him our school's Boo Radley. She wasn't totally wrong.

"Wouldn't miss it," Owen deadpanned. He glanced at me for a moment, then rounded the corner, the sound of his broom brushing against concrete slowly fading.

"You're coming too, right, Allison? It's gonna slay." And Chloe wiggled her fingers at me, walking off before I'd even answered her.

I stepped into Dad's office, knocking on the door frame. "Dad?"

"Hey, Alice." My dad twisted around in his seat, his posture reminding me of boys my age twisted around in their desks. The overhead light caught the gray in his hair and the shadows under his eyes, making him look both old and young at the same time. "Claire with you?"

Ninety-five percent of what my dad said to me was "Claire with you?" or "Have you seen Claire?" In case you were wondering if we were close.

"Locker room," I said. "Uh, I was wondering . . . did you have time to look at my application yet? For the Mercer internship?" The Summer Research Internship at Mercer School of Medicine was one of the most prestigious internships for high school students in the country, the kind of thing that made college admissions boards drool all over their laptops. It was also a pipeline into Mercer's premed program, which I'd had my heart set on since I was a tiny nine-year-old playing Operation in my spare time and dreaming of one day pulling the bones out of real people.

I wanted to be a forensic pathologist. That was a doctor who investigated the cause of sudden or unexpected deaths, and sometimes even testified in court if foul play was suspected. Read: dream job.

Since my dad worked at Mercer, I was hoping he might be able to give me some tips on what the committee might be looking for.

For a second, his expression was so totally blank that I knew he hadn't just forgotten to read my application; he'd also completely forgotten that I'd asked him to look. Maybe he even forgot he had a second daughter at all.

Then he flashed a smile. It was his homecoming-king smile, his class-president smile. Dad had been the king of everything back in high school. When he smiled like that, it was so easy to see why.

Claire had inherited that smile. I had not. "I didn't forget, Alice; I swear. I'll look at it tonight."

I was walking away from Dad's office, my brain still entirely focused on my application, when I turned the corner and walked right into Wesley James Hanson III.

And I mean I walked *right into* him. Like in a movie. Like that scene in *Scream* where Sidney was running from Ghostface and turned the corner and ran into Billy.

I wondered if he was waiting for me.

"Alice," Wes said. "Hey."

He stared at my lips for a moment. My mouth felt suddenly very dry.

"Hey," I said.

Every inch of his skin was tan, like he'd somehow just gotten back from the beach, even though we live two thousand miles from the nearest real beach. He was chewing a toothpick as he spoke to me, and something about this was incredibly seductive.

I could see him in a horror movie. I could see him in *any* movie. He had that thing that never went out of style, that rich-kid, bad-boy thing. He was Skeet Ulrich, Heath Ledger, Timothée Chalamet.

He was . . . wearing a Hello Kitty barrette.

"Hello Kitty," I said, because apparently I can't think a thing without saying it.

"Yeah." He touched the barrette. "It's from a collab she did with Minnie Mouse. See how she's wearing Minnie's red polka-dot bow?"

She was, in fact, wearing a polka-dot bow. "That's . . . cool," I said. But I was thinking, *Lucky kitty.*

I'd been wanting to touch Wes's hair since the day I met him.

Wes moved the toothpick to the corner of his mouth with his tongue. "I watched that movie you told me about. *The Invitation*? It was intense. Thanks for the rec."

The Invitation, 2015 film about a really messed-up dinner party.

I felt myself loosen a little, like I always did when talking about horror movies. "Right? Like, how the whole first half of the movie was all about building this really claustrophobic feeling of tension, so you just kept waiting to see what was going to happen and making up these ideas in your head about what was . . ." I trailed off as Wes leaned in closer, plucking a golden leaf off my jacket sleeve.

He'd been doing this sort of thing more frequently lately. Finding little reasons to touch me. An eyelash on my cheek. A tag sticking out of my shirt. Every time I felt his skin against mine, it was like striking a match. That instant sizzle.

"I was gonna say it was scary," he said, letting the leaf flutter to the ground. "You know a lot about movies, don't you?"

I looked up at him, barely daring to breathe. He'd gotten closer to me when he'd leaned in to get that leaf, right inside my personal space. This wasn't *friends* close. This was *something more* close.

"I do," I said. I could smell that cowboy scent of him all over again. It rendered me momentarily mute.

"I'm thinking about asking you to watch one with me sometime," he said, searching my face.

I blinked. "You are?"

"Yeah, I'm actually pretty nervous about it." He smiled, all shy.

"Well, fear's good for the soul," I said, and his smile widened.

"That it is." He scratched the back of his head. "So, what do you say? You doing anything later tonight?"

One of my favorite Wes rumors was that he spent the last four years writing and directing horror films in South Korea, and that he had to hide out here because his last film pissed off the North Korean government and now he was on a watch list.

If you'd asked me at the beginning of the summer, I'd have told you it was more likely that *that* rumor was true than that Wes would ask me out on a date.

Sometimes life was amazingly unpredictable.

I was still trying to remember how to form words when an obnoxiously cheerful voice from behind me said, "Oh, *hello.*"

I closed my eyes. The temperature of my face rose to one thousand degrees.

Wes glanced over my shoulder. "Oh, hey. You're Alice's sister, right?"

I could feel Claire stiffen behind me. My sister had never in her life been referred to as *Alice's sister* before. In my nightmares, I was usually naked when she interrupted one of my conversations with

Wes and stole him away from me. I suppose I should've been grateful that I wasn't naked now. If you're about to watch the love of your life become completely infatuated with your sister, it's best to be fully clothed.

I tried to focus on that as Claire dropped her arm over my shoulder and said, "Yes, Claire is . . . me. *Hi.*" Of course she sounded charming when she said this. I noticed the subtle tightness in her voice only because I know her better than anyone.

"Wes." Wes looked back at me, waiting for me to say something, but for some reason the thing that popped into my head at that moment was this story I once heard about how the movie *Saw* was inspired by a news report about a man who broke into people's houses to tickle the feet of sleeping children.

Do not say that out loud, Alice.

"So. *Wes*," Claire said. "How do you know my baby sister?"

Wes looked at me again, then back at Claire, frowning. "She watches movies here after school sometimes."

"That she does, Wesley; that she does." Claire looked at me. And now they were both looking at me. It was my turn to speak, but I couldn't speak, because all I could think about were my perfect vintage loafers, now *Claire's* perfect vintage loafers. It hadn't even been her fault that she'd ended up with them. They'd just looked so much better on her. Everyone said so. She wore them one time, and after that, whatever magic they'd had when I first tried them on was gone. What was the point of wearing amazing shoes when I knew I would never look as good as Claire looked wearing them? I'd given them to her the next day.

I really didn't want Wes to be like those loafers. Claire could have any guy she wanted; when was *I* going to meet another guy who looked like Heath Ledger and liked horror movies and appreciated my off-the-wall fashion choices?

Never, that was when. Wes was one of a kind.

I studied his face, expecting to see the dumbstruck expression that every male and a solid percentage of females got when interacting with Claire.

But Wes was still looking at me, somehow resisting the gravitational pull that was my sister's perfection.

Maybe he didn't like perfect? I mean, he paired argyle socks with athleisure. Maybe perfect was too boring for someone like him.

His brows furrowed, a little expectantly, and I remembered that he'd just asked me out on a date. *Me*, not Claire.

My heart did a leap. I should probably answer him.

"About the movie," I said. All casual. "I think I could be into that."

"Cool." He said the word a beat too quickly, a smile touching his lips. He pulled out his phone. "Can I text you later?"

Claire blurted, like she couldn't help herself, "Her number is 402-555-4605."

I resisted the urge to roll my eyes. Claire had never totally figured out how to behave when she wasn't 100 percent the center of attention. To be fair, she didn't have a lot of practice.

"Thanks, I think," Wes said, still looking at me as he typed my number into his phone. "I'll hit you up."

And away he went, leaving his sweaty cowboy smell behind again.

Claire waited until he was out of earshot before turning back to me, all wide-eyed with indignation. "You have *so* much explaining to do."

Her voice was a little jealous, a little awed. I felt a skip of pleasure.

I was always the one jealous of Claire. It'd never been the other way around before. "Do I?"

"How long have you been keeping your love affair with Wesley James Hanson the Third from me?"

"Calm down; there's no love affair. We just . . . talk."

"Yeah, sure, uh-huh." She said this just a touch too fast. Man, she really was jealous. I almost felt guilty. Then I looked down and saw my perfect loafers on her feet.

Claire didn't even like vintage clothes. She'd wanted to try the loafers only because she'd seen someone wear a similar pair on TikTok.

She unwrapped a piece of gum and put it in her mouth, then went to toss the wrapper in the trash and missed. She must not have noticed, because she kept walking, leaving the wrapper on the floor behind her.

I heard the sweeping sound of a broom and looked up as Owen appeared in the hall again. He leaned over and plucked the wrapper off the floor.

I was still a few steps away, so I don't think he saw me. He was staring after Claire, an annoyed expression on his face. As I watched, he lifted his hand, fingers folded to look like a gun.

He aimed it at the back of Claire's head, cocked his thumb, and murmured, "Pow."

CAN'T BE MORE THAN THIRTY MINUTES NOW

Claire and I had just pulled into the parking lot in front of Lacy Farms when I finished giving her the (extremely abbreviated) story of what had gone down between me and Wes. I watched the numbers on the dash switch from 6:59 to 7:00 just as the engine clicked off, almost like Claire had timed it. Which was totally something she would have done. She'd always been superstitious in really weird, small ways. Like, if we made it home without hitting a red light, it meant I was going to ace my bio quiz tomorrow, or if she texted Alex Kramer at exactly 12:34, it meant he was going to fall madly in love with her. According to Claire, the world was gameable.

"Sart hre." Claire leaned over the steering wheel, reading the few remaining letters on the weatherworn sign marking the Lacy Farms corn maze. "Do you think it's a code?"

I stared down the dark, dark path and tried very hard not to shiver because if I did, Claire would never let me hear the end of it.

"I do think it's a code," I told her, all solemn. "It means skip the cheugy, scary corn maze and go right for the party. You could be drinking lukewarm beer in less than five minutes." Sometimes, if I just asked Claire for what I wanted, she'd surprise me and do it.

She narrowed her eyes. "I thought the point was to go through the maze to get to the party."

"Eli told me there's another entrance around back. Leads right to the party, and there's zero chance of finding sweaty boys carrying chain saws." Eli was the kind of person who liked to make a point of knowing things other people didn't. It was one of his superpowers. For instance: Everyone knew Chloe Bree had rented the entire cornfield at Lacy Farms for her annual Halloween party. But only Eli knew she'd talked the track-and-field guys into dressing up and hiding in the stalks to scare the shit out of people as they made their way through.

"Is Eli always such a baby?" Claire asked, throwing her car door open a little more dramatically than necessary. She was looking across the field now, to where Millie and X were hanging around the corn maze entrance, talking to Sierra Clayton, the best-looking girl in our grade.

X was wearing the traditional Omaha East werewolf mask. Our mascot is a wolf, so every year, the kids at our school buy the same werewolf mask for Halloween as a weird show of school spirit. I don't know when it started, but it's a thing now. And Millie was still all decked out like Velma from *Scooby-Doo*.

I groaned. "I knew everyone would be wearing a costume."

"Here." Claire plucked the cat ears off her head and put them on me. "Now you're a . . . grungy nineties cat?"

"I don't think that's a thing."

"Okay . . . then you're . . ." Claire's eyes lit up. "Oh my God, you're an *alley cat*. Get it?"

Okay, I couldn't help laughing at that. "But now *you* don't have a costume."

"Oh, don't worry about me. I don't mind making the sacrifice if it means my baby sister gets the most perfect costume of all time."

Claire cut her eyes to me, bold red lips pursed. "Are you really not going through the maze with me?"

"You don't actually have to be a serial killer to hurt someone with a chain saw, you know," I said, following her. "A drunk high school boy could manage just fine." Common sense; it's like the main rule of being a Final Girl, but Claire just rolled her eyes.

"Come on, Allie, what kind of person skips the scary corn maze? On Halloween? That's the entire point of the party." She raised her artfully disheveled eyebrows, daring me to tell her that I was exactly that kind of person, always have been and always will be.

It wasn't even about fear—it was about being smart. Anyone who'd ever seen a scary movie knew to skip the corn maze, just like we knew not to venture down into a basement or up into an attic, to drive past hitchhikers and heed the warnings of toothless old men at gas stations. If you watched enough horrible things happen on-screen, you could figure out how to avoid them in real life.

The *Halloween* theme started playing from my pocket. I pulled out my phone and glanced at it, but Claire was watching, so I stuck it back in my pocket without reading it.

Claire grinned. "What? You aren't going to read Wesley James Hanson the Third's text in front of me?"

Ignoring that. "I'm going to go talk to Millie and X."

Claire was already most of the way to the maze, but she turned around and started walking backward so I could see just how ridiculous she thought I was being. "Come on, Alley Cat. You're not seriously going to let me go through the scary maze on my own, are you? If you don't come with me, I might die." And then she grabbed her neck and made these gross gagging noises, like she was being choked, before disappearing into the corn.

If you don't come with me, I might die.
Those were the last words my sister ever said to me.
Really.

I read my text. I was expecting a cool-guy, one-word text—*hey* or *sup*—but Wes sent me this:

> You gain strength, courage, and confidence by every experi-
> ence in which you really stop to look fear in the face. You are
> able to say to yourself, "I have lived through this horror. I can
> take the next thing that comes along." You must do the thing
> you think you cannot do.
>
> —Eleanor Roosevelt

I smiled, then read it again.
What a weirdo.

X, Millie, and I made our way around the maze to the back entrance, following the sounds of voices down a single camping-
lantern-lit path to a big clearing in the corn. A ton of people from
school were already there, but Claire wasn't with them, so we
grabbed SOLO cups of warm beer and talked about how annoying
it was that all Sally Hardesty did in the original *Texas Chainsaw* was
scream, that *Scream*'s Sidney Prescott was iconic, and that the best
slashers of the '70s and '80s were the ones where the Final Girls
actually fought back.

"Maybe that's what our podcast is about," Millie said. "Like . . . we can teach listeners how to be a Final Girl?"

"How to be a *good* Final Girl," X added.

Ten minutes passed. Then fifteen.

Twenty.

Millie and X went to refill their cups. I sent Claire a text, but she didn't answer. She hadn't answered the last three.

SHOWTIME

If this were a real slasher, this is when the music would start. The camera would close in on my face.

"Buccinator muscle," I murmured under my breath. It was this weird thing I did when I wanted to get out of my own head. I would try to remember the names of the different muscle groups I'd had to learn in the college-level anatomy class I took over the summer. As I waited for Claire, I ran through the jaw, picturing the long, pink slabs knitting together beneath my cheeks. "Masseter muscle, temporalis muscle . . ."

The sun had fully set by the time I'd finished, and the only light came from the camping lanterns. I peered into the entrance of the maze, holding my breath like you do when you drive by a graveyard. It was dark inside. Seriously dark. I couldn't see more than a few inches in front of me. Looking down, I couldn't see my own shoes. I turned the flashlight app on my cell on, but that almost made it worse. Now there was a two-foot-wide circle of bright white that left everything outside of it even darker, filled with twitching shadows and things that went still the second I moved the beam to look directly at them.

Somewhere in the corn, the hard metal-on-metal grind of a chain saw roared to life.

I froze, fear twitching through me, then took a breath. Claire was just messing with me, right? To punish me for being too chicken for the maze. The whole thing was such a horror-movie cliché. If I were smart, if I were following my own damn rules, I'd turn around and go back to the party.

But this was real life. No matter how well you know the rules, no matter how smart you think you are, you're never prepared for your life to turn into a horror movie.

"Claire?" I called, walking into the maze.

A breeze blew through the corn, shaking the stalks. The sound was like a low, snickering laugh. But no one answered.

"Okay, Claire, you got me," I said, going a little farther. Dead leaves crunched beneath my sneakers. Wind played with my hair. Something rustled in the corn, followed by the dragging sound of footsteps.

I took a right at the fork in the path, and the light from my phone bounced over a short dress, a pale face.

Not Claire—Chloe Bree. In a true homage to *The Texas Chainsaw Massacre*, she'd made it look like her arm had been cut off at the shoulder. A pale stump of flesh and a broken, yellowed bone protruded from the strap of her dress, and fake blood gushed down the side of her body and clumped in her long, pale blond hair.

I felt a kick of fear and had to bite my lip to keep from gasping.

It looked so real.

"I . . . uh, admire your commitment to the theme, Chloe," I told her, swallowing.

She didn't answer. There was a glazed, drunk look to her face. Her eyes were all glassy, like she'd just thrown up, and her hair was soaked with sweat and fake blood. She took a single step toward me, and her legs knocked together.

I reached out to steady her. "Whoa, did you have a little too much to drink?"

Chloe opened her mouth, and I saw that her teeth were slick with blood. She looked down at her shoulder, drew a long, sobbing breath—

And *screamed*.

The Wilhelm scream is a stock sound effect that's been used in films, television, and video games since the '50s. It's been in Star Wars, *Game of Thrones*, even a few Pixar movies.

And now, apparently, my life. Because that's exactly how this sounded, like a horror-movie scream.

Blood oozed over Chloe's lips and chin, thick drops of it that looked black in the light of my phone. That blood wasn't fake. The smell of it was so strong, it clung to the insides of my nostrils. I could taste it in the back of my throat—

I don't remember running. My body seemed to move on its own, legs lifting me and propelling me through the corn, heartbeat thudding like crazy in my throat. I had to get out of there. I had to call the police; I had to get an ambulance for Chloe. Long icy-cold breaths knifed through my lungs. Cornstalks whipped my face and arms. Twigs snapped beneath my shoes.

And then I turned another corner of the maze, and there she was.

Claire knelt on the ground, crying. She had blood in her hair, and there was blood and dirt streaked across her face, but she didn't appear to be hurt. Not yet.

A guy stood over her. Tall and skinny, with lean, ropy muscles; pale skin pockmarked with acne scars; long dark hair. I recognized him. I knew I recognized him.

Owen, I thought. It was Owen, the janitor guy from the gym.

What was he doing here?

Owen had a mask balled up in one hand, and his other hand was groping his stomach, which was already dark with blood. There was something sticking out of him, something small and pink, and it took me a second to realize that it was the little pocketknife Claire carried in her purse for self-defense.

The next few things happened very quickly.

First, Claire looked up and saw me standing in the corn. A relieved smile flickered over her lips, and she started to say my name. "Al—"

And then my foot caught on something lying across the field, and I fell, hard. The ground slammed into me, pushing my lips back into my teeth. The taste of blood hit my tongue.

I groaned and glanced down, wanting to see what had tripped me.

It was a chain saw.

The same chain saw that this monster had used to cut off Chloe's arm.

I heard noises then. Grunting and a sort of wet, meaty sucking sound. My head hurt like hell, and I could barely move, but I managed to look up just as Owen jerked my sister's knife out of his stomach.

"No," I moaned. I tried to push myself back to my feet, but I was too slow. My arms were shaking too badly, and I couldn't quite regain my balance.

I couldn't reach them in time; I couldn't stop him.

And so I watched as Owen Trevor Maddox lurched forward and stabbed my sister once, right in the chest.

I watched him kill her.

HALLOWEEN, ONE YEAR LATER

Cold air whips into my jacket as I stand at the bottom of the staircase that leads up to my school. It smells like autumn, like rotting leaves and dead things, and I have to breathe through my mouth so I don't gag. It's already dropped below forty degrees. Much too cold for October.

I hold my jacket closed with one hand and use the other to dig my cell out of my pocket, frozen thumb shakily jabbing at the green play button on the screen.

Two familiar voices instantly buzz to life in my ear, as annoying as fruit flies:

"Did you just burp?" says X, his voice deeper than it sounds in real life. I adjust the volume on my AirPods.

Millie says, "No, it was a cough. Why? Did it smell like a burp?" Her voice is better. It's deeper, and it does that vocal-fry thing that people seem to hate, but I actually don't mind. She sounds like she's smoked a million cigarettes and washed them all down with shots of whiskey, which couldn't be further from who she is.

X says, "No, it didn't smell, but I just burped, too, and I thought we were twins."

"Burp twins! I love it."

"Is that gross? Are we gross? I don't care. Okay—" There's a pause as X takes a deep breath. "So, this week, Millie and I are finally, *finally* going to talk about the murder you've all been asking us about for the last year."

X adds, "It happened last year in a cornfield right outside our hometown, Omaha, Nebraska."

"Before you ask us," Millie breaks in, "we already know that you're all thinking, 'But wait, isn't Nebraska just one hundred percent cornfields?' And the answer is no. Omaha—where we're both from—is, like, this little suburby city."

"Go watch the 1999 movie *Election* with Reese Witherspoon if you can't picture it. It was filmed in Omaha."

"Right," Millie says. "So anyway, this story hits pretty close to home, which is why it's taken us so long to cover it. Claire Lawrence wasn't just our classmate; she was the older sister of one of our best friends, and it felt sort of weird to talk about her murder before now."

My stomach dips at that. *One of our best friends.* Millie doesn't say the rest: that the three of us have barely spoken in the last year, that we can hardly be considered "friends" anymore. I hear it, though. It's a scab I can't stop picking at.

"The guy who's been charged with her murder is about to go to trial," X says. "And we agreed that it would be even weirder if we just didn't mention Claire at all, so we thought there might be a way to talk about this while still being respectful."

"Exactly," Millie says. "It's important to both of us to be respectful of her family."

Family. What a laugh. My parents split up just a few months after Claire died. We sold the house where I grew up, my dad started drinking, and the only thing my mom ever says to me anymore is "When are you going to be home?" Some family.

I close my eyes, reminding myself to breathe. No part of this podcast is "respectful."

"Here goes." X breathes out, the sound exploding in my earbuds. "Claire was this totally beautiful eighteen-year-old girl. I'm talking movie-star beautiful. She had a sort of Emma Stone thing going on. She was really pale and thin, with giant eyes and great hair."

"She did have really good hair," Millie says.

"It's the color, right? That red."

"It's hard to pull off red hair as a teen girl."

Oh, please, I think. They know her hair was dyed.

"Which brings us back to rule number one," Millie cuts in. "Guys, I've said it before, and I'll probably say it every episode. If you want to be a Final Girl, you've *got* to blend in."

"Look, we know it's not woke to admit this anymore, but it's just so true," X adds. "Watch any slasher—the pretty white girl *always* dies first."

"I know the common assumption is that the Black character always dies first. I actually thought that, too, so I did a little research," Millie adds. "*Time* did a study, and according to a random sampling of horror films, fifty-two percent of the time it's a white female who dies first, twenty-four percent of the time it's a white male, twelve percent of the time it's a Black male, and eight percent of the time it's a Black female."

"I think the Black body count is so low because they forget to include Black people in these horror movies," X points out. "Black people die first outside the horror genre all the time."

"Yes, exactly. And you'll notice that Asian men or women aren't mentioned at all, despite the fact that Japanese and Korean horror have been influencing American horror for decades."

I'm the one who sent them that article. A year ago, I would've been more than happy to talk about death stats in horror movies, but now I ball my hands into fists and shove them deep into my pockets, hating both my old friends so much I can hardly breathe.

A few months after Claire died, Millie and X started the podcast *How to Be a Final Girl.* They analyze true-crime cases like they're scary movies, walking listeners through the crimes and explaining all the choices a true Final Girl would've made.

That's their whole gimmick. Learn from Final Girls. *Be* a Final Girl.

I know I shouldn't be so surprised that they went ahead with the podcast. We'd been talking about doing it for a full year before Claire died. But it still stings that they took my idea. *I* was the one who was always saying the rules of scary movies were perfectly applicable to real life, and that if everyone just lived like they were in the middle of a truly gruesome slasher, things would turn out okay.

And now they're using my own words to explain why my sister got murdered.

It's disgusting.

"I actually want to talk about our villain before we go any further," Millie is saying when I start listening again. "Nineteen-year-old Owen Trevor Maddox was arrested for Claire's murder, but he hasn't been convicted yet. His trial starts this week. According to the only witness, Owen attacked another girl, Chloe Bree, with a chain saw before going after Claire—"

"Ugh, I still can't think about that without wanting to hurl," X says.

"I know, right? So anyway, Chloe didn't die, but Owen didn't know that, so he went after Claire next. But Claire had this little pocketknife on her, and she stabbed him with it in self-defense. Serious Final Girl move, right? But then Owen pulled the knife out of his own stomach and stabbed her with it, killing her. Allegedly."

"Allegedly?" X sounds skeptical. "Don't tell me you think he's innocent?"

"*I* don't think anything," Millie says. "But the only evidence the cops have against Owen is one eyewitness testimony. The witness watched Owen stab Claire with Claire's knife, but she didn't see anything that happened before that. She didn't see Owen go after Chloe with a chain saw, and she didn't see Owen attack Claire or Claire stab Owen. So all that's conjecture."

"You think someone else went after Chloe with the chain saw?"

"I already told you that I don't think anything! I'm just putting the evidence out there. But Chloe has no memory of the attack itself, and our thing is that life follows horror-movie rules, right? If this were a scary movie, the whole Owen thing would feel way too easy, like a giant misdirect. I feel like I have to at least mention—"

Fuckingstupidbitch. I yank the AirPods out of my ears, resisting the urge to throw them, to scream. I knew this was coming, but I'm still completely unprepared to actually listen to my former friend Millie defend the monster who butchered my sister. I can't even think Owen's name without remembering the way he looked standing over her body, her blood smeared across his face, her knife still clutched in one hand.

The Owen Trevor Maddox truthers are a contingent of idiots who've convinced themselves that the guy I *saw* stab my sister isn't actually a murderer. He was just in the wrong place at the wrong time, or maybe I'm lying or I hallucinated the whole thing.

Maybe it's crappy to blame X and Millie. All this conspiracy bullshit started way before their podcast even came out. Owen has spent the last year claiming innocence, but his lawyers have refused to let him do any press that might interfere with their defense, so people have been coming up with all sorts of wild stories about what really happened that night.

And it's not like *How to Be a Final Girl* is some huge national hit or anything. It's pretty popular locally, though. Almost everyone in our school listens. So when they put this episode out, they had to know it was going to make everything worse.

I shiver, forcing the thought out of my head, and stuff my Air-Pods into my pocket. I hurry up the crumbling stone staircase that leads to Omaha East, the school itself looming over me in all of its Greek Revival, stone-columned glory.

I'm halfway to the front doors when a girl flies past me, nearly knocking me off my feet. I stumble back a step, swearing. The girl stops and turns.

I'm momentarily stunned into speechlessness.

It's Sidney Prescott, from *Scream*. Like, *actually* Sidney Prescott. Same pouty Neve Campbell mouth and shoulder-length brown hair; same overcurled '90s-style bangs. Same face.

I blink a few times, trying to get my eyes to catch up with my brain. I must just think she looks so much like Sidney because of how she's dressed in the exact same oversize gray sweatshirt that Sidney wears when she runs into Ghostface for the first time.

"Sorry," Sidney mutters, and then she's running again, racing through the school's front doors so fast that I actually turn and look down the school's steps, expecting to see Ghostface appear from behind a bush, holding a butcher knife.

"Asshole," I mutter. But I can't help being a little impressed with the girl's costume. You'd think I'd be over scary movies after what happened to Claire, but it's the opposite, actually. Horror movies are the only things I can stomach anymore. Movies that end happily, with people falling in love and achieving their dreams and starting families and shit, they make me want to hurl.

Give me a good slasher any day of the week. I want to see lives ruined. People destroyed. I want to listen to other people screaming. It's the only time I can drown out the screams still echoing through my head.

School hasn't started yet, so the Omaha East halls are only slightly crowded: overachievers wearing elaborate costumes made out of cardboard boxes and papier-mâché heading to their zero-hour classes; drama nerds decked out in stuff they pilfered from the costume closet, here for before-school rehearsal; kids with cars who drive in early so they can find a parking space napping in front of their lockers, rubber masks hiding their faces. Our school has always been big on dressing up.

I don't like walking down the halls at this time of day. Claire's most alive here. I can practically see her racing up from the auditorium, still in stage makeup and her Juliet costume, stealing my last sip of coffee, the rest of my doughnut.

I push the memory away and keep my head ducked as I make my way to my locker, hoping to get in and out without anyone stopping to offer condolences or ask me what I think of the trial. After Claire died, all anyone wanted to talk to me about was the cornfield and Owen and what I saw. I went from being the quiet, bookish girl that no one really noticed to the only witness in the most horrific crime this city had seen in decades. It was like being famous, if being famous totally sucked. I couldn't walk into school without getting swarmed. People mostly moved on over the summer, though. Unfortunately, all of that's going to change today.

Today's the day they never show in horror movies. It's what happens after the credits roll, after the Final Girl foils the bad guy.

Today's the day the trial of Owen Trevor Maddox begins.

Eli's already at his locker, nursing a can of Sprite Zero Sugar. Eli's Mormon, so he doesn't drink alcohol or caffeine, and he's cut sugar, too, because "sugar is the new tobacco," according to Medscape.

He looks up as I approach, fuzzy eyebrows lifting in surprise. "Are you actually here?" he asks, frowning. "Why are you here? Weren't you going to skip?"

"Did you seriously hit me with three questions before I even got my locker open?" I say. Ever since we were kids, Eli and I have tried to talk to each other using only questions. It's our game. How long can we keep going until one of us breaks?

"Do you expect me to be sorry?"

"Do you expect *me* to give up so easily?"

"Is that a trick question?" Eli fires back.

"Were you expecting one?" I ask, and Eli smirks.

He's not in costume. Or at least not any more than usual. He's like a character from one of those teen dramas where everyone sprinkles their vocabulary with four-syllable words and even the unpopular kids dress like they're runway models. His look has always been nerd chic. Think sweater-vests and bow ties and loafers with tassels on the toe, all found after hours of careful rummaging through the good Goodwill, out west.

He's currently wearing oversize librarian frames, tortoiseshell, with a little gold chain that goes around his neck.

I know that if this were a movie, Eli would slot fairly easily into the gay-best-friend trope, but I think that's just because people are uncomfortable with guys exhibiting an interest in stereotypically "girly" things like fashion and baking. Not that it matters, but he isn't gay.

Honestly, the question thing can go on for a while, so I'm going to jump ahead to when Eli asks if my shoes are vintage and I blurt "Yes!" even though I'm thinking *How did you know?*, I groan, and Eli does a little victory cheer.

"Yesterday you said you weren't going to come in," Eli says. I can hear the *Didn't you?* hovering at the end of his sentence, but he presses his lips together to stop himself from uttering it. He already won; he doesn't have to rub it in.

"Ms. Perez told me I'd get a failing grade if I didn't hand in my homework in person." I manage to yank my locker open and stop an avalanche of books before they come crashing to my feet. "So here I am."

"I'm into whatever look you're going for, even if you are here under protest," Eli adds, looking me up and down. "It's very *Craft*-era Fairuza Balk."

I wasn't trying for that, but I still appreciate the comment. I'm wearing a black dress for court, and I've borrowed Claire's— formerly *my*—vintage loafers, to honor her, sort of. I suppose I've got a slight goth-schoolgirl look happening.

"Thanks," I say. Nineties-era fashion has always been the point at which our interests intersect. We used to hit Scout and Thrift

America and all the other good vintage stores every weekend, but I can't remember the last time we did that.

Eli leans against his locker, absently pushing the padlock back and forth with one finger. It looks like he wants to say something else.

"Spit it out," I tell him.

"It's nothing. It's just . . . Millie and X are at our table. You should stop by and hang for a bit. They miss you." He says this in a voice that's trying very hard not to sound hopeful, which just makes me feel guiltier.

Omaha East is a massive downtown school. There are at least five hundred students in each grade, which means you only ever really get to know the people in the same classes with you. I've known Eli since kindergarten, so we've always been a package deal, but for the last three years we've made a point of hanging with the other honors kids, Millie and X, and, sometimes, Sierra Clayton. We'd all study together during free periods and take over the corner table in the cafeteria before school, books spread between us as we tried to get a little early-morning reading done before our first classes. Eli, X, and I were locked in a three-way tie for class valedictorian, our GPAs so close that a single point on a single quiz would've been enough to sway things one way or another. Someone would usually bring coffee and doughnuts from O-Town Dough, and we'd all share notes and flash cards and conspire about how we were going to ace Mr. Belvedere's pop quiz or gossip about the pretentious way Madame Feldman said "*tous les jours.*" God, it was nice, like having our own tiny private world.

But that was before Claire died. Before Millie and X started *How to Be a Final Girl*. Before my parents split up and my dad started drinking and everything in my life turned to crap.

Thinking about my old friends now causes a deeply sad feeling to open up inside me. Nostalgia or anger, all of it mixed up with grief over Claire. Before I can stop myself, I think of what Millie said on the podcast:

If this were a scary movie, the whole Owen thing would feel way too easy, like a giant misdirect.

I have to hold my breath to keep from screaming.

My senior year wasn't supposed to be like this. Nothing was supposed to be like this.

Your Friends Aren't Really Your Friends

Omaha East's cafeteria is inside the school's enclosed courtyard. The courtyard used to be open-air, but they closed it up when people realized how ridiculous it was to expect students to shiver through frigid Nebraska winters in order to get to a science class on the other side of the building.

The rest of Omaha East might be grungy and falling apart, with shoddy air-conditioning and cockroaches in the basement, but the courtyard is actually pretty epic. It reminds me of one of those impossibly cool high schools that seem to exist only in teen movies. X and I used to talk about how amazing it would be to film a slasher here, how the flickering gas lamps in the courtyard are the perfect touch for a really good Act One jump-scare scene.

I push that thought out of my head and instead run through everything I want to say as I follow Eli to our old table. I'm going to do it; I'm going to tell Millie and X exactly what I think of their stupid podcast.

Or at least that's the plan. But then I hear Millie's voice.

". . . remember how she painted herself *green*?" Millie has an abnormally loud voice at the best of times, but when everyone is talking in hushed, early-morning whispers, it actually echoes, like she's using a megaphone.

A shudder goes through me. Eli and I stop behind her, but Millie's facing the other direction, so she doesn't see us.

X, sitting across from her, does. "Millie," he murmurs.

Millie must not hear the warning in his voice. "You remember that, right? It was for *Wicked* auditions? God, that was cool."

Eli shoots me a sideways glance. I ignore him, too focused on the pit opening up inside my chest.

Millie's talking about my sister, of course. I should've figured everyone would be talking about her today. Specifically, she's talking about how Claire got cast as the lead in *Wicked* when she was just a freshman. Omaha East is serious about the performing arts; people who don't even have kids here buy tickets for our fall musical. Freshmen never get cast in speaking roles, but Claire was determined. She knew she was good enough, but she was worried they'd bury her in some chorus role, so she made it clear she was going out for Elphaba by slathering green body paint all over herself during auditions.

What Eli and Millie probably don't remember was how her skin was stained green for a week afterward. She had to do this really intense bleaching treatment to get all the green out. It made our hall smell toxic for weeks.

"Hey, Allie," X says pointedly. Millie stops talking in the middle of the word *amazing*, and I hear her chair groan as she turns to look at me. A blush appears on her naturally tan skin.

X and Millie are dressed up like Bonnie and Clyde, with fake gunshot wounds and everything, probably some sort of inside reference from their podcast that I don't get because I normally refuse to listen on principle. Millie's had her hair cut short since the last time I saw her, and it's half-hidden by her beret.

I stare at the beret so I don't have to meet her eyes.

"Alice," Millie breathes. "I'm so—"

"It's fine," I murmur before she can apologize. Dimly, I remember that I was going to say something to her about the podcast, but I can't remember what it was. My head's too full of Claire and bleach and *Wicked*.

I want to ask Millie if she remembers how Claire sneaked us into the wrap party, even though we were only in middle school and so embarrassing. How I felt so proud of her that night, like she was a real celebrity and not just the star of a high school play. My famous sister, Claire.

I clear my throat so none of the emotion I'm feeling comes out in my voice and say, "I'm not staying. Ms. Perez wanted to see me . . ."

The world's most awkward silence gathers between us like a dear friend. Why, hello, awkward silence; so nice to see you again. What exactly are you supposed to say to the people who used to be your best friends and now talk about your dead sister on their obnoxiously well-liked podcast? *I listened to your last episode, and it made me want to vomit blood, but the new mics are sounding pretty good.*

Oh God. I wish the floor would open up and swallow me. I wish this were like a movie I was watching on Netflix and I could just fast-forward through this scene.

What did I think coming over here was going to accomplish? This isn't scripted; I'm not going to magically figure out the perfect thing to say to make things go back to the way they were.

X flashes me one of his megawatt smiles. Normally, I can't help smiling back at him. But I think of his voice buzzing in my ear (*Watch any horror movie—the prettiest girl always dies first*) and feel the corners of my lips tighten.

X's smile falters. "Uh, Millie was just going to tell us all about Sierra's new secret boyfriend."

It's an offering, his way of trying to make this not awkward, as though that's even possible.

Play nice, I think.

"Um, Sierra has a boyfriend?" I don't know Sierra too well, but this is actually sort of interesting. It's a pretty open secret that she hasn't dated anyone since she started high school. This shouldn't be a scandal. I mean, *I* haven't dated anyone, either. But Sierra . . . how do I put this? Sierra has D cups. So, according to the gross adolescent mutants who go to our high school, her being single is basically a Shakespearean tragedy. Never even occurred to them that she might not be interested in their misogynistic asses.

"Secret boyfriend. Key word being *secret.*" Millie shoots X a look, but she doesn't seem particularly annoyed. Millie loves gossip. You don't tell her something unless you're ready for the whole world to hear about it. If Sierra doesn't know that by now, it's her own fault the secret's out.

"Does he go here?" I ask.

Millie hesitates—her final concession to the fact that this is supposed to be a secret—and then expels a long breath, giving in. "No, I think he went to Mercer. She told me she met him at the gym."

"He's a college kid?"

Millie shakes her head. "Used to be. Sierra said he got kicked out."

I go still as X makes a joke I don't catch, and Millie rolls her eyes and says something about how we don't live in *Riverdale.* I barely hear them. I stopped listening after "he got kicked out."

Eli, who knows every one of my secrets, stiffens beside me, realizing what I've already worked out. His face falls as he glances at me. "Allie—"

I hold up a hand, stopping him. I'd completely forgotten what I came here to do, why I thought this was a good idea. I feel like my lungs are filling with water. Like I'm drowning.

"I— I gotta go," I murmur, backing up.

X stands. "Alice, wait."

My body is frozen, even as my brain whispers, *Run away, run away.*

"I just wanted to say that we, uh . . ." X trails off, looking at Millie.

"We wanted to say that we're sorry," Millie adds. "About the podcast. Some of our followers are truthers, but we don't think you're lying or anything."

"Right. Yeah," I say. And with that, I turn and hurry for the door on the opposite side of the room, cheeks burning.

"Alice, hold up," Eli calls. I hear his shoes slap against the stone floor behind me, and then he's grabbing my shoulders, spinning me around. In a low voice, he asks, "You think Sierra's dating Wes?"

I shrug, trying to look like I couldn't care less, which probably just makes it clear that I care a lot.

Eli told me that he'd heard Wes got kicked out of Mercer at the end of last year. Something about a fight or maybe an illegal casino night he was running out of his dorm. The rumors weren't totally clear, which is very on-brand for Wes.

I really don't want him to be dating Sierra.

Trapezius, I think, running through the names of the muscles in the back. *Deltoid* and . . . and I can't remember anything after that. Something pricks my eyes, but it's probably just dry in here. I'm not crying. I used up all my tears after Claire. I don't have any left.

I haven't spoken to Wes since Claire died, our almost-relationship just another thing on the long list of casualties from that night. But I still feel a twist in my gut when I think of him dating Sierra. I have the sudden urge to kick a chair, to slam a door.

When am I going to stop being surprised by all the things I've lost, all the things that suck now that never sucked before?

"Are you going to be okay?" Eli asks.

"Yeah," I say automatically. I don't have even the slightest idea what "okay" feels like anymore, but I'm going to keep moving and thinking and talking, and I guess that's close enough.

Eli looks like he wants to say something else, but all that comes out is, "Yeah, that's good." He pushes his glasses up his nose with one finger, adding, "You should avoid the third floor. I heard some of the Final Girls are hanging out there."

A chill moves through me. The Final Girls are what the *How to Be a Final Girl* fans all call themselves. Over the past week, they've become obnoxiously insistent that Owen Trevor Maddox is innocent.

It wouldn't bother me so much if they didn't keep trying to talk to me. Like they think they can convince me that I didn't see what I know I saw. I feel another rush of hate toward Millie and X. Assholes.

"Thanks," I tell Eli, and I step into the hall, letting the cafeteria door slam shut behind me.

Final Girls Do It in a Cornfield

Ms. Perez's office door isn't locked. It creaks open when I knock.

She has her coffee cup halfway to her lips, but she sets it back down on her desk when I poke my head into the room. "Alice," she says brightly. "You came."

"You threatened me with a failing grade if I didn't." I hover awkwardly, still halfway in the hall. Ms. Perez's closet-size office is a time machine: cartoonish purple-and-pink flowered curtains, oversize coffee mugs, and an actual honest-to-God lava lamp sitting on her desk. It looks like the dorm room from *Urban Legend*. (Another '90s slasher. Gory. Terrible. I've seen it twelve times.)

Ms. Perez completes the picture: At thirty-five, she's not even one of the younger teachers here, but she still dresses like a college student. Her oversize button-downs are always a tad wrinkled, her dark hair swept up in a perpetually messy bun. The only sign that she puts any effort into her appearance is her makeup, flawless red lips and perfectly winged eyeliner peeking out from behind sensible black-framed glasses.

"Last year you wouldn't have needed that incentive to turn in your homework." Ms. Perez takes the paper from my hand and plucks a red pen from the jar on her desk, biting off the cap.

"You're going to correct that in front of me?"

"Your classwork isn't where I'd hoped it would be this year," she says through a mouthful of pen cap. "You seem . . . bored." As though to punctuate the statement, she draws a firm red X through my first problem.

I frown down at the paper, unable to stop myself from wondering what I did wrong. "How can you think I'm bored if I'm missing problems?"

"Sometimes we don't put forth our best efforts when we aren't being challenged." Ms. Perez glances up at me, light reflecting off her glasses so that I can't quite see her eyes. She spits her pen cap onto her desk, sending it rolling into a potted plant. "It looks like you spent about five minutes on this."

Less than that, truthfully. I did the entire assignment before Michael Myers finished killing his family in the first five minutes of *Halloween*. I shrug. "So?"

"So I thought you needed to take calculus if you wanted to be on the premed track in college. I expected to see you in my AP class, not slumming it in Algebra Two."

I can't help the lump that forms in my throat. AP Calc was the plan, just like the summer internship at Mercer was the plan, followed by a full ride through their premed program and, if I was feeling brave, medical school somewhere cool and far from the Midwest. The University of Washington or NYU or (dare I even dream) Johns Hopkins.

But that was before. Before Claire died, before my family imploded. My forensic pathologist dream feels like kid stuff now, like wishing to be a ballerina or an astronaut or the president. Now my big goals include seeing Owen Trevor Maddox behind bars, watching every horror movie on Netflix, and getting through high school, in exactly that order. Everything else is background noise.

"I'm not doing premed anymore." I study the smudged crescent of lipstick Ms. Perez left behind on her coffee mug so I don't have to look at the disappointment on her face.

It's not like Ms. Perez and I are close or anything. She was my Honors Algebra 1 teacher freshman year, and she was encouraging, I guess. She always said she was impressed by how quickly I could commit new formulas to memory, and when I told her I wanted to be a doctor, she gave me the information on the Mercer internship, but that's all. It's not like she's the Hannibal Lecter to my Clarice Starling. She's just a teacher. She doesn't have any right to feel disappointed with me just because I changed my mind.

And yet she sighs deeply, like I just told her I'm going to dedicate the rest of my life to alpaca farming.

"Here." She slides a bowl of individually wrapped Life Savers across her desk. "It's too early. The sugar will wake you up."

I take one, fumbling with the wrapper. "My mom's waiting outside. I should probably go meet her."

"The trial starts today, doesn't it?"

I nod, and then I unwrap the Life Saver and stick it in my mouth before she can ask me any more questions, letting the sour-green-apple taste spread over my tongue.

"Good luck," Ms. Perez says. "I mean it. I can't imagine how difficult it's going to be to sit through something like that."

I heard somewhere that people say "I can't imagine" only about things they can imagine perfectly and wish they couldn't.

"Thank you," I mutter, and step out the into the hall.

"And, Alice?" Ms. Perez calls after me. I hesitate, glancing back at her. "If you change your mind about AP Calc, there's still a spot for you. All you have to do is say the word."

For some reason, that's the thing that really gets to me. Ms. Perez still thinks there's a chance that I could have the future I always dreamed of. She thinks it's as simple as enrolling in the right classes, going to college, moving on.

I don't know how to tell her that there isn't any moving on. Not for me. My life ended the night of Chloe Bree's Halloween party, when I let my sister go into that corn maze alone. The memory of it plays through my head on a loop.

Her heading toward the corn. *If you don't come with me, I might die.*

And me just . . . walking away. At that moment, it didn't matter how many scary movies I'd seen or how well I knew the rules and the clichés. I just let it happen. I let my sister die.

I chew through the rest of the Life Saver, trying to ignore the lump forming in my throat. I would give anything in this world to go back to that moment. To change it. But I can't, and I have to live with that knowledge forever. My sister's dead and it's all my fault. The world is forever altered, forever worse, because of something I did.

"I won't change my mind," I say, and then I hurry back into the hall, beelining for the stairwell as tears turn my eyesight blurry.

I don't cry in front of people. It was the one rule I made for myself after Claire's death. No public displays of mourning, no falling apart at school. I didn't want to be that girl, the grieving girl, the one whose entire identity was wrapped up in her sister's murder.

I make it down three stairs, four, when—

Bam.

It's Sidney again, the same girl who practically knocked me over on the front stairs. This time she slams right into me. The air leaves my lungs in a *whoof*, and then she's in my face, talking so fast I can barely make out her words.

"Holy mother of fuck. I *swear* I didn't see you there. Are you okay? Did I get you good? You aren't bleeding, so it can't be that bad . . . or, wait, *are* you bleeding? I don't see blood, but sometimes that shit can be internal—"

"I'm fine, it's fine," I say, waving her off. I do my best to wipe the tears from my face without her noticing, more embarrassed by the fact that I've been discovered crying than hurt.

"You sure?" The girl looks even more like Sidney Prescott up close. She has the exact same strong jaw and good eyebrows, the same faint spray of freckles all over her cheeks. I haven't seen her around before, I realize. But like I said, the school's massive, so that doesn't mean much. She could be a freshman, or she could be new, or maybe she's actually Neve Campbell and she's enrolled here undercover for a role. Reese Witherspoon did that over at Papillion High to prepare for *Election*.

No, she's way too young to be the real Neve Campbell. I wonder if people are constantly telling her she looks like her? Probably not. No one my age knows that Neve Campbell is the actress who played the Final Girl in *Scream* unless they're obsessed with old horror movies, like me.

Sidney or whatever her name is stares at me for a moment, head cocked like she's waiting for me to answer a question.

"I'm sorry, did you say something?" I ask.

"I asked you if you're sure that you're okay." Her voice is so sincere that there's a part of me that wants to answer her for real. *No, as a matter of fact, I am not okay. I haven't been okay for three hundred and sixty-four days. I'll never be okay again.* I can practically feel the words forming on my tongue. They taste sour and sweet, like green-apple Life Savers.

And then I look down. At some point in the last hour, Sidney took her sweatshirt off and tied it around her waist. She's wearing a T-shirt underneath. It's black, with the words FINAL GIRLS DO IT IN A CORNFIELD written in red ink that's supposed to look like blood.

Disgust and anger curdle inside me. Some inside joke from Millie and X's podcast, I'm sure. Which means she's one of them, an Owen Trevor Maddox truther. She thinks that the piece of shit who murdered my sister should walk free.

I'm not a violent person. I've never understood how someone could kill another human being. But right now, at this moment, I feel hate roaring through me. It's a feeling I've only ever experienced when I think about Owen Trevor Maddox.

This girl, this incredibly stupid, incredibly lucky girl gets to go to school and dress up like fictional characters and wear stupid T-shirts and listen to podcasts and come up with stupid conspiracy theories about murderers.

And my sister will never do any of those things again, because she's dead.

I could strangle her. I really think I could.

I settle for jamming my shoulder into hers and muttering "Your T-shirt is disgusting" as I walk past.

Keep Away from Bad Boys

A huge group of people have gathered on the steps outside the courthouse. Most of them are carrying signs: JUSTICE FOR CLAIRE! and REMEMBER CLAIRE! and things like that. I feel a lift of something unfamiliar when I see them. Hope, maybe? I don't think this trial will change anything—Claire will always be dead—but all these people who didn't even know her made signs and showed up to tell the world that this kind of thing is evil and should be punished. That has to be worth something.

Or maybe they just want to be on TV, a cynical voice inside me whispers. And just like that, the hope is dead. Goodbye, hope. I suppose it was nice while it lasted.

Traffic's brutal. I'm still in the car with my mom, slowly inching closer to the courthouse parking lot, when I spot Wesley James Hanson III. He's camped out beneath a tree a few yards from the crowd, long legs stretched across the dry grass, hair falling over his face.

He looks . . . different than I remember. Scruffier, angrier. Gone are the little out-of-place details I used to love, the argyle socks and the pearls. I can imagine this version of Wes getting kicked out of school for fighting and gambling much more easily than I can imagine him wearing a Hello Kitty barrette or texting me Eleanor Roosevelt quotes. It's like he's a different person entirely.

I recognize him because he's wearing the same navy peacoat he wore every day last fall, collar turned up against the wind. No one else I know has a coat like that. It looks like it cost more than my parents' car.

My stomach does a weird kind of spasming thing when I see him, cycling through feeling sick and then excited and then nervous before finally settling on cautiously horrified. It sort of feels like menstrual cramps.

As I watch, he tips something toward his mouth. Coffee?

I lean forward, eyes narrowing as I peer through the window. Nope, not coffee. It's a flask. Jesus, it's not even nine in the morning.

"I'm going to get out here and walk," I say.

Mom turns to me, blinking like she's only just remembered I was sitting next to her. "What?"

"I'll see you inside, okay?" The car's not moving, so I throw my door open and climb out, head ducked as I weave through cars and past the crowd, over to where Wes is sitting. Sprawled across the dead grass, he looks like a character from a prestige drama. A disgraced prince, maybe, or the bastard son of some politician.

If I were writing this moment into a script, I wouldn't be able to resist adding a little internal monologue. *Alice knew she should turn around and walk in the other direction* . . .

He spots me coming when I'm still a few yards away and leans his head back against the tree trunk, an unreadable expression on his face. It's the first time we've been this close to each other in a year, but if he's surprised to see me, he doesn't let it show.

"Hi," I say, stopping about three feet from where he's sitting.

"Hi," Wes says through a yawn. His hair is long and curly and wet. I want to tell him it's going to frizz in the dry air, but why would I do that? He doesn't care. He probably did it on purpose. He's the kind of guy who's hot enough to pull off hair that looks like shit.

"I, um, I heard . . ." I'm going to ask him about Sierra, but then his dark brown eyes zero in on my face like a spotlight, and I completely lose my nerve. "I heard you got kicked out of school," I say instead.

Wes drops his eyes, letting them linger on my bare legs. It makes me think of the first time we talked, when he complimented my suspenders, and for a second, I think he's going to say something about my loafers—*Claire's* loafers. I can see it so clearly, how he'll say something flirty, and then I'll say something flirty, and then I'll ask if he's seen any good movies, and it'll be just like it was last year, just like it was before everything went to shit.

Something inside of me tenses up. I thought I was done wanting things, but maybe not. Maybe I want this.

But after an artfully long moment, Wes just shrugs. "It was a misunderstanding."

"Oh."

He shifts his eyes back up to my face. "Is that why you came over here? To ask me about school?"

"No."

"Because you haven't talked to me for a year. And I texted you." Wes studies me. "A lot."

The timbre of his voice is lower than usual and a little gravelly. I look down at him, frowning. He sounds upset, but his expression is normal enough. Maybe I imagined it.

I don't know what to say. He sent me seventeen texts over the last year. I read all of them at least three times. There were quotes from songs about loss, old presidential speeches, and kids' books. My favorite was this Shel Silverstein poem about two people who were blue and didn't know it because they hid their blueness from the world. I sort of thought the blue thing was a metaphor, like maybe Wes was talking about us, how we were both weirdos. Maybe that's why he liked me.

At some point, he stopped sending me quotes and started sending me questions. *Hey, are you mad at me? Hey, do you want me to leave you alone?*

I could never bring myself to write back. Not once. Every time I looked at my phone and tried to come up with something, I'd think about how I wanted to ask Claire what I should say. But I couldn't. Claire was never going to text a boy ever again. She was never going to have another crush or another kiss or another date. She was in the ground.

And once I started thinking about all that, it seemed unfair that *I* would get any of those things. That I should be happy, even for a second.

I wet my lips. I should say something. It's been too long since I've spoken. But when I search my mind, I come up blank. I used to find it so easy to talk to Wes. Or . . . well, I guess not *easy*, but . . . natural, sort of. Being this close to him would cause every nerve in my body to fire at the same time, but I always knew which words to use to make him laugh or think or roll his eyes. It was thrilling, like discovering I was fluent in a foreign language. Most of the guys I knew from school were like Eli and X, geeky and smart. Wes is different. Or he *was* different. I don't know what he is anymore.

I shift my eyes to my feet and then back up to his face. Wes is staring at me like I've grown a second head, but I can't figure out how to end this conversation without looking stupid.

"Then why did you?" Wes asks after a million years. I've grown up, died, and been reincarnated as another nerdy girl who has absolutely nothing to say.

I blink. It's been so long that I've forgotten how to speak. I'm pretty sure my larynx has closed up. Maybe reincarnated me wasn't born with a larynx.

"What?" I croak. A miracle.

"Why did you come over here?"

Oh, that. I release a short, unamused laugh. "I honestly don't know."

Wes is quiet for an uncomfortably long time. He reminds me of something carved from a hunk of wood or a big slab of stone. He's a sculpture, proof that even ancient Romans understood the value of a bad boy.

Was he this stoic last year? I don't think so. I want to ask him what's changed, if he's mad at me or mad at the world. I want to know if he still has the Hello Kitty barrette. But I feel like I don't have the right to ask any of those things anymore. Maybe Sierra didn't like the barrettes and the socks and the nail polish. Maybe that's why he's so different.

After a while, he stands, groaning slightly as he dusts the dirt from his jeans. I brace myself, expecting him to just walk away, making it perfectly clear where I rank on his list of priorities. Instead, he offers me his flask.

I hesitate. It's really early. And I'm supposed to testify later.

Screw it, I think. I take the flask and drink—

And immediately start coughing.

Wes is watching me, a smile curling his lips. "Too strong for you?"

"It's orange juice," I say, swallowing.

"Yeah, well, I skipped breakfast."

"You don't have a normal water bottle?" I ask, then realize he probably doesn't. Wes would never buy something so practical for himself. I hand the flask back to him. "Thank you."

"Anytime," he says. But he's looking over my shoulder now, distracted. I turn, following his gaze.

A flash of white-blond hair leaps out of the crowd, followed by a glimmer of red the exact color of blood. I flinch as the blond girl lifts her arm, something about that small movement triggering a memory:

I'm not standing under a tree with Wes anymore. I'm in the corn maze, and Chloe Bree is stumbling toward me, her eyes vacant, blood gushing out of the stump where her arm used to be . . .

I blink three times, fast, and the memory of Chloe Bree fades. The real-life Chloe Bree is standing on the courthouse steps just a few yards away, though, wearing a T-shirt with the words I WAS NUMBER 1 written across it in red.

Her empty shirt sleeve flaps in the wind, and I can't help but stare. Chloe lost her softball scholarship after Owen cut her arm off. She's given interviews saying she wished he'd just killed her, that it's worse for her living this way. I sort of understand where she's coming from. My dad always said Chloe was the one to watch, that she was good enough to make the Olympic team if she kept up with her training. Of course, that's not going to happen anymore.

Two other girls stand beside her. Like Chloe, they're both wearing T-shirts instead of carrying signs. Their shirts read I WAS NUMBER 2 and I WAS NUMBER 3.

Oh God, I think, and a shimmer of horror moves through me as I look from the girls' T-shirts to their faces. I know who they are. Everyone knows who they are.

They're Owen's victims.

Or they would have been his victims, if it wasn't for Claire.

Three days after my sister's murder, the police found a manifesto uploaded to this incel blog, AlphaMaleNet. It was ninety pages of misogynistic ramblings, complete with a list of three names:

Chloe Bree.

Erin Cleary.

Sierra Clayton.

The police traced the manifesto back to Owen Trevor Maddox. The names, they concluded, were his future victims. The theory goes that Owen had been planning a murder spree starting on Halloween night, with Chloe Bree in the corn maze. Only Claire had been in the corn maze too, and she'd stopped him.

This part is all conjecture, as Millie and X so helpfully pointed out. Chloe doesn't remember anything about the attack itself, only waking up with her arm missing. I'm the only witness. If it hadn't been for the manifesto, Owen might've actually gotten away. The police figure that Claire saw Owen go after Chloe with the chain saw and stabbed him with her pocketknife to stop him while Chloe escaped and found me. Owen had been planning on going after the other two girls on his list after killing Chloe, but Claire ruined his plan, so he killed her instead. She stopped the horror movie before it could happen. She was a hero.

Now Owen's would-be victims are lined up outside the courthouse, forcing everyone to remember what he would've done if my sister hadn't stopped him.

Looking at them, I'm struck by a horrible thought: Why did my sister have to die for them? She wasn't even on that list. She should've been safe.

"Figured this place would be a circus," Wes mutters, eyeing the girls lined up on the courthouse steps.

I follow his gaze to Sierra and feel a drop in my stomach, any doubt I had about whether they're together vanishing. She looks beautiful and brave standing on the courthouse steps, like some sort of warrior princess. She's small and curvy, with long dark curls, the lead in a Marvel movie, the kind of girl every guy immediately falls in love with. If Wes is the always-stylish bad boy, she's the girl who belongs on his arm. You'd never find a girl like her slumming it in some horror flick. Not like me.

She's so much more Wes's type than I ever was. He's probably here to support her. He barely even knew Claire.

"Why do you think Owen chose them?" I ask. It's the one thing that wasn't in his manifesto. Why Chloe and Erin and Sierra? What did the three of them have in common? "I mean, I don't think they were friends."

Wes turns back to me, his eyes searching mine. His expression is complicated all of a sudden, mysterious things zipping past his dark eyes.

After a long moment, he shrugs and looks away. "Who knows? People hide all sorts of—"

"Alice? Alice Lawrence?" A reporter has spotted me and separated from the crowd of people gathered around the courthouse steps. "Alice, can I ask you a few questions?"

He doesn't wait for me to answer but waves over a short, skinny guy carrying an oversize camera. My pulse picks up.

Shit.

"I— I should probably go," I murmur, already backing away. Wes stares at the reporter, frowning.

The reporter and the cameraman are only a few feet away now. I catch a BC on the official-looking press credentials dangling from their necks, which means national news, not local. I get to make a fool of myself in front of the whole country instead of just my own state. Fantastic.

When Wes looks back at me, the line of his mouth is tighter, his eyes narrowed. I've never seen him like this before, but his face settles so easily into the expression that I know instantly it's one he wears often. Maybe even always. He looks like a wild dog. He looks *feral*.

I think of every single violent rumor I've heard about him.

He steps between the reporter and me, seeming to grow a few inches as he straightens to his full—considerable—height. "I'm going to need you to back up, man."

"Wes, don't," I say, touching his arm. His body is rigid beneath my hand, and I have a fraction of a fraction of a second to think, *Holy crap, he really is carved from stone.*

The reporter grins. "Come on, Alice, tell your guard dog to stand down." He tries to move past Wes.

I conjure the dirtiest look I can manage. "Screw you."

"Wait, are the two of you dating?" he says with a snicker. "That'll make a great opening line. 'Sister of murder victim finds love with'—"

Wes's knuckles flash. There's a popping sound and the reporter drops. It happens that fast.

"Oh my God, *stop!*" I grab Wes by the arm and attempt to pull him back, but it's impossible. He's all muscle, and he has no intention of going anywhere. It's like trying to move a tree or a boulder. I say, my voice full of warning, "Wes, *stop!*"

Wes glances at me and the wild-dog look fades from his face, but not quick enough.

I really don't know him at all, I think.

He takes a step back, hands lifted. "You stay the hell away from her," he says, and spits on the grass next to the reporter, who's moaning now and clutching his nose. Then, looking back at me, he adds, "You're gonna want to get inside before the cops show up."

Watch Your Head

I'm panting when I meet my mom and the district attorney's assistant, Nora, at the courthouse's back entrance, like I've just run a mile. I don't know whether Wes was joking about the cops showing up, but he's right. I'm not sticking around for that.

"Alice? Good, you're here. You ready?" Nora is tall and beautiful, with light brown skin, freckles, and impossibly shiny hair. She reminds me a little of Meghan Markle—*Suits* Meghan Markle, not Princess Meghan Markle. "You guys both ate, right? Do you need a granola bar or something? An apple? I think there's a vending machine around the corner . . ."

My mom shakes her head, and Nora turns her huge dark eyes on me, waiting.

"I'm fine," I mutter. Usually I grab a piece of toast before heading out the door, but this morning, I got up early to rewatch *Halloween,* and I don't actually remember whether I ever pulled my eyes away from the screen long enough to eat. I can still taste the orange juice from Wes's flask.

Nora shuffles us through the door, her high heels clacking against the marble floors. Now that we're inside the courthouse, today feels more real than it did before. Specifically, the part where I'm going to see my sister's murderer again. Owen's bail was set high because of the violence of his crime, but I read in the news about some advocacy group that did a fundraiser to send him home.

I cried the day they let him out. For twenty-four hours, I was convinced I was about to star in Claire's murder: the sequel. I was that sure Owen was coming for me next, that I was going to see him around every street corner, that he was hiding on the other side of every closed door. But then I heard he went to live with his brother in Crawford, which is this tiny town all the way on the opposite side of Nebraska.

And now he's back. He's back, and in just a few minutes, the two of us will be in the same room for the first time in a year. I've been trying not to think about that.

"Are you sure you're not hungry?" Nora is asking, frowning. "Because once we get inside, things can get a bit—"

We round a corner, and her words are lost beneath a sudden roar of shouting voices and footsteps. There are reporters everywhere. They all have brightly lit cameras and microphones, and as soon as they see me, they swarm.

"Alice, have you been called to testify against Owen Trevor Maddox?"

"Alice, how do you feel about seeing your sister's murderer?"

"Alice, there are people who doubt what you say you saw."

Alice! Alice! Alice!

I put a hand to my face, shielding my eyes from the lights. I feel dizzy all of a sudden. My eyesight blurs, and my knees buckle. I'm sure I didn't eat that piece of toast after all, and I'm suddenly desperate for food, any food. The granola bar or apple that Nora promised, or anything from a vending machine, or even just a single swallow of water, something to keep my hollowed-out stomach from turning itself inside out.

"Alice? Alice, how are you doing?"

It's Nora again. I shake my head, my way of saying *Not good* and *Get me out of here* without having to use my words. Luckily for me, she's done this before, so she understands. She nods once, curtly, and begins cutting through the reporters, a modern-day Moses parting the Red Sea.

"They can't follow us into the courtroom," she says, and I nod. I have a destination now—the courtroom. I picture the windowless walls and the wooden chairs in my head until I can practically feel them around me. The doors are straight ahead. Just a few more feet . . .

And then something happens. The crowd turns like the tide, heads moving away from me, voices lowering and then rising again. Only they aren't saying my name anymore. They're saying his.

Owen! Owen! Owen!

I inhale and hold the breath inside my lungs, turning on instinct. He's easy to find in the crowd, all those cameras pointing at him, lights flashing so that he seems to be glowing.

Owen Trevor Maddox. He looks just like he does in my nightmares, just like every bad guy in every slasher movie I've ever seen. His long black hair has been pulled into a ponytail at the back of his neck, and he's wearing a suit and tie, his dark eyes carefully trained on the floor. In the light coming off the cameras, his acne scars look more pronounced, and I can see a patch of dark hair on his chin that he missed shaving.

And then, like a predator suddenly made aware of the presence of food, Owen's nostrils flick and he lifts those eyes and looks at me, right at me, almost like he can sense me standing on the other side of the crowd, closer than I've been since that night in the cornfield.

The breath I'd been holding escapes from between my lips in a steady stream, air leaking from a balloon.

Those eyes. I'd forgotten how black they were, like two pools of oil. There's nothing inside of those eyes, no emotion, no remorse.

They're evil, I think, and the hair on the back of my neck stands straight up. Pure evil.

Owen keeps looking at me until the courtroom doors fly open and someone, some man in a suit, ushers him inside. The air in the hall seems to shift the moment he leaves, like how the pressure changes after a storm blows through.

Oh God—

I'm going to be sick.

I pull away from my mom and Nora and race down the hall to the bathroom. Damp air and tile the color of overcooked salmon greet me when I slap the door open. I stumble into a stall and crouch over the toilet, fingers curling around cold porcelain as I heave. My stomach churns, and a sour taste clings to my tongue, but nothing comes up.

My head spins. I close my eyes.

You can do this, come on, pull yourself together, you have to do this . . .

Outside my stall, a door opens and closes. A faucet switches on. I open my eyes, instantly alert.

I'm no longer alone in here.

I give my head a firm shake and flush the toilet. Water swirls around and around the bowl. I suck down ragged gasps of air as I watch it slip down, down, down the drain. And then I stand and push the stall door open.

Sidney is at the sink, washing her hands. She's still wearing her FINAL GIRLS DO IT IN A CORNFIELD T-shirt.

"You." I spit the word like it's a curse.

She looks up, catching my eye in the mirror above the sink. "Hey, Alice, I thought I saw you run in here."

"You know my name now?"

"You're the only witness in the biggest crime this city has ever seen. Everyone knows your name." She jabs the dryer with her elbow and starts shaking her hands dry. "You're Beyoncé."

"Whatever," I mutter, making my way to the door.

"You're about to put an innocent person away for the rest of his life." Sidney raises her voice so I can hear her over the dryer. "You sure you're okay with that?"

I freeze with my hand resting on the bathroom door, my blood boiling.

"There's no evidence against Owen," she continues. She's done drying her hands and now she leans over the sink, uncapping a tube of ChapStick. "They couldn't prove he bought the chain saw or the mask. You know they even looked under that chick Chloe's fingernails to see if she, like, scratched her attacker or whatever? And they didn't find any of Owen's skin cells or his DNA. Nothing."

Just leave, I tell myself. Ignore her.

"Your testimony is the only thing they're using to convict him. Are you really comfortable with that?" She smacks her lips, caps her ChapStick. "You really think you're gonna be able to sleep at night?"

I shouldn't engage, I know I shouldn't engage, but it pisses me off when people get things so completely wrong.

"No other evidence?" I say, finally turning around. "What about his manifesto? All his future victims? How do you explain that?"

The girl cocks an eyebrow at me, dark eyes glinting, and I realize too late that this is exactly what she wanted me to say, that I've played right into her hands. "How do you know Owen wrote that manifesto? The cops traced it to a computer in a public library."

I grit my teeth. "Owen was the last person who logged on to that computer."

"Wrong again." The girl's smiling now—actually smiling, like this is all some big joke. She takes a second to adjust her bangs. "They know *someone* logged on to that computer using Owen's username and ID, but they can't prove it was him."

"I know what I saw." I feel calm enough, but my voice trembles, and there's a steady stream of sweat inching down my back. "Nothing you say is going to change my mind. Owen Trevor Maddox killed my sister. He deserves to spend the rest of his life rotting in a cell."

Sidney isn't smiling at me anymore. She looks sad and serious and, somehow, so much older than she did a moment ago. There are tiny little creases around her eyes and frown lines framing her mouth like two parentheses.

I feel a twinge of nerves. There's no way she's a high school student. I don't know why I ever thought she was.

"What exactly are you doing here?" I ask her.

"I'm not trying to convince you of anything, Alice; I swear," she says. "I just want you to understand the magnitude of what you're about to do. Your testimony is the key piece of evidence in a case that will forever change someone's life. If you're wrong, there won't be a single day that goes by that you don't regret it."

She's right, of course. Sending someone to prison for murder is heavy stuff, the kind of thing that stays with you.

But the thing is, I'm *not* wrong. I was there and this girl wasn't. I experienced my sister's murder, and she heard about it on some podcast.

"The only regret I have is not going with my sister into that maze when she asked me to." I tighten my grip on the bathroom door, and the cold metal digs into my palms, steadying me. "If I'd have done that, Claire would still be alive. And I could've killed Owen myself."

It's something I fantasize about often. I hear my sister's last words—*If you don't come with me, I might die*—and instead of walking away, I laugh and follow her into the dark.

If I'd done that, I would have been with her when she saw what Owen did to Chloe. I could have helped her. *Saved* her.

Sidney tilts her head, her eyelids dipping low over her eyes.

She says, "It'll be helpful if you remember that you asked for this."

I frown at her. "Is that supposed to be some kind of a threat—"

The bathroom door swings open behind me, smashing into the back of my head. Pain blisters through my skull.

And then.

Well. And then everything goes dark for a little while.

"Allie? Allie?"

The name pulls me up from unconsciousness. *Reporters again*, I think, groaning. They must've found me in the bathroom. I can just imagine the sort of pictures they're taking of me right now as I lie unconscious on the salmon-pink tile floor. The headline will read: *Only Witness in Claire Lawrence's Murder Faints in Bathroom while*

Arguing with Seriously Misguided Person. Or possibly something even more humiliating.

"Come on, open your eyes."

I keep my eyes clenched shut.

Maybe they'll think I'm dead.

"Allie, come on, I barely touched you. Are you really hurt? Do you need me to call Dad?"

Wait . . . *Dad?*

The voice continues. "Because if I call Dad, he's going to think you got a concussion, and he'll make you go to the emergency room for sure, and then we'll spend the whole night in the hospital just because you got a teensy-tiny little bump on your head. Do you want that, Alley Cat? Do you?"

Alley Cat. The nickname shoots through me like a spark. There's only one person in the entire world who calls me Alley Cat.

Called me Alley Cat.

I open my eyes.

She's leaning over me, red hair spilling over her shoulders, anime-character eyes wide and annoyed.

My sister, Claire.

She's alive.

Stay Out of the Cornfield

It's dark, but Claire's leaning close enough that I can make out her expression. It's a familiar one, or it used to be: lips pressed together hard, eyes a touch too wide, faux annoyed. I know what she's thinking even though she hasn't said the words out loud. They could be a cartoon dialogue bubble above her head.

Are you really still lying on the ground? Really?

I'd almost forgotten about this, how it used to feel like we could read each other's minds.

I stare up at my sister, hungrily watching each twitching muscle, the flare of her nostrils, her shifting eyes. This is Claire, distilled into a series of microscopic expressions. It seems impossible that she was ever like this, a constantly moving, changing person. For the last year, she's existed only in my imagination, a character in a scary movie, running the same lines over and over again.

Now her brows pinch in the middle, and the corner of her mouth curls. "Alice? Come on, this is getting seriously weird."

I sit up without realizing what I'm doing and reach for her face, half expecting it to break apart the second I touch it, like a reflection in water. But the skin beneath my fingers is really there, and it's really warm—

And then Claire jerks away from me. "Hey, watch the hands! You know I did a sheet mask this morning."

"Sheet mask," I murmur. A memory rises in my head, something I haven't thought of in a year: Claire dancing around in the bathroom before school, getting ready. She's got a sheet mask plastered over her face, and when I tell her she looks like Hannibal Lecter, she chases me, waving another mask.

"Your pores are screaming for help!" she shouts. "Save your skin!"

I blink and *poof*, the images vanish: just another Claire memory. I thought I'd used them all up by now, but I'd forgotten about that one.

"How are you . . . here? What's going on?" I look around, blinking.

And here's a fun new twist: I'm no longer in the courthouse bathroom. I'm lying on the ground outside and it's dark out. Seriously dark. No-moon, no-stars dark. I can't see more than half a foot in front of my damn face, and when I go to push myself to my feet—

Eww. Something slimy beneath my palm. Wet leaves, maybe? I flinch and pull my hand back. "Where are we?"

Claire blinks at me. "Are you okay? Maybe you hit your head when I ran into you?"

"You ran into me?"

"Yeah," she says slowly. "You came to find me, and I was running the other way because, wow, this is scarier than I thought it would be, and it was dark and—" She claps her hands together. "I'm sorry, Alley Cat; I didn't realize I hit you that hard."

I frown, thinking of the bathroom door at the courthouse, how it slammed into the back of my head. That must be why this is happening. I have a concussion or something, and now I'm having a hallucination. An incredibly realistic, incredibly vivid hallucination.

I bring a hand my head, feeling around for a bump or blood or even the slightly tender beginnings of a bruise.

I feel . . . hair. And scalp. No bump, though. And nothing hurts.

"How's your head, genius?"

"Don't call me that," I mutter, a reflex. Claire's always calling me *genius* in that superior tone of hers because she secretly hates that I do so much better on tests than she does.

Or she was always calling me *genius*. *Was.*

How badly did I hit my head?

Claire stands, brushing something from her black tights. I stare at those tights for a moment. And then I look up, taking in her short black skirt, her black sweater, the little pink cat nose she painted over her real nose.

My eyes flick back to her sweater.

The last time I saw that sweater, it was drenched in blood.

My throat closes up. It's a horrible thought, a glitchy thought, the neurons in my brain short-circuiting. I squeeze my eyes shut until it goes away.

Okay . . . so Claire's dressed like a cat because tonight's Halloween. And we're outside in the dark because . . .

A breeze moves past my face, bringing the earthy smell of dirt and leaves, the smoke from a distant bonfire. If I listen, I realize I can hear the sounds of people laughing, people talking . . .

Because we're in the corn maze, my brain supplies. We're in the corn maze at Lacy Farms, on the night Claire died. I should've known. I've had this nightmare a million times.

Did I get knocked out back at the courthouse? Am I lying in a hospital bed right now, struggling to regain consciousness?

I grab a chunk of my leg and pinch, hard.

Shit, that hurt.

Claire sticks her hand in my face. "Come on, girl, I want to get through this thing quick. Word on the street is that Kylie Mack is gonna try something with Amy Sullivan later, and if I'm not there to see it with my own eyeballs, I'll have to hear about it through the gossip mill like a peasant."

I smirk in the dark. I completely forgot that she used to talk like this, like she was some old-timey queen and all the rest of us were just commoners, her subjects, that we should be thrilled she's allowed us to bask in her regal presence. I used to think it was so cheesy. Now my eyes get teary. This is one hell of a dream.

I take her hand, allow her to pull me to my feet. She smells like oranges, like the Glossier bodywash she uses every morning, and also, very slightly, like burned hair. That smell, it causes another memory: Claire before school, Lizzo blasting from her Bluetooth speaker, the smell of singed hair filling the hall as she works to get the ends ever-so-slightly curled, doing it over and over again until it looks natural, perfectly windswept, like a character on a CW show.

This doesn't feel like a dream.

Claire blinks at me. Her eyelashes look nineteen feet long, part superior genetics, part falsies, part really expensive mascara. "Allie? You're looking at me like I have some crazy-gross zit popping on my nose. Am I getting a zit? You're my sister, so you have to tell me."

"You're . . . um . . . you're not getting a zit, I swear." My voice actually breaks. Oh God, I'm going to cry. I inhale, try to get myself together, but it's too late, I can already feel the sob working its way up my throat, threatening to explode . . .

Dream or hallucination or whatever the hell this is, it's the most real Claire's felt in a year. She's saying things I forgot she ever said, teasing me just like she used to tease me. I can smell her damn hair.

Before I can stop myself, I grab her and squeeze.

Claire stiffens in my very sudden, very unlike-me embrace. But because she's Claire and physical touch is her love language, she relaxes into it. She lowers her head so that it's leaning against my head and pats me on the back, her hand moving in slow circles. "There, there, Alley Cat. I told you this thing was scary."

"Yeah, totally," I mutter.

"See, aren't you glad you came after me?"

"I came after you," I repeat, still feeling slow.

"I mean, you let me wander around in the dark for a good fifteen minutes first, but I knew you'd come after me in the end." Claire gives me an extra-tight squeeze. "In exchange, I promise I'll protect you from all the corn-maze baddies. Sound fair?"

I squeeze her tighter, and her skinny shoulders feel like they might actually give way beneath my arms. I can feel the safety pin holding her bra strap in place through her sweater. She used to pin the strap to the inside of her clothes so it wouldn't slip down her shoulder throughout the day. I forgot how much she used to hate when it did that.

This doesn't feel like a dream, I think again. There are too many things my sister did that I'd forgotten about, things she said that I haven't thought about in months. The sheet mask. The safety pin. The smell of her hair. It's crazy how much you forget about a person when you don't see them every day. All the little details that make up who they were drip out of your head like water falling though cupped hands.

"Weird," I murmur, my voice muffled by hair.

"Hey, how about a little confidence?" Claire says, hurt creeping into her voice. "I'm capable of fighting off baddies. It's not that weird."

More memories now, coming at me faster: I see Claire running into my bedroom after hearing me scream, smashing a spider that had crawled in through the crack in my window with her bare hands. Claire, always the first to accept a dare, to walk into the dark or stand too close to the edge or wave her hand through the flame. My sister was fearless. God, I miss her.

"Yeah, yeah, I know that, Claire." My voice is cracking again. I take a step away from her, wiping my cheek with the back of my hand. "You're basically Erin from *You're Next*." Erin is the best of the Final Girls.

Claire opens her mouth to say something about my horror-movie obsession when a scream—strangled, desperate—cuts her off.

The Wilhelm scream.

My heart stops. Claire and I move at the same time, our bodies twisting around, heads jerking, both of us staring wide-eyed directly into the wall of corn. The scream seemed to have come from the other side, and like all truly horrific screams, it ended too soon, a scary movie suddenly put on mute. The silence it leaves behind is pulsing.

The two of us stand in that silence for a long moment, neither saying a word. Then Claire glances at me. She tries a smile, but it's a wobbly, unsure smile. So unlike her. "It's a scary corn maze, remember? People are going to scream."

I swallow, an uneasy prickling growing beneath my skin. My brain struggles to put something together. Last year, when Chloe Bree looked down and saw that her arm was no longer attached to her body, she screamed exactly like that.

But that doesn't make sense. I'm supposed to be there when Chloe screams.

My convo with Sidney comes back to me in snags and pieces.

The only regret I have is not going with my sister into that maze when she asked me to, I think. If I'd have done that, Claire would still be alive.

That's what happened. In this dream, hallucination, whatever the hell it is, I followed Claire into the maze. I was with her instead of Chloe. I stopped her from running into Owen, from getting killed.

But that would mean that Claire never stopped Owen. It would mean Owen is still here.

That he's in the maze with us right now.

Was That a Chain Saw?

Fear itches up the back of my neck. My heart becomes a bass drum. I suddenly understand why every horror movie soundtrack is so similar. It's the sound of fight-or-flight, the sound of heartbeat in your ears and blood surging through your brain, telling you, *Run, run, run.*

"Claire," I murmur, barely a whisper. "We have to get out of here. Like, right now."

"That's what I've been trying to say." Claire's voice is much, much too loud. I'm suddenly too aware of the silence on the other side of the corn wall, how it seems to be listening. "I feel like we've done the maze, and now it's time for beer and a party and Kylie and—"

"Claire," I snap, interrupting her. "Shut up. We have to go now."

Something about my voice must convince her that I'm dead serious, because she stops talking, her brow furrowing. I don't think I've ever told Claire to shut up before. "Of course, Alley Cat, whatever you want."

I turn in place, trying to remember how I made it through this maze last year. Every direction looks the same. Darkness layered over corn. Dead ends and wrong turns.

I swallow hard. "Do you remember how to get out of here?"

"Yeah, it's just a left and then . . ." Claire trails off. "And then . . ." she says again, but it's clear she doesn't know.

A sound cuts into the silence: a metal-on-metal growl, the same sound I hear in every one of my nightmares.

A chain saw.

My brain stops working. I pick a direction and run, pulling Claire along behind me. Twigs crack beneath our shoes, and it makes me think of chain saw blades crunching through bone, eating through Chloe's arm.

"Allie—slow down."

Blood in my ears, sweat in my eyes. I can't see anything. The stalks are too high, their leaves blocking what little moonlight has managed to seep through the clouds. The wind picks up, shivering through them, and a low moan sweeps across the fields.

I will never accuse Sally Hardesty of screaming too much in *Texas Chainsaw* ever again.

I clench my eyes shut, thinking, *Wake up*, but I see my sister kneeling in the dirt, looking at me with so much relief, hoping I'd come to save her. I see Owen pulling the knife out of his own stomach, stabbing her with it—

My eyes flick back open.

Run, run, run.

Around one turn, and another. I hear voices now, laughing, music. We're close to the party, close to people, to safety.

I don't slow down. I've watched enough horror to know this moment, the moment that you think you're home free, is the most dangerous. It's *Scream*, Drew Barrymore watching her parents' car inch closer, nanoseconds before Ghostface leaps out of the darkness with a knife. It's Chris Hemsworth's motorcycle slamming into the invisible barrier when you think he's going to make the leap and escape in *The Cabin in the Woods*.

I tighten my grip on Claire's arm, and she says, "Allie, come on, you're hurting me."

I take one last turn and—

It happens just like it did the first time around: my ankle catching on something, the ground slamming into my chin, blood on my tongue.

Everything is exactly the same.

Except, this time, Claire's right behind me. I hear the panting sound of her breath, her voice high-pitched and unnatural. "Shit, Allie, are you—oh my God."

It's the way she says those words that scares me. Not like she's swearing, but like she's praying. I forget about the pain in my lip, the taste of blood on my tongue. The only thing I can hear is my own heartbeat pounding in my ears. I push myself up, trying to steady my breathing. I blink and blink again, and that's when I see the blood.

It's everywhere. Splattered across my shirt and my jeans. Smeared over my palms. I must've fallen into a pool of it.

"Oh my God," Claire says again. She sounds hysterical. "Allie . . . Allie . . . oh my God!"

Now's when I'm supposed to look over my shoulder to see what tripped me. But I can't move my neck. I can't move anything.

My hands start to shake.

Do it now, I think.

Blood still pounding in my ears, I look.

Chloe's body is sprawled on the ground behind me, facedown,

her dress hitched up just above her thigh. She has one arm twisted behind her back and the other—

I press a fist to my mouth, my stomach churning.

Oh God. I'm going to be sick.

Chloe's other arm is no longer attached to her body. It's lying next to me in a pool of blood that looks black and bottomless in the dark. I can smell it, the wrongness of it. It smells like decay, like rot. Like death.

And that's when I realize something that really should've been apparent from the beginning.

I should never have been able to smell Claire's hair or her body-wash. I shouldn't be able to smell this blood.

You can't smell things in dreams.

Which means that this, whatever's happening . . . it's real.

No One's Gonna Believe You

"Allie? What do we do? Allie? Come on, talk to me." Claire's voice seems to reach out and grab me from somewhere far away. I inhale so quickly that the oxygen burns my lungs.

Get it together; you know what comes next.

I do know what comes next. Even if I hadn't lived through this exact moment before, I've seen it in a thousand horror movies. It's the break into Act Two, the lull after that first really big scare. I flash back on every conversation I've ever had with Millie and X. This is the moment when the Final Girl proves she's not like other girls. She's smarter, braver. This is the moment when the audience decides whether she deserves to live or die.

But I don't feel smart right now, or brave. Even though I know what I'm supposed to be doing, it takes all the energy I have to haul myself to my feet and pull out my phone, fingers stiff against the slick screen.

The 911 operator's voice is rote, mechanical. She tells me an officer will be there soon. And then the line goes dead.

Claire's hovering behind me, saying something that I catch only in bits and pieces. "—can't be real, right? It's a joke, like a Halloween joke, right? Chloe just set this up to fuck with us, right, Allie? Allie? Allie, talk to me—"

I shake my head, too numb with fear to answer her. I stay frozen for maybe ten more seconds, skin crawling as I stare down at Chloe's body.

Then a soft rustling in the cornfield. Wind moving through the stalks.

Footsteps.

Reality slams back into me. Owen is still here in the cornfield with us.

He could be watching us right now.

I flinch like I've been hit. This is basic stuff, Slasher Films 101. If I were watching a movie version of this moment, I'd be shrieking at the screen right now. *Get out of the cornfield, you idiot!*

I grab Claire's arm, hauling her out of that field. I remember the way now. Or my body does, the same way your fingers can start working the combination on your locker before you stop to think about what it is. I turn left, left, and then right, and we're out, the party sprawling before us. I grab the first kid I see, some freshman whose name I don't know.

"There's a girl back there . . ." I press a balled fist to my mouth, choking back a sob. "She's . . . I think she's dead."

The next twenty minutes are chaos. No one believes me. Like Claire, they all think it's a joke, the beginning of some elaborate Halloween-night prank Chloe set up to fuck with us. I have to say the words *Chloe Bree is dead* at least three more times before people start doing anything, and even then, they're pretty reluctant.

Music switches off, and voices grow louder, higher. Someone stands on a bale of hay and announces that there's been an emergency and everyone needs to clear out, and then someone else shouts that everyone should stay, that the cops are going to want to question us, and then someone *else* shouts, "Trick or treat, bitches," and everyone starts applauding and laughing.

I can't deal. I find a metal folding chair and collapse into it a second before my legs stop working completely. My eyes fall closed, and I see Chloe's pale blood-splattered hair and missing arm.

I know a lot of people who like horror movies but can't handle the gore. Millie always used to tell me that once she'd seen those gruesome images, she could never get them out of her head. My trick was always to look for the clues that it wasn't real. Horror-movie blood is always way too red, and horror-movie skin looks like rubber and foam if you look closely enough.

I can't do that with Chloe, though. Her body, what Owen did to it, I'll remember that for the rest of my life.

I force my eyes back open, not wanting to even blink in case she's still waiting on the inside of my closed lids. The cold air makes my eyes tear.

Blue and red lights flash in the parking lot, announcing the arrival of the police. For a while, time doesn't work like it's supposed to. It kaleidoscopes in on itself, spiraling around me in fragments of too-bright light and sound. Claire hands me something in a SOLO cup. I take a tentative sip—water—and cringe, swallowing in the exaggerated way of a child being force-fed medicine.

"This is unreal," Claire says, sitting next to me. "I can't believe this is happening." She turns those oversize eyes on me, and I release a small, choked laugh.

Unreal? She doesn't know the half of it.

I swallow another mouthful of water, moving my gaze down to my lap. *Not a dream*, I think again, the same thought I had when I first saw Chloe's dead body. But if this isn't a dream, it would mean that I'd somehow *wished* my sister back from the grave, that I'd traveled back in time to the night of her death. It would mean that Owen got away.

That his murder spree was just beginning.

I lick my lips, feeling suddenly panicky. *This can't really be happening*, I try to tell myself instead. If it's not a dream, there has to be some other explanation. A hallucination, my brain short-circuiting. Maybe I'm lying in a hospital bed right now, tubes in my nose, a machine keeping me alive.

But every explanation I come up with feels less true. Like how if you say the word *table* over and over again, it loses all meaning. Maybe I'm having a stroke. I'm pretty sure people can smell things when they're having a stroke. It's messed up that this comforts me.

"Hey, look," Claire murmurs. "Eli's here."

I turn, following Claire's gaze to the far end of the clearing, where Eli is standing with a crowd of our classmates. He's easy to spot, because while everyone else is dressed in dark colors and costumes, Eli wears an ugly Christmas sweater unironically. He always says Christmas starts immediately after Halloween ends.

I was already with the police, so I didn't see Eli that night, but I know from talking to him later that Millie called him right after Claire died. He raced right over to pick her and X up and take them home.

It's a small, strange detail that just makes everything that's happening seem so much more real.

"This can't be real," I mutter under my breath.

Claire blinks at me. "What?"

"Nothing. I'll be right back." I glance at Claire. "You okay on your own for a minute?"

Claire shudders. The camping lights set up around the cornfield aren't bright enough to illuminate her whole face, so I can't quite make out her expression. Her mouth is drawn and tight, darkness hiding her eyes. She's never scared easily, but even she seems to be working hard to keep herself together.

"*Okay* maybe isn't the word I would use," she says with a shaky laugh. "But yeah, go."

I grab her hand and squeeze. "I'll be right back, I swear."

Eli is deep in conversation with X and Millie, their voices low, conspiratorial murmurs.

"... heard she made it look like her arm had been *cut off*," Millie is saying.

"Yeah, apparently she got some help from one of the drama club—" X sees me coming and breaks off to say, "Alice, isn't this unbelievable?" But he has an earth-shattering smile on his face while he says it. *Not cool, X.*

"Uh, yeah, it is," I say, confused. I know X likes true crime, but he still sounds more delighted by the brutal murder of one of our classmates than he should be. To drive this home, I add pointedly, "It's horrible."

Eli turns at the sound of my voice. "*Thank you. That's* exactly what I've been trying to say. Chloe took things way too far this time. They're saying she went all-out with that arm." He seems to notice the blood splattered over my clothes for the first time and says, "How did you get that to look so real?"

Blood surges up my neck, making my face hot. "What are you talking about?"

"Are you part of Chloe's big Halloween prank?" Eli asks, smiling. "Did you help her fake her grisly murder?"

My eyes fall closed, a rush of anger and frustration welling up inside of me. "How can you think this is fake? The *cops* are here."

Frowning, Eli murmurs, "Well . . . don't you think that's part of it?"

He's doing our stupid question thing again. I could kill him.

"This isn't a joke!" I snap, and Eli flinches, looking hurt.

"Alice, come on, this is Chloe," X adds. "She rented an entire cornfield for her Halloween party. You honestly think she's above hiring a few people to play cops?"

"They might even be real," Millie adds. "Nat Howard's brother's on the force, remember? He pulled me over once because he thought I was driving drunk, but really there was just a bee in my car."

For a moment the sheer romantic-comedyness of Millie's life distracts me from what's going on. *Of course* she got pulled over because there was a bee in her car. I can't help but picture how her inevitable love story will play out in three predictable acts, and it takes me a second to remember what we're actually talking about, the horror movie that is my life instead of the romantic comedy that is Millie's. I don't have the energy to try to convince them this is real, not when I still don't understand *how* it's real. I peer down into the plastic cup of water I'm still holding, thinking, *What is this? What's happening? How, how, how?*

"Ms. Lawrence?"

The voice startles me. I jerk around and find a man wearing a uniform that looks like something he got from his older brother's closet standing over me. His hair is too long, his jaw shadowed in stubble.

He looks more like a high school student than a cop. He could be auditioning for the part of a dopey, bumbling police officer.

I frown as I study his face. Was he here last year? I can't remember.

I can't remember anything about the night of Claire's murder. Except for the actual murder, of course.

"Ms. Lawrence?" the dopey police officer says again, and I blink, coming back to life.

"Alice." My voice sounds distant, like I'm hearing it through thick glass. I tighten my grip around my cup. My fingers are trembling.

"Alice," the man repeats. "Good to meet you. My name is Officer Howard. You mind coming with me?"

Officer Howie, I think. Officer Howard is too grown-up, too official-sounding for Nat Howard's older brother.

"You *are* part of it." Eli goes wide-eyed, looking utterly thrilled. "I can't believe you yelled at me!"

I'm too shocked to figure out how to respond, so I just shake my head and follow the cop. Behind me, I can hear X reciting a recipe he knows for how to make the most realistic-looking fake blood. "All you need is one part flour, one part red food dye, one part chocolate syrup, and two parts corn syrup . . ."

I wish this were fake. The bottoms of my shoes feel sticky, but the blood clinging to the soles isn't made of chocolate syrup. It's real blood: Chloe's blood. I release a nervous breath in a little burst that sounds like a laugh.

Officer Howard shoots a look over his shoulder, taking a second to eye the stains on my clothes, just like Eli did. "You okay?"

"Head rush." I try for a smile, but my lips feel grotesquely tight across my teeth.

"Yeah, well, you've had a bad shock." We stop walking once we've reached a relatively empty corner of the clearing, and Officer Howard turns to face me. "You probably want to go home and get into bed, but I'd like to ask you a few questions, if that's okay? While everything's still fresh in your memory?"

"Yeah, I can do that."

"Great. Can you start by walking me through what you were doing just before you found the body?" A notebook has appeared in Officer Howard's hands. It looks comically small between his thick fingers.

I almost laugh. *Well, Officer Howie, I was in a courthouse bathroom a year from now, preparing to put the creep who did this behind bars for the rest of his life when some psycho wearing iconic '90s Final Girl Sidney Prescott's face asked me about regret...*

Obviously, I can't say any of that.

Choosing my words very carefully, I tell him about the party and following my sister into the corn maze, finding Chloe's body.

Officer Howie's eyebrows go up as I talk. He looks like he's a heartbeat away from putting a hand on my shoulder and telling me to keep my chin up. "And did you see anyone else in the corn maze tonight? Anyone suspicious?"

All of a sudden, an almost overwhelming feeling of relief crashes over me. I know the answer to this question. I did see someone in the cornfield.

"Yes," I say immediately. "I saw—" And then I break off, thinking of what Sidney said in the bathroom right before all of this happened.

You're about to put an innocent person away for the rest of his life. You sure you're okay with that?

I close my mouth, hesitating. If this were a movie, I'd discover that I was sent back in time to learn a lesson, right a wrong. Owen wouldn't really be the killer! It would be someone entirely unexpected. Millie! My mom. Maybe even me!

No, I think, gritting my teeth together. This is ridiculous. I *saw* Owen stab my sister. Some fangirl in a courtroom bathroom isn't going to convince me to doubt my own memory.

If it means saving two other lives, I'm completely comfortable sending Owen to prison for the rest of his life. I can end this nightmare right now.

"This kid ran past me right before I found Chloe's body," I tell Officer Howard. "His name is Owen Trevor Maddox."

The cop looks up from his notebook, moving just his eyes. "Is that right?"

I nod, suddenly nervous. It's not really a lie. I did see Owen, on a different version of this night.

Officer Howard flips to the next page in his notebook. "Approximately what time was this?"

In my head, I see the numbers on Claire's dashboard flip from 6:59 to 7:00. "A little after seven," I say. "Like 7:20, maybe?"

"Did you see anyone else enter or leave the maze at any other point tonight?"

"No. But it was pretty dark."

A female cop approaches and taps Officer Howard on the shoulder. "Excuse me," he says, and turns, the woman murmuring something into his ear.

My phone starts playing the *Halloween* theme. I tug it out and glance down.

The contact on my screen makes me stop breathing.

WESLEY JAMES HANSON III it reads in all caps, three heart-eyed smileys trailing behind the words like groupies. Claire had changed it as a joke.

I'm so distracted by the contact name that it takes a moment for my eyes to flick to the message beneath it:

we still on for tonight?

I feel a hard twist in my gut, remembering. The movie. Our date, or whatever it was. Of course, that never happened. Instead of going out with the boy I'd been fantasizing about all summer, I spent the night sobbing in the police station.

Only not tonight, not in this hallucination or dream or whatever the hell's going on. I let my fingers linger on the screen for a moment before, with a sigh, forcing myself to type back: sorry, have to cancel. Irritation prickles through me as I hit send. It was hard enough to do this the first time around.

Officer Howie is nodding at the other cop when I look up again. "Right, okay," he says to her. Then, turning back to me, he adds, "Here's my card." Something small and white flashes between his fingers. "If you think of anything else, please give me a call."

I take the card from him, feeling dazed, sad about Wes, and a little like I'm being blown off. "Is that it? Aren't you going to go look for Owen?"

Officer Howie's expression doesn't change. "We'll certainly take your lead into consideration, Ms. Lawrence, but we have to examine all—"

"Lead?" I can feel the blood rushing into my head, making my face hot. "No, you don't understand; I *saw* Owen tonight." I can hear my voice rising. "He's seriously dangerous."

I think of Owen's manifesto, those girls standing on the courthouse steps, their T-shirts reading I WAS NUMBER 2, I WAS NUMBER 3. If I can't make this cop believe me, their deaths will be my fault.

"No," I say, inhaling sharply. "You have to listen to me. You have to stop Owen before he hurts someone else."

Something in the air shifts. Officer Howie's eyes narrow, and I realize what he's going to say a second before the words leave his lips.

"What makes you think he's going to hurt someone else?"

Obviously the Cops Aren't Going To Help You

Officer Howie's eyebrows pull together, and his mouth gets small and puckered like he's chewing on an invisible toothpick. Somehow these two things come together to make him look much, much more intimidating than he did a second ago. He even seems taller, as impossible as that is. Staring back at him, I feel suddenly uneasy.

"Do you have reason to believe someone else might be hurt tonight?" he asks me.

"No," I say too quickly. Then, backtracking: "I mean, I don't know."

"I think it might be a good idea for you to come down to the station with me, Ms. Lawrence," he says. "Is there someone we can call to meet you there? A parent, maybe?"

My palms have started to sweat. I rake them down my jeans, wanting to kick myself. How could I be so stupid, blurting out that Owen's going to go after someone else like it's common knowledge? I know he's going after Erin only because of his manifesto, which the police aren't going to find for another three days.

By then, Erin and Sierra will be dead, too.

"What?" I laugh, a weird nervous tic. "Um, why would I have to call my parents? Am I, like, a suspect?"

"No, of course not. But I don't think you're being completely honest with me, and I'd like to ask you a few more questions. Since you're a minor, it would probably be a good idea for you to have a guardian present."

A tremor moves through me. "But you need to find Owen." I try to inject as much urgency as possible into my voice. "He's the one you should be questioning. He did this."

"You know what's sort of strange?" Officer Howie scratches the back of his head with his pen. I find myself wondering if the aw-shucks, kid-brother routine is just an act, if he's using it to knock me off guard. "I've spoken to about twelve other kids who were in that maze at the same time as you, and none of them saw this Owen guy. Just you."

I swallow hard. Another mistake. It was one of the reasons my testimony was so important today—or the real today, the today in my timeline—because no one else saw Owen in the maze. Even Chloe couldn't remember her attacker.

"He—he was wearing a mask," I try.

"Then how did you know who he was?" When I don't answer, Officer Howie pulls his phone out of his pocket. "You can call your folks from the car. Let's go."

My heartbeat kicks up a notch. "Am I being arrested? Do I, like, need to get a lawyer?"

"You want a lawyer with you to answer some questions?" Officer Howie shakes his head like he's disappointed in me. "I suppose I can call one up if you like. It might take him a few hours to get down to the station, though."

A few *hours*? My heart's going faster now, practically vibrating in my chest. I don't have that kind of time. Someone needs to find Erin and tell her that she's in danger. That needs to happen *now*.

Every second I spend talking to Officer Howie is a second too long.

I reach up to brush a strand of hair behind my ear and yank down on my earlobe, one of many fun new nervous tics I developed after Claire died. My mouth feels dry and tight. I try to buy myself time to think by gulping down the rest of the water she got for me when, across the field, Claire suddenly starts screaming.

"Oh my God! Blood! There's blood on my skirt! It's hers!"

It's a real bloodcurdling number, very slasher film. I'm impressed.

I turn too quickly at the sound of her voice, accidentally emptying the rest of my water onto Officer Howie's oversize uniform.

"Shit!" He takes a step back, grabbing the front of his shirt with one hand and peeling it away from his skin. He turns away from me, shouting for forensics.

It's just for a second, but it's long enough for me to think of Owen's manifesto, the list of victims he'd intended to murder before my sister stopped him.

Chloe Bree. Erin Cleary. Sierra Clayton.

I can't waste any more time here, and I *definitely* can't let myself get hauled to the police station for hours of questioning. Someone has to warn Erin that she's next.

I have to warn her.

Officer Howie's still shouting over his shoulder, distracted, trying to peel his wet shirt off his chest. It's not the perfect time to make an escape. Officer Howie's only a few feet away, and he looks fast—something which I am very much not. But beggars can't be choosers and all that, so I move back. When he still doesn't turn around, I start to run.

"Hey!" he shouts. "Ms. Lawrence, we're not through here!"

I think of how he probably has a gun, and for a moment I'm sure I'm going to pee my pants.

Oh my God, what am I doing?

I am not a Final Girl. I *watch* Final Girls in movies. That's my greatest skill.

And yet I dart through a cluster of classmates, sending them stumbling in all directions, hoping it'll slow him down. Officer Howie might be faster than me, but I'm smaller. I hear him swear as I swerve around a corner.

Claire's Jetta is one of the last cars still in the parking lot. I throw the driver's side door open and slide in, and I'm just about to hit the ignition when I remember that I don't have the key; Claire does.

"Shit!" I slam my hands against the steering wheel, frustration building inside me. My head feels like it's full of those Styrofoam packing peanuts people use for their breakables when they're moving. Everything is white and crowded and—

I just ran away from a *cop*. What the hell was I thinking? Of all the awful, privileged-white-girl moves I could've made tonight . . .

Oh God . . . I can't breathe . . .

I hear a sound—a twig breaking—and jerk my head up, entirely expecting to see Officer Howie racing across the parking lot toward the car, a trail of officers behind him, guns already out.

But it's not the cops who are running toward me—it's Claire. She throws the car door open and slides into the passenger seat, tossing me her keys.

"What are you doing?" she asks, frowning. "Go, before that cop guy catches us!"

Relief slams into me. "Yes, ma'am," I say, and hit the ignition. This time, the car growls to life. I throw it into drive and peel out of the parking lot like we're already in the middle of a high-speed chase, tires squealing on the pavement.

"So," Claire asks, flashing me one of her signature slightly mischievous grins. "What did you think of my distraction?"

I stare at her, not getting it. "Your what?"

"My distraction. The screaming? The blood?" Her eyebrows go up. "Come on, Alley Cat, that was one of my best performances, like, ever. I was totally channeling Sarah Michelle Gellar in *I Know What You Did Last Summer*. You know, the scene where she wakes up and all her hair's been cut off?" Claire demonstrates screaming again.

I'm still staring at her, and I must be slow or something because I have no idea what she's talking about. "Wait—the screaming and stuff, that was on purpose?"

"You did our signal." Claire pulls her earlobe twice, looking a little hurt. "So I got you away from the creepy guy. Did you think I'd ignore you just because it was a cop?"

I blink a few times, understanding crashing over me.

The signal. I'd totally forgotten about that.

Claire came up with the signal my freshman year after she dragged me along to my very first high school party. I hadn't wanted to go, but she'd insisted, telling me I needed to spread my wings, get out of my comfort zone. From what I could tell, that mostly involved wearing eye makeup and a low-cut top.

It's time for you to embrace your inner hottie, I remember her saying. *But if someone creepy starts talking to you and you want an exit strategy, just catch my eye and give me one of these*—she tugged on her earlobe twice, just like now—*and I'll get you out of there, got it?*

Of course, guys never talked to me, not even the creepy ones, so Claire quickly co-opted the signal for herself, using it as a way to make a quick exit from whatever hot-but-not-very-smart person she'd just gotten bored with. And there were so many hot-but-not-very-smart people. She must've used the signal a dozen times in her last month of life alone, but I never needed it. Not once.

Now my eyes feel wet. It didn't occur to me that she'd never stopped watching for it. All that time, all I'd ever had to do was pull on my damn ear, and my big sister would've been waiting in the wings, ready to swoop in and save me.

"No, I, uh, totally knew you'd come through," I say, horrified to hear my voice cracking a little. Before I can stop myself, I reach over and squeeze her hand. "Thank you."

Claire shoots me a look. "No one messes with my little sister. Besides, that wasn't, like, a *real* cop. Davey Howard used to hang out in the kitchen like a creep whenever Nat had her friends sleep over."

My mouth feels suddenly dry. "We should probably talk about the dead girl we just found in the cornfield," I say, glancing at my sister.

Claire's eyebrows go up. "How about we start with you telling me why we're going all *Fugitive* and work our way back from there?"

Don't Split Up

Lacy Farms is on the far edge of town, so it's a while before the scenery changes, the one-lane highway turning into two, cornfields becoming suburban sprawl, stop signs and traffic lights popping up like fireflies.

I use the time to tell Claire as much as I can about what's going on, trying to walk that oh-so-thin line between being honest and not sounding like a total nut.

Here's where I land: "I sort of know who killed Chloe, and I know who he's going after next."

Claire says nothing for several long moments. The only sign she gives that she's heard me and is trying to process what I've told her is the way she's blinking too fast, like she has something caught in her eye.

"I . . . don't think I understand," she says finally. "Did you see something weird in the corn maze? Like, before I caught up with you?"

"Not exactly."

More blinking, and then Claire gives a decisive shake of her head. "Okay, then, did you have some sort of premonition? Did he confess to you in a dream?" Her lips slowly inch into a smile, my only clue that she's teasing me.

"No, no one confessed, but—" A light bulb goes off in my head, and I close my eyes, a groan escaping my lips.

Confess.

Owen had always planned to confess to his crimes. He was going to go on his killing spree and kill himself, and then, three days later, his famous manifesto was supposed to go live, providing the world with all the horrible, misogynistic details of why he'd resorted to murder. Of course, my sister ruined that for him. But not in this timeline.

I can't wait for Owen's manifesto to hit the internet—two more people will be dead by then. But maybe I don't have to.

"Owen wrote this thing," I blurt out. I haven't actually read Owen's psychotic manifesto, but they covered it in the news. "A manifesto, I guess you'd call it. He left it open on his computer at the library, and I accidentally read some of it. I— I thought it was just a sick joke." That last part was a total lie, but Claire doesn't know that. "But then we found Chloe—"

"Hold up," Claire says, cutting me off. She's studying my face, her eyes a touch wider than usual. "This thing you read, Owen actually admitted he was going to kill Chloe?"

"And Erin Cleary and Sierra Clayton, yeah." *Explain that one, Sidney,* I think.

Claire swears under her breath. "And you didn't go to the cops and report his ass?"

I feel my jaw tighten. *Why, yes, that is a bit of a plot hole.* "I . . . thought it was a prank."

Claire glances at me, her expression unreadable. For a moment, I'm sure she's going to call my bluff. Why would she believe my stupid story, anyway? What kind of person would leave something like that out in the open in a public library where anyone could read it? I watch her from the corner of my eye, my entire body going tense.

But she just releases a heavy exhale and says, "That's so messed up."

Relief floods me with so much force I almost sob. This is why I love my big sister. She's always believed me, even when no one else did, even when I was lying. I never realized how important it is to have someone who believes in you.

"After we found Chloe, I tried to tell Officer Howie—*Howard*— about it, but he clearly didn't buy it, and then he started getting all suspicious and telling me he was going to take me down to the police station to answer more questions. If he did that, I couldn't warn Erin she's in danger."

"So now we're going to . . . what? Try to stop Owen?" Claire hesitates, shooting me an anxious look as I pull up next to a stop sign. "Seriously?"

I roll my lower lip between my teeth, suddenly nervous. I hadn't actually thought this part through. My brain had gotten as far as *Find Erin, warn her she's next,* but it hadn't taken the tiny step forward to the obvious problem with this plan.

Owen will be coming for Erin, too. If we go looking for her, we're almost definitely going to find *him.*

The tension in my gut twists even tighter. I think of how Owen looked the night I saw him murder my sister. His face hard and mean as he yanked the pocketknife out of his stomach and lunged.

A tremor moves through me. I don't want to go anywhere near him ever again. But what other choice do I have? If I don't do something, Erin's going to die.

"Yeah," I say, desperately trying to keep the nerves out of my voice. "That's the plan."

Claire's watching me now, eyebrows drawn together thought-fully. It's impossible to tell what she's thinking, but I can't help wondering if she's just a little bit proud of me. Claire's always been the brave one. The bravest thing I've ever done is go to a midnight showing of *The Exorcist* with X, and that still gave me nightmares for weeks. In real life, I'm the girl who checks every piece of Hal-loween candy for puncture marks, even though I heard on a true-crime podcast that the thing about poisoned Halloween candy was a hoax. I'm not normally the type to run toward the danger. The whole point of obsessively studying slashers is to know what to look for so I can run the other way.

"Erin Cleary," Claire says after a moment. She blows air out through her teeth. "She's in that gated community off Seventy-Second Street, right?"

"Is she?" I didn't actually know Erin before the night of her would-be murder. She was just another girl in a sea of straight-A, star-volleyball-playing, girl-next-door-pretty-type girls. Omaha East has girls like that in spades. If we were the same year, Erin and I might've been friends, but Erin's a senior, and in this timeline, I'm still a junior, so we don't have any classes together.

"How do you know where she lives?" I ask Claire. After the mani-festo came out, Erin got crazy famous, at least in Nebraska. But be-fore that, she was kind of under the radar. Claire didn't usually hang with girls like that.

"She had that party after the girls' volleyball team won state last year, remember?" When I frown, confused, Claire adds, "Dad told us about it? You didn't go because you had that big math test the next day."

Now I wrinkle my nose. I still don't remember the specific night

Claire's talking about, but skipping a party to study for a test does sound like me.

Or it sounds like the old me. The me who loved studying and books and wanted to be a doctor. New me doesn't even get invited to those parties, so there's no reason to feel bad about skipping them.

"Do you think she'll be home?" Claire asks, glancing at me.

"Yeah." After Claire's murder, Erin told the story of how she had spent her night to anyone who would listen. Apparently, her parents had taken her older brother to visit colleges that weekend, so she'd been all alone in their big house out at the edge of town.

I don't know how I'm ever supposed to sleep there again, she'd exclaimed tearily, even though Owen was all the way in Crawford by then, and as far as I knew, no one else was trying to kill her. So, yeah, I know she'll be home.

But Claire frowns. "Wasn't she at the gym earlier?"

"Was she?"

"We saw her there, remember? When we were getting ready?"

"Claire, that was hours ago."

"But I see her whenever I swing by to pick up Dad on a Friday night, even if it's super late. She could still be there." Claire glances at me and then back at the road. "We should split up."

A shiver moves through me. She did *not* just say that. "Claire, come on, haven't you ever seen a horror movie? You're never, ever supposed to split up."

"*This* isn't a movie; it's real life." Claire's eyebrows go up, challenging me. "We can't risk Owen finding Erin at the gym while we're on the other side of town wandering around outside her house."

I glance at my sister. The curl has fallen out of her red hair, leaving it limp and sweaty around her face. Her eyes are smudged with mascara, and a few of her false eyelashes have come off, the tiny black crescents looking kind of sad now that they're no longer attached to her lids.

I feel a pang seeing those false eyelashes. I wonder what happened to them after she died. Did some intern peel them off at the hospital morgue? Or did they wait until she got to the funeral home for that? I can still remember how she looked lying in that casket at the funeral. Her makeup demure, understated. Mauve lipstick, brown eyeliner. No bold lipstick or false eyelashes, no curl in her red hair. She would've hated it so much.

I might not fully understand the rules of the bizarro alternative reality I've landed in, but I can't help the truly terrible thought that occurs to me: the Claire in this timeline is on borrowed time. It's like the truly terrible *Final Destination* franchise; you can cheat death for only so long before it comes looking for you.

I can't let her out of my sight tonight, not when I just got her back.

I tighten my grip around the steering wheel. "We're not splitting up, okay? It's way too dangerous."

Claire twists in her seat so that her whole body faces me. It's a clear sign that she's gearing up to argue.

But then the *Halloween* theme starts playing from my pocket, cutting her off before she can start: my phone. I groan and pull it out, squinting at the screen.

"Dad's calling," I explain, hiding a grimace. Our dad is the last person I want to talk to right now. "I'm not going to answer."

I catch an edge of aggravation in Claire's expression. "You can't do that," she mutters, taking the phone from me. I have to resist the urge to roll my eyes. Of course she can't. Claire's the definition of a daddy's girl. She touches the phone screen, putting the call on speaker. "Hey, Dad."

"Claire," our dad's voice booms, "I've been trying to reach you. You left your cell in the locker room again. Some girl found it and dropped it off at the lost and found."

I'm hit with another memory from tonight: Claire primping in the locker room before the party, snapping selfies for Instagram. I'd forgotten that she always used to leave her phone in random places.

Claire squeezes her eyes shut. "Sorry?"

"We talked about this. I need to be able to get ahold of you when you go out. Where are you? I'm in the car now; I can bring your phone to you."

I shoot her a look, and she says quickly, "Uh—I'm going to be with Allie all night. Can't you just call her if you need me?"

He releases a low breath. "I guess that's fine. Allie? Are you there, too?"

I'm surprised that he wants to talk to me, and it takes me a second to lean closer and say, "Hey, Dad."

My father's voice changes subtly now that he knows he's talking to me, his tone becoming more serious. "Allie, hey, so I just wanted to let you know I'm doing a coaching session tomorrow at noon, but I'll be around before that if you still want to talk about your application."

"Application?" I don't remember what he's talking about at first, and then it all rushes back: the Summer Research Internship at Mercer School of Medicine.

The application is due next week. Or it *was* due next week. I'd been working on it all fall, but after Claire died, I blew it off. I vaguely remember seeing that some senior from Lincoln High got it.

"Oh," I say now, blinking. I forgot I'd asked Dad to look over my application before I sent it in, a rare moment of father-daughter bonding.

I find myself wondering briefly what might've happened if Claire hadn't died. If he'd have been proud of all the work I put into that application. Even in this bizarro time-slip version of reality, I can't help wanting to make my dad proud. Messed up, isn't it?

Claire cuts in, "We're still on for squash tomorrow, right?"

"I made sure to book time at our favorite court before I left the gym," Dad says, the eagerness returning to his voice now that he's talking to his favorite daughter again. "We have a slot at four fifteen tomorrow afternoon."

"Wait, you just left the gym?" I ask.

"A few minutes ago, yeah."

I glance at Claire, hoping to win this argument once and for all. "I bet it was empty, right? No one's working out this late on Halloween night?"

"You'd be surprised; there are always a few nuts who come in every holiday—" A beep cuts him off, the sound of an incoming call on his end of the line. "Ah, that's your mom. Don't stay out too late!" And the phone goes silent.

"He said there were still people at the gym," Claire says, a pleading note to her voice. "One of them could be Erin. Owen's the janitor; he has to know she works out there on the weekends. Allie, it'll be the first place he checks."

"Then we won't have to worry about running into him, because I'm telling you, Erin's at home."

Claire groans. "You can't possibly know that."

Wanna bet? I think.

Claire's still staring at me, her eyes slightly narrowed. For a second, I'm sure this is going to turn into a stupid fight. Claire and I used to get into the worst fights about the silliest things: misremembered movie quotes and who borrowed whose sweater and whether we accidentally gave the other a dirty look. I don't think I could stand to fight with her tonight; I really don't.

Maybe she's thinking the same thing because she blows air out through her lips and says carefully, "I think we need to do something for morale."

I blink at her. "What?"

"I know that what's going on tonight is very serious," she says, leaning over to switch on the radio. "That's exactly why we need to hype ourselves up."

A song comes on, the familiar chords seeming to fill every inch of the car. Claire's eyes light up.

"This," she says, emphatically. "This is exactly what we need. It's fate."

I groan because that's what she's expecting me to do, but I can't help the twitch at the corner of my lips—almost a smile. The song is Taylor Swift's "Shake It Off." It came out when I was, like, ten, and I loved it so much that I'd played it on repeat, belting the words at the top of my lungs. Of course, as soon as I started middle school, everyone said Taylor was basic, and I wanted to be cool, so I pretended I thought she was basic, too.

Claire was not okay with that. "You are not everyone," she'd told me. "They're all sheep. You are a stallion."

Even at ten I knew that stallions were boy horses, but gender is a construct, and besides, I got what she was saying. Ever since then, we blast Taylor whenever she comes on the radio. It's our thing.

Claire cranks the volume as high as it will go. "Sing with me," she says, bouncing in her seat. "It'll get our heart rate up. Adrenaline is good when you're running from serial killers."

I have to admit, it's hard to argue with that kind of logic.

We pull to a stop outside Erin's gated community at the exact moment the song ends. ("It's a sign!" Claire says as I cut the engine.)

"I have to text Eli to get Erin's phone number," I tell Claire, dropping her car keys into her open hand. Eli has everyone's number. He's basically a human-shaped search engine. "Unless you know it?"

"I don't know it," Claire murmurs, frowning down at the keys.

"Do you know her address?" I climb out of the car and turn, expecting to see her climbing out the other side.

But she's scrambling over the partition separating the passenger and driver's seats.

"Claire? What are you—" I reach for the door, but she hits the lock before I can get it open.

"I tried to reason with you, Alley Cat," Claire says, adjusting the rearview mirror. "But you didn't want to listen, so we have to do this the hard way."

I tug on the door handle even though I can clearly see that it's locked. Anxiety rises inside me. "Claire, what are you doing? Open the door!"

"I'm going to the gym to warn Erin," Claire explains, meeting my eyes through the window.

"Claire, you can't do that." I slap a hand against the glass. "Claire, come on! Open the damn door!"

"It's like you said: Owen's probably at the gym, so you'll be perfectly safe out here."

"It's not *me* I'm worried about!"

"I'll be fine. I've seen all the same movies you have, remember? I know the rules. And I'll try extra hard not to get killed, okay?" Claire says this jokingly, but I can tell by the way she chews on the corner of her lip that she's scared as hell.

Fear and anger roar up inside of me. She *should* be scared. If history's any indication, she's the one in real danger tonight, not Erin and definitely not me.

"Claire!" I shout again.

"I'll be back to pick you up in twenty! Promise!" She wiggles her fingers at me and drives away, headlights illuminating the night like distant ghosts. A chill moves through me as they turn a corner and disappear, leaving me all alone in the dark.

I let my eyes fall closed, releasing my frustration in a loud exhale that sounds more like a growl. This is just so exactly like Claire. She's so stubborn, always convinced she's right.

I turn toward the black wrought iron fence that surrounds Erin's neighborhood, trying to tamp down the anger rising inside me. Claire might've taken off, but Erin's still here. And she still needs my help.

There's a call box at the gate, buttons lined up next to little plaques of people's names. I find the button for CLEARY and push. A distant chime sounds.

I look around as I wait for her to answer. The neighborhood seems oddly deserted, just two cars parked across the street, a station wagon and an ancient-looking Jeep with a bumper sticker that reads PROUD PARENT OF A MONROE MIDDLE SCHOOL HONORS STUDENT. A few crunchy leaves have fallen from the trees, dotting the sidewalk around me with orange and yellow and red. I kick them, and they scatter across the road like confetti.

The chime dies. No answer. I turn back to the call box, frowning. That's weird.

"Come on, I know you're in there," I mutter, hitting Erin's call button again.

Another few minutes pass with no luck. Could I have gotten this wrong somehow? Could Erin be at the gym after all? I feel a kick of fear for Claire.

No. No, I know Erin's home tonight. I pull out my phone and text Eli, like I meant to before. Do you have Erin Cleary's number and address?

I tap the side of my phone with my thumb while I watch three little dots appear on my screen. Then vanish.

"Come on," I murmur, nerves flaring inside me. Owen could be at Erin's house right now. She could be fighting for her life.

I glance at the fence surrounding the neighborhood. It's about as high as my shoulder, with pretty whorls and swoops that would make super-convenient footholds. It really seems more decorative than practical. It's probably intended mostly as a deterrent because it clearly wouldn't keep anyone out if they really wanted to get to the other side.

I slip my phone into my pocket and pump my hands open and closed a few times for courage.

I've never even climbed a tree before. I'm the definition of an inside person. Stairs can be tricky for me, if I'm not paying close enough attention. It used to be a family joke, how Mom and Dad could always tell whether it was Claire or me on the staircase by whether or not they heard the thud of someone falling.

I know this, and yet I grab hold of the fence and slip my foot onto one of the swirls of iron. Lift myself up off the ground. I swallow. *That was easy enough.* I pull myself up a little higher and a little higher, arm muscles I didn't even realize I had already burning, and then I'm crawling over the top of the fence and dropping onto the other side.

The impact of landing causes pain to prickle through my legs, a little groan to escape my lips. But at least I don't fall.

My phone plays the *Halloween* theme. I check my screen and see five new texts from Eli.

erin's dead to me after she started dating that asshat kyle stahlicker. remember when he called me a loser last year? he's truly our school's worst Kyle.

never mind found it 402-555-0909. Addy is 7105 south mountain rd

why do you need it tho?

how do you even knob Erin?

*sorry KNOW ducking autocorrect

I shove the phone into my pocket without answering him and look around. From this side of the fence it's clear that Erin's neighborhood is much bigger than I was expecting it to be. I can't see any houses, just huge trees, their leaves forming a canopy over dark, winding roads. There are a few streetlights, old-fashioned-looking gas-lamp things, like something out of Jack the Ripper's London. They're pretty, I guess, but not very practical. They cast small bits of sidewalk in flickering circles of yellow light and leave the rest of the neighborhood in perfect, absolute dark. No wonder Jack the Ripper was such a prolific killer. You can't see *shit*.

I feel my first prickle of fear.

Anyone could be hiding in that dark.

I start walking, focusing on the steady thump my sneakers make against the sidewalk so I don't have to think about how creepy it is to be wandering around here in the dark. Erin's place can't be far. I'll just follow this road until I get to it.

Something cracks behind me. The sound is sudden and then there's silence. I stop walking and whip my head around.

No one there.

The trees seem bigger, though, like they grew a few feet while my back was turned.

I swallow, tasting something bitter trailing down the back of my throat.

It doesn't matter that I can't see anyone. If this were a horror movie, the killer would be hiding behind a tree, ready to slide out the second I turned my back. I can practically hear the swell of music, a subtle cue to the audience that some serious shit is about to go down.

I'm going to kill Claire for leaving me here alone.

"Okay," I murmur. "Just get to Erin's and warn her. Easy." I hunch my shoulders up around my ears and force myself to turn back around, walk faster. My legs feel jerky and stiff.

There's another sound behind me, a shuffle on the concrete. It could be footsteps, or it could just be a squirrel racing across the road, but I tense up and glance back again. Still nothing. The shadows just beyond the trees seem darker, though. They seem to pulse. Something flickers at the corner of my eyes and I twist around, heart jackhammering in my chest. But there's nothing there.

My stomach clenches like a fist. I'm playing right into the murderer's hands, acting just like a horror-movie victim. I need to be smarter than this. If I were watching this scene right now, what would I be screaming at the screen?

Weapon. I need to find a weapon. Swallowing, I pull my house keys out of my pocket and weave them between my fingers, like Mom taught me to do whenever I had to walk home alone in the dark. It's for self-defense, but I'm not entirely sure how it's supposed to work. I guess you're supposed to dig the sharp part of the keys into your attacker's cheek? Or maybe you're supposed to throw your keys at him, as a distraction? It's occurring to me now that I should've asked for more details.

I glance over my shoulder again, convinced that this time, I'll see Owen standing behind me, that chain saw clenched in his hands.

Still no one.

I fumble my keys. They clatter to the pavement in a jingle of metal, the sound shocking me so much, I let out a little yelp of surprise. So stealthy, me. I scoop the keys up again without bothering to slow down, stumbling over my own legs in my desperation to keep going.

That sound behind me is way too much like footsteps now. It's the telltale drag and slap of soles on pavement, muffled, like whoever's there is trying to be quiet, to creep up on me.

Nerves crawl up my spine. I quicken my pace again, practically running now—

The footsteps behind me speed up, too.

I clench my eyes shut. Oh God.

I push my body into a run. My fear feels like a physical thing, like two hands grasping my throat, choking the air from my lungs. I'm light-headed, dizzy, and I try to run faster, but my knees knock together. My whole body is shaking.

Light flickers at the end of the block, a car rolling up to the corner.

Relief slams into me. *Oh thank God.* A car means people, safety. I stumble out into the street, waving both hands over my head. "Hey! Hey, please stop, I need—"

But the car swerves around me in a blare of horn and speeds down the block. I watch its headlights flicker through the trees in growing horror.

I'm all alone again.

Somehow, impossibly, the sidewalk looks even darker than it did a moment ago. I look around, trying to figure out how this could be, when I realize that there are even fewer gas lamps here.

Fear makes my legs weak.

I turn back around and start walking again, eyes peeled for any sign of a house in the trees, for any light or sign of movement—

And then a hand drops onto my shoulder.

Flash
Sideways

I whirl around, a horror-movie scream locked and loaded in my throat—

And find Sidney Prescott standing behind me. Her forehead is creased in a look of deepest concern, and she's got her hands propped on her hips. "What the *hell* are you doing wandering around in the dark?" she demands. "Don't you know there's a murderer on the loose?"

Breath explodes from my lips in a sudden exhale. I double over, hands going to my knees, willing my still-racing heart to steady. "Oh my God, it's you."

The fear doesn't leave my body, though. I can feel it knotted in my muscles, buzzing up the backs of my teeth. I wet my lips. "I thought—"

"Yeah, yeah, I know what you thought." Sidney gives a slow shake of her head, and the feeling that I've disappointed her intensifies. "Haven't you ever seen a scary movie? Don't walk alone at night is, like, rule number one."

She's right, obviously. I know she's right, but I'm not going to tell her that. Not after she just scared me so badly, I nearly wet myself.

"*You're* walking alone at night," I point out instead.

Sidney just shrugs, her lips curling into a lazy catlike smile. "I suppose I am. Whoops."

"What the hell is going on? Did you . . . *do* something to me? How—"

"Hold on." Sidney's hands come up in front of her chest, like I'm a spooked animal she's trying to keep calm. "I can explain everything, but like I said before, there's a murderer on the loose, so maybe let's not do it outside in the dark."

"You know somewhere else we can go?"

She flashes a wide grin and moves to the side, gesturing to the curb behind her. "Why don't you step into my office?"

Her "office" is a white van idling on the curb, leaking exhaust. It's nondescript in the most literal sense: no windows, no logo, no identifying characteristics of any kind. It's what most people would refer to as a creepy-ass murder van.

I blink at the van once, then twice. I would swear on my formerly dead sister's life that it hadn't been parked at that curb a moment ago. And yet.

I glance back at Sidney. "You cannot expect me to get into that thing."

She looks confused. "You don't like?"

"You just told me off for walking alone at night, and now you're asking me to get into a van that strangers probably use to lure small children on their way home from school. Nope."

"Alice, if I wanted to abduct you, all I'd have to do is . . ." Sidney lifts a hand, goes to snap her fingers—

"Okay, okay!" I say, stopping her before she can send me to some even more bizarro version of the past. I have no idea how she did whatever she did to me, but I know I can't risk her making tonight even weirder. "I'll come with you. Just put your hand down."

She lowers her hand and I exhale, adding, "Do you have a name? I'd like to stop thinking of you as Sidney from *Scream*."

"I don't mind Sidney, but if it bothers you"—she gestures to her T-shirt, the words FINAL GIRLS blazing in red—"you can just call me this."

I frown. "You want me to call you Final Girl?"

"Why not?" Final Girl starts toward the van, calling over her shoulder, "And you know you were going the wrong way, right? Erin's place is way on the other side of the complex."

The inside of the creepy murder van is lit red by the dozens of chili-pepper-shaped lights hanging from the windows. They make everything—the steering wheel, the car seats, the smooth lines of Final Girl's T-shirt—look strange and sinister, like we're in an episode of *The Twilight Zone*.

The effect is somewhat ruined by a huge poster of the Adam Sandler movie *Click* taped to the inside of the back door.

"*Click*?" I ask as I climb inside the van. Adam grins at me from the poster, holding a glowing blue remote.

"That movie was straight fire," Final Girl says, settling herself into the driver's seat. "Have you seen it?"

I'm so confused. "Um . . . no. It's the one about the magic remote control, right?"

Final Girl nods and says, without a trace of irony, "Based on a true story."

I honestly can't tell whether she's joking. "Wouldn't *Scream* or *I Know What You Did Last Summer* be more on-brand?"

"You think I like those movies because I look like this?" She makes an elaborate show of buckling her seat belt before motioning for me to do the same. "Safety first, Alice. Did you know that out of the 36,096 people killed in traffic accidents in 2019, forty-seven percent weren't wearing their seat belt?"

"Uh, no, I didn't know that." I pull the passenger door a little too hard and it slams closed, sending a shudder through the van. The *Click* poster ripples.

Final Girl watches me, one eyebrow raised, until I find my seat belt and click it in place. "The Final Girl makeover is for you," she says after a moment. "Because you like horror movies. I figured it would make this whole experience a little easier."

Final Girl's second eyebrow joins the first, both disappearing under her '90s-girl bangs. She says, like I'm an idiot child, "You *have* noticed that your world is a bit different from the last time we met, right?"

It takes everything I have not to roll my eyes. "Yeah, I got that far, thanks."

"Well? What do you think is happening?"

I stare back at her, thinking of my realization in the cornfield, the smell of blood making it clear that this isn't just some dream. It's real. The word repeats in my head like a song. *Real, real, real.*

But I can't think of how to say it out loud. The idea that this is really happening, that I've somehow been sent back in time, it's just too crazy. I wet my lips, staying quiet.

Final Girl is still watching me, waiting, her big brown Sidney Prescott eyes unblinking. "Isn't it obvious?" she says when I don't answer her. She spreads her hands, waiting for me to fill in the blank, and when I don't, she says, "I'm an angel."

This is *not* what I expected her to say. In fact, this is so far outside the realm of what I expected that I release a nervous chuckle, waiting for the punch line. It doesn't come.

"You're an angel," I repeat.

"We like to drop in from time to time to even the scales of good and evil," she says, like this is a totally normal thing to say, something she expects me to accept without question.

I blink at her, waiting. Still no punch line.

"And you look like Sidney Prescott from *Scream* because I like horror movies?" I say.

"I'm usually a lot more glowy than this," Final Girl explains. "And there are wings . . . It's a whole vibe. Trust me, it would just freak you out."

"Nope," I blurt before I can stop myself. *Nope, nuh-uh, no way.* There's no such thing as angels. Everything in life has a logical explanation; a rational, reasonable explanation. It's the whole reason I'm into science, the reason I want to go into medicine. If you look hard enough, everything is figureoutable. I just have to think.

I close my eyes, pinching the bridge of my nose between two fingers. My brain is white noise. No thoughts, just static. After a moment, I exhale and say, "No. You look like that because I . . . because I was just listening to that stupid podcast, *How to Be a Final Girl.*"

That makes sense, in a sort of twisted, dream-logic way. Millie and X were explaining how Claire could've survived by acting like a Final Girl, and now I have a real-life Final Girl in front of me, and my sister's all alive again. Checks out.

But Final Girl frowns. "You think a *podcast* sent you back in time?"

An incredulous laugh hiccups out of me. "*No.* I think I hit my head, and now I'm having a really messed-up hallucination."

Final Girl puts her van into drive and pulls away from the curb, making sure to check both her mirrors even though there hasn't been anyone else on this street since we started talking. "I take it that means you don't like your gift?"

"Gift?" I glance at her. Something about the way she talks bothers me. Sometimes she seems like just another teenager, someone from school, even. But other times, like now, it's clear that there's something more to her, something older. Something *other*.

Angel, I think, and shudder.

"You said your greatest regret was not following your sister into the corn maze last Halloween. So, I've arranged for you to take a look at what would've happened if you did."

I screw up my nose. "Sort of like a bizarro version of *It's a Wonderful Life*?"

"It's actually a trope called a Flash Sideways." She winks at me. "You're welcome."

I think of the smell of blood, Claire's orange-scented bodywash. *Real.*

"Gift," I say again slowly. "What exactly does that mean?"

"It means that I've sent you back to the night of your sister's murder to see what actually went down." Final Girl's eyes dart over my face, like she wants to make sure she has my full attention. "You were so sure you knew exactly what happened that I figured it couldn't hurt for you to see it play out for yourself. Nothing you don't already know, right?"

So I was right. This is about whether or not Owen killed my sister.

It would be a little more suspenseful if I hadn't *seen him do it with my own eyes.*

I glance out the window. We've just rolled past a house with dark windows. Several jack-o'-lanterns grin from the porch steps, their candlelit eyes seeming to wink at me. Like they're in on the joke, too.

I stare at those jack-o'-lanterns, my heart beating in my chest like a closed fist. Nothing about this night has felt like a dream or a hallucination. I can smell dead leaves and fireplace. My tongue still stings from when I bit into it.

I glance back at Final Girl, trying to ignore the fear creeping through me. She seems pretty damn real, too.

A million questions race through my brain. How am I supposed to even begin to accept that something like this is possible? And even if I do, why is it happening now, to me?

Or maybe that's not the right way to think about it. Maybe things like this are happening all the time, all around us, and I've just never noticed before.

I shiver, feeling suddenly dazed by the possibilities. The quantum mechanical implications alone could keep me going for weeks.

Does this mean time travel is possible? What about necromancy? Because Claire was dead, we buried her, and now—

The scientific part of my brain is on fire, but I don't know how long Final Girl's going to let me interrogate her, and—if I am going to accept that this is really happening—there are only a few questions that matter.

I swivel around on my seat, facing her. "Okay, let's say I believe you about this being a gift. Does that mean I can change things? Like, can I actually change the past?"

"You mean can you save your sister's life? Sure." She shrugs, actually *shrugs*, like this is no big deal. "It's your gift; you can do whatever you want. But we're playing by Cinderella rules, okay? There's a time limit. And you can die—that one's important. This isn't a video game; if you die here, then you die for real, which would be a shame because you've got some things to figure out."

My next question dies on my lips. "Wait, what things do I have to figure out? I thought this was a gift?"

"No such thing as a free lunch. You gotta figure out the truth while you're here. If you do, you get to keep whatever changes you make tonight. But if you don't, all this goes back to normal."

The truth. Meaning I have to go through with this charade about figuring out why Owen went all stalker-killer in the corn maze. And if I don't, Claire will go back to being dead, my parents will go back to being split up, and I'll go back to being the girl who lost all her friends, who gave up her crush and college and all her plans for the future.

I feel something heavy settle in my gut. I've known for a year now that Claire was more than just my sister, that she was the glue holding my life together. But I hadn't realized until this moment how bad things had gotten, how far I'd let everything fall.

I don't want to go back to that world.

Is it really possible? Can I undo everything tonight?

"Figure out the truth," I say on an exhale. "Okay. I can do that."

"But you only have until midnight, in case that wasn't clear with my Cinderella comment. Clock strikes midnight and you go back to the courthouse, back to the future."

"Unless I die." I exhale, suddenly nervous. The whole "don't die" thing seems super easy until I start thinking about how Owen already took down Claire. Claire, the strongest, bravest person I've ever known.

I don't stand a chance.

A pained expression crosses Final Girl's face. "Seriously, don't die. I really cannot overstate how important that is." She points to her T-shirt. "You gotta be a Final Girl, got it? You gotta figure out who the killer is, but you have to be smart about it. Do that and you can change history."

I close my eyes and give my head a shake, like the negative thoughts might just rattle loose. "Okay. I think I've got it."

Final Girl pulls into a winding driveway at the end of the street, and a house appears from between the trees like a fairy-tale castle, white columns and Juliet balconies and big floor-to-ceiling windows. All of them dark.

"Erin's place," she explains, stopping at the curb. She leans across my lap, opens the car door for me. "Good luck."

You Know You're Already Too Late, Right?

White gravel crunches under my feet as I make my way down a straight, tree-lined driveway. Erin's house is massive. It looks like four smaller houses all smooshed together, with multiple chimneys piercing the sky and a wraparound porch. Cool blue light reflects off black windows, dozens and dozens of them, too many to count.

I didn't realize my shoulders had crept up around my ears until they drop back down to where they're supposed to be, the sudden release like an exhale.

So. Erin is crazy rich. Okay.

I jog up the steps to the front door and hit the bell. A faint musical sound echoes though the house: Beethoven's Fifth. I make a face as I listen, unnerved. That song is a strangely disturbing doorbell, the chimes too hollow, echoing for far too long.

I wait a few minutes after the bell dies, listening for footsteps or a voice calling that the door is open. Nothing. I pull out my phone and dial the number Eli sent me, but it doesn't ring. A glance at my phone screen shows that I don't have cell service.

Hi Erin, this is Alice Lawrence. I'm outside your front door, I type out, figuring sometimes a text will go through even if a call doesn't.

It isn't until after I hit send that I realize that might kind of freak her out.

Can you text Erin and tell her to answer her front door? I text Eli.

Luckily, this goes through. Being Eli, he responds immediately: OMG is this part of Chloe's prank? Is Erin the next "victim"????

I knew I hated Halloween for a good reason.

Please just do it? I write back.

Eli sends twelve wide-eyed confused-looking emoji faces back.

"Come on," I mutter. I'm about to hit the doorbell again when the *Halloween* theme starts. I glance down at the screen, expecting to see another string of annoyed emojis from Eli.

But it's not Eli. It's Wes.

heard about what happened in the cornfield you cool?

My breath goes still, fingers hovering above my phone screen. This is . . . unexpected. Not just because Wes doesn't seem to think that what happened with Chloe was a prank, but because it's against the Wesley James Hanson III brand to show concern of any kind. He's all manly expressions and quiet stoicism, his real emotions hidden far below the surface of his (perfect golden) skin. It's one of the reasons the nail polish and socks and barrettes always fascinated me so much: the weirdo accessories were like a tantalizing peek into his inner world.

A little thrill moves through me, despite everything.

Still breathing, I type back, and shove my phone back into my pocket without waiting to see whether he responds. I can't obsess over Wes right now. He'll only distract me, and I can't afford to be distracted if I'm going to find Erin before Owen does. I have to "figure out the truth" like Final Girl told me to. Erin isn't the only one whose life depends on it.

I hit the doorbell again, and Beethoven's Fifth echoes through the seemingly empty house, giving me chills.

Why *the hell* isn't she answering?

I shield my eyes and peer through the glass pane to the side of the door. A black-and-white marble floor stretches through the entryway, leading to a curving staircase, a modern-looking chandelier winking from above. Standard rich-people stuff. But no people.

A pit opens up inside my stomach. This can't be happening. Claire can't be right about Erin being at the gym tonight. I can't have gone through all this just to send her straight to Owen all over again. I dig my fingernails into my palms, feeling like I'm about to scream.

And then I catch movement from the corner of my eye, a ribbon of smoke snaking out of one of the upstairs windows.

My heart slams into my chest before my brain can work out what I'm seeing. Did Owen set a fire? Was that how he'd planned to kill Erin? By burning her perfect house to the ground?

But I don't smell smoke. And when I squint and look a little closer, I realize that it's not actually smoke I'm seeing—it's steam. Erin's not answering the door because she's taking a shower.

I swallow, suddenly uneasy. Isn't the victim in scary movies always taking a shower when the killer arrives? I think of the famous scene from *Psycho*, Marion Crane taking a shower in black-and-white. The killer pulls back the curtain, a knife flashing—

I start pounding on the front door. "Erin? Hello, is anyone there?" I jiggle the handle. Locked.

I look through the window again, my eyes ticking off the heavy shadows on the other side of the glass, the shallow wedge of space between the back of the staircase and the far wall, the darkness beyond the door that leads to the hallway. All perfect places for someone to hide.

Nerves prick the back of my neck.

He could be inside right now.

I take a slow step away from the door. My legs wobble. I grab for the porch banister to steady myself, but my hands are shaking so badly that it takes me two tries to actually grab hold of it. All I can think of is the fact that Owen could be inside right now. That he could've heard me.

I glance at the road behind me, realizing that I want to run. Badly. I'm not proud, but when you've seen as many horror movies as I have, you know when it's about time for a good chase scene. Things have been quiet for too long. I feel like I'm being hunted.

In my head, I see Owen standing over my sister in the cornfield, his jaw tight. He reaches for the knife in his gut and yanks it out, lunges—

A sick shudder moves through me. I can't live through that again.

Final Girl told me not to die, so shouldn't I get the hell out of here?

And yet, I hesitate. She also said that I need to figure out who the killer is, that I have to be smart. I don't think a real Final Girl would leave another girl to die, even if it meant saving herself. She'd figure out how to get inside. Warn her.

I close my eyes, an exhale whooshing out of me.

How do I get inside?

I open my eyes and glance back at the house. There are windows everywhere. The entire house is basically made of glass. One of them has to be unlocked. I try to open the ones directly beside the front door, but they don't budge, so I peer through the glass again, squinting to see if I can make out anything inside.

This time, I don't get caught up looking for hiding places. I see all the way through the house to a sliding glass door leading to a deck around the back.

Staring at that door, I feel my muscles snap tight, the minuscule hairs along my arms and the back of my neck standing straight up.

That door . . . it's open. Just a few inches, like someone slid it closed without checking to make sure it latched behind them. The curtain beside it flutters lightly in the breeze coming in from outside.

I close my eyes, bringing a hand to my forehead. A layer of sweat coats my skin, and it feels sticky beneath my fingers. My mouth is so dry it feels like my tongue might crack.

If Owen got inside the house through that back door, then I can, too. All I have to do is make my way around to the back of the house.

Through the dark, dark trees.

And the yard that faces the woods.

Alone.

Easy peasy, right? No sweat.

My legs tremble as I hurry across the yard and around the side of Erin's house. I try to ignore the way the darkness seems to pulse and how the trees could be hiding anyone. Wind rattles the branches around me, making the leaves shiver.

Wind in Nebraska isn't like wind anywhere else. There are no mountains or tall buildings to stand in its way. It travels over thousands of miles of emptiness, and if you aren't used to it, you'd think you were about to be pulled from the earth, Dorothy style, and flung across the sky.

I'm used to the wind, but tonight the sound it makes as it passes through the trees is like rattling bones. It makes the windows in Erin's house tremble almost as badly as my own arms and legs.

I tighten my hands into fists as I pick my way up the steps to the back patio, fighting the desire to run in the opposite direction, to text Claire and demand that she come pick me up right the fuck now.

The sliding door is just ahead. I grab the latch, pull.

It slides open—

Then jerks to a stop.

"What the . . ." I try again, yanking harder this time, but the same thing happens. I look down, noticing a two-by-four wedged between the door frame and the wall, stopping the door from sliding all the way open.

My gut sinks all the way down to my feet.

Okay, I think, swallowing. I've done my part. I really and truly tried, but there's just no getting into this house. Maybe that means Owen wasn't able to get in, either. Maybe all this stress was for nothing.

But I stay staring at the two-by-four, thinking. What kind of rich people wedge something like that into their sliding glass doors? It looks totally out of place. Maybe Erin heard about what happened to Chloe from one of her friends, got scared because she was here all alone, checked all the doors and windows to make sure they were locked, and then found something to wedge the sliding door shut, just to be sure no one would be able to get in.

Or else Owen did it after he came in, so no one would be able to follow him.

A second-floor light switches on, drawing my eye. I back away from the sliding glass door, gaze moving upward, barely daring to breathe.

A shadow appears behind a curtained window. It moves around the room, then vanishes. A moment later, the light in the next room switches on, and the shadow reappears. I hear the faint sound of music, muffled by the windows.

"Erin!" I shout, cupping my hands around my mouth. "Erin, open your window! Please!"

The wind picks up, swallowing my voice. Between that and the music, there's no way she's going to hear me. I look around for a rock or a stick, something I can throw at her window—

Then, from the corner of my eye, movement.

I freeze, my skin crawling. It was a small movement, barely a flicker, but my heartbeat stops inside my chest. My eyes slide back to the glass door, scanning the darkness inside.

It's a kitchen. I see a massive marble island, bar stools, a gleaming stainless steel fridge. Someone left the oven light on, and the faint gold glow illuminates a gas stove top, leaving the shadows beyond even darker.

I take a step closer to the glass, hoping for a dog or a cat to come padding out of the dark, explaining the movement I'm sure I saw. But everything is still.

My eyes settle on a door on the far side of the kitchen, leading to the pantry or the basement or a closet.

It's open, just a crack.

My chest constricts.

Was it like that before?

I try to inhale, but a sob hitches up my throat so that the breath comes in two short gasps, leaving me light-headed. I ball my hand into a fist and press it to my mouth, thinking, *What do I do now? What the hell do I do?*

The upstairs light flicks off, leaving the house dark again. For one second, two, everything is still.

I pull my phone out of my pocket, fingers trembling as I dial 911. I press send ...

No service.

Of course there's no service.

"Shit!" I could throw the damn thing. What's the point of living in some fancy housing development if you can't even get cell service?

I hear the music before I see movement. It's EDM, something loud and crashing and mechanical, the bass practically vibrating through the floor. The kitchen light flicks on, illuminating a figure in the doorway. I flinch—

It's just Erin. Like a true horror-movie victim, she's wearing something slutty: an oversize Omaha East Volleyball T-shirt, no pants.

(Look, I'm not slut-shaming or anything—if I were home alone, I wouldn't be wearing pants, either—but if I were watching this scene in a movie, I'd be rolling my eyes so hard they'd fall out of my head. Of *course* she's not wearing pants. Gotta make sure all the fourteen-year-old boys watching at home have hard-ons while a teenage girl gets murdered.)

Erin carries a bright red Bluetooth speaker into the kitchen and places it on the island, bobbing her chin and dancing around as she starts rummaging through the cupboards.

I bring a fist to the glass and start to pound. "Erin! Erin, open up!"

She doesn't seem to hear me over the music.

"Erin!" I scream, so loud my throat feels scraped raw.

Erin stops dancing and pulls her head out of the cupboard. She turns around, eyes moving toward the sliding door.

I pound harder, my hand quickly growing numb. "Erin! Open up!"

She flinches now, her eyes widening. It's bright inside the kitchen, dark out in the yard. She can't see me.

She yanks a drawer open, fumbles inside. I see a flash of steel and jerk backward, fear jackknifing through me.

She has a butcher knife.

"Who's there?" Erin calls, voice shaking. She takes a single step toward the glass door. "Kyle, if this is some kind of fucking joke—"

A figure appears behind her. He's wearing the same cheesy werewolf mask that X was wearing back at the cornfield, only he's paired it with a full-on shaggy wolf costume.

He looks massive, bestial.

I feel a sick twist of fear noticing that he doesn't have his chain saw anymore. Now he's holding a golf club. I glance back at Erin and slap my palm against the glass. "Erin, Erin, he's—"

Erin's still staring out the sliding door, frowning slightly, butcher knife trembling in her hand. She takes a step closer. "Hell—"

The killer's already swinging his golf club. He hits her directly in the back of her skull with a sick splat.

Blood sprays the glass. Erin's eyes go wide and her mouth falls open, her teeth already coated in red.

Her pupils flicker through the darkness. Focus on me.

"Help . . . me . . ." she says.

And then she lurches forward, dropping to her knees. Her face slams into the door, legs jerking beneath her.

You Should Probably Be Running

The killer calmly removes the golf club from Erin's skull, the sound muffled by the glass and the electronic music still pounding from the speaker.

I'm frozen with horror, unable to move, unable to think.

The killer looks up, peering straight through the glass door to find me in the darkness.

Slow waves of blood surge up my neck. I'm suddenly aware of the sweat under my armpits, the fact that my body is so rigid I'm practically shaking. I can see, beneath the sagging, shapeless eyeholes of the werewolf mask, the dark glint of the killer's eyes.

Fear roars up inside me. I take a single clumsy step backward. Something catches my ankle, and the deck slams into my back, pushing the air from my lungs in a sudden, hard whoosh. Above me, the swirl of darkness and distant stars.

I'm stunned for a moment, pain blistering through my head. The trees around me are silent, not even a whisper of wind in the branches. Somewhere not too far away, a twig snaps.

Then the muffled sound of EDM clicks off.

Footsteps walk toward the door.

I hear Final Girl's voice in my ear, as clearly as if she were crouching beside me.

Don't die.

My arms are wobbly with fear, but I manage to get them underneath me and push myself back to my feet, my breath scraping up the insides of my lungs.

The killer is directly on the other side of the door, head cocked in amusement. Looking right at me.

He watches me from the other side of the glass, and I feel my stomach drop. I stumble back a step as he reaches for the door and pulls.

It jerks open an inch—

Then stops.

In an instant, both of us look to the side and see the two-by-four wedged between the glass door and the wall, blocking it.

Five seconds of extra time. That's all it buys me. I don't know if it's long enough, but luckily my body starts moving without any input from my brain. I don't think; I don't plan; I just run.

Down the deck stairs, stumbling to my hands and knees when I reach the ground. Twigs bite into my palms and rip at my jeans, but I scramble back to my feet, run faster. All I can think about is putting as much distance between myself and Erin's house as humanly possible. I pick a direction without thinking, throwing myself into the deep woods surrounding her backyard.

Pebbles roll beneath my sneakers, making it hard to keep upright. I'm so focused on not falling that I nearly barrel directly into a tree, managing to change direction only at the last possible second. A branch claws at my face, leaving a stinging feeling behind on my skin. I keep going, trying to move faster, faster, but my legs just can't manage to do what I tell them to. They feel numb, like I'm a doll just removed from the packaging, still stiff.

This feels like every nightmare I've ever had come to life. I'm not

fast or sporty. I'm a thinker, not an athlete. All those beautiful summer days when other kids were outside playing sports, I was watching scary movies in bed with all the curtains closed like the capital-F
freak that I am. My body doesn't get that this is life or death, not at
first. My legs shake so badly they can barely hold me upright, and
my arms—what are you supposed to do with your arms when you
run? I waste precious seconds waving them around my body, as
though I can physically pull myself through the air, like swimming.
(Ha, as if I *swim*.)

Wind explodes in my ears, making it impossible to hear the killer
behind me. But I know he's there. I can feel the heat of him, gaining
on me. I can hear his breathing, his footsteps crashing through the
brush.

I close my eyes and pump my arms, thinking, *Faster. Faster.*

Far off, I hear the soft tap of rain in the trees, but I can't feel a
drop. On the other side of the woods there's a deep, rumbling laugh.
I scream in response, but then the sound dies, and in the sudden
quiet, my brain starts working again.

Thunder, I realize. It was just thunder.

A fresh gust of wind blows through the trees, rustling the leaves.
The rain sound is spreading now, echoing against the hard-packed
dirt. I feel cold pricks on my arms and the back of my neck. The
dirt beneath me grows soggy, fresh mud slopping up over my shoes,
cold flecks hitting my ankles.

And then, suddenly, I see a glowing orb of moon just ahead. I'm
out of the woods. The ground below me changes, transforming
from dirt to concrete, and the shift is so unexpected that I stumble,
one hand scraping against the curb as I manage to right myself at
the last second.

There's a heavy breathing sound in my ears, but I can't tell if it's me or if it's him, if he's that close.

I think of the golf club he killed Erin with, the club he's probably still holding. I picture it swinging through the air, wind whistling around it. I imagine how it might smack into the back of my head, how my skull would collapse in on my brain, my blood spraying like Erin's blood sprayed. The damage would be so deep that I might not even feel it at first.

The gate and fence surrounding Erin's property loom up ahead of me.

Oh thank God.

I push myself harder, hit the fence at a run, not even stopping to think that I should not be doing this. I'm not coordinated, not strong. I do not run and jump and climb fences.

I grab the fence and pull myself up, muscles screaming—

And then a hand curls around my ankle and down, down, down I go.

Come On, It's Way Too Early in the Night to Die

So, I think, in the seconds after the cold, damp fingers curl around my ankle. *This is how I die.*

I lose my grip on the fence and stumble back to the ground, thrashing and fighting out of the killer's grip. He lets go of my ankle, but he's still looming overhead, blocking me in.

All that time I spent watching horror movies, screaming at the victims to actually *do* something, kick or run or grab a stick and swing, apparently it was all a big fat waste.

Because now that I'm faced with my very own serial killer, what do I do? I cower against the fence, hands thrown up to protect my face, like I might become invisible out of sheer desperation. Every survival instinct I have shuts off. With the last flare of awareness in my short-circuiting brain, I manage to clench my eyes shut, knowing I'm not strong enough to watch the golf club swing at my face, ending my life.

I just hope it's quick.

"Alice?"

It takes a minute for me to focus on the voice beneath the shrill roar of screaming in my ears.

I'm screaming, I realize, closing my mouth. The sound cuts short, my throat scraped raw.

A hand grasps my arm. "Alice? Hold up, what's going on?"

I blink a few times. There's no werewolf mask hiding the face in front of me, but it's still a moment before I can make sense of the dark hair, the sharp jaw, the flipped collar of an all-too-familiar navy peacoat.

"Wes?" I choke out, utterly confused.

Wesley James Hanson III takes a step away from me, breathing hard. "Shit," he mutters, running a hand back over his hair. It had already been messy, but now it's frizzing around his face, the mane of an angry lion. I notice that he's painted a tiny orange-and-black jack-o'-lantern on the nail of his ring finger.

"This is so weird," he says, blinking. "I was just thinking about you, and here you are."

Under normal circumstances, I'd be replaying the words *I was just thinking about you* over and over in my head, but I'm way too freaked to do that now. I blink, pulling my gaze away from the jack-o'-lantern's tiny black smile. "What are you doing here?"

"I live just over there." He jerks his chin toward a row of very expensive-looking houses on the other side of the road, their winking porch lights barely visible through a thick row of trees. "Now you go."

I glance past him to the pulsing darkness of the woods behind him. It's stopped raining, and wind stirs the branches. Another gust and the leaves scatter with a wet, rattling sound.

Owen could still be back there. Waiting.

"We have to get out of here," I say. The tremor has crept back into my voice, and my palms feel damp with sweat. "Is your car close?"

Wes's brows knit together. "Yeah . . ."

"Cool, let's go." I grab his arm and reach for the fence again, my foot quickly finding a swirl of iron to step up on—

"Wait, I know this cool trick." Wes gives me a look that involves a lot of eyebrows and then turns to the keypad and punches in a few numbers.

Gears crunch and squeak. I jump back to the ground as the gate eases open—

Wes waves his hands in the air, a magician performing a trick. "And . . . *open*. Neat, right?"

I'm barely listening. A flicker of movement at the corner of my eye. I jerk around, staring hard at the woods. Blood thumps in my ears, but if the murderer's still there, he stays hidden.

Cars whiz past in a stream of water-blurred headlights. The rain has started up again, so light that it's more like moisture hovering in the air around than a drizzle.

I dart after Wes, down the sidewalk and across the street, to the tired-looking Jeep with the PROUD PARENT OF A MONROE MIDDLE SCHOOL HONORS STUDENT bumper sticker.

I've never seen Wes's car before. It's at least three different colors, one of which is rust—*most* of which is rust—and it seems like the kind of car you buy when you're an entitled rich kid trying very hard not to look like an entitled rich kid. I don't have the heart to tell him it's not working.

"Monroe Middle School?" I ask.

"Oh, yeah. I had to donate to the bake sale to get one of those."

"And here I assumed you had to have a Monroe Middle School honors student to get one of those."

"Yeah, well, I know people." Wes glances at me as he fumbles for his keys. "It's pretty trashed—"

"It's fine." As if I care about how clean his car is right now. I pull my phone out of my pocket and dial 911.

A man's voice answers. "Omaha Emergency Services—"

"Hi . . . uh . . . there's been a murder at Seventy-One Zero Five South Mountain Road; please send help." I end the call before he can respond. Officer Howie already wants to talk to me about Chloe's murder. I'm guessing he'll be much more motivated to find me and drag me into the station once he learns that I was around for Erin's murder, too.

That I watched the whole thing.

I shudder, feeling sick.

Wes has stopped fumbling with his keys, and now he's staring at me. There's a moment of tense silence, filled only by the sound of rain tapping the top of his Jeep. I think he's waiting for an explanation.

Me too, I want to scream. *I'd like an explanation, too.*

"Alice," he says, when I don't say anything. "What's—"

"Once we're in the car." I cast another nervous glance over my shoulder, but the street is still quiet, empty. Thank God. "Come on, we really have to hurry."

"Okay." Wes turns back to the car, gets the door unlocked. I jog around to the passenger side as he lunges across the seats to hit the lock for me. And then I'm hurling myself inside and pulling my door closed as he starts the engine.

Music screams from the speakers. It's angry. And . . . German, I think.

I spare a fraction of a second to think about the rumor that Wes is a German soft-core porn star and then quickly push it out of my head again. Not the time.

"Sorry," Wes murmurs, turning the volume down. One dark curl has fallen across his forehead, like a question mark. "Police station?"

I barely hear him. I exhale, collapsing against my car seat without answering. Now that we're moving, I allow myself a single moment of sweet, sweet relief.

The killer didn't get me. I'm still alive.

For now.

The moment passes quickly, and then I'm thinking of Claire. I pull my sister's number up with shaking fingers and text: where are you??

"Alice?" Wes says. I lift my eyes to his face. He says in a careful monotone, "Do you want me to take you to the police?"

"No," I say. I expect him to argue with me, or at least ask me *why*. But he just switches on his turn signal. If I told him *I* was the killer and that I needed his help burying the body, I have a feeling he'd have had the same reaction.

I turn my attention back to my phone, hit send, and drop it onto my lap, my head falling into my hands.

It's as though all the horror of what's just happened crashes over me at once, stealing what little remains of my energy. My shoulders slump, body curling in on itself.

Breathe, I think, staring into the darkness of my cupped palms. *Just breathe; the worst is over.*

A moment passes, and then another. Wes balances a palm against the steering wheel and cracks the knuckle in his thumb.

"So," he says after a moment. "I like the ears."

I frown at him, and then my hand flies to the top of my head, where Claire's cat ears are still perched. I'd completely forgotten I was wearing them.

"Thanks," I say, dropping my hand back to my lap. "I guess you're too cool for a costume?"

"I'm wearing a costume."

"You are not."

Wes moves his coat aside, revealing one of those HELLO MY NAME IS stickers on his shirt. He's written *Anthony Perkins*.

I smile. "*Psycho*. Nice," I say. Then, exhaling, "Aren't you even a little bit curious about what's going on?"

Wes glances at me, then back at the road. "I figure you'll tell me when you're ready."

"Ready—" My phone buzzes, distracting me. I snatch it off my lap, but it's Eli, not Claire.

I texted Erin but she never wrote back, probably because she's too busy sucking face with the school's worst Kyle.

Claire's fine, I tell myself. She's at the gym, far away from the murderer. But I stare at my phone screen like I'm capable of burning holes through the thing with my eyes, unable to move or even inhale.

If she's so fine, then why the hell isn't she texting me back?

"Could you drop me off at the gym?" I ask, looking back at Wes.

"I'm not just leaving you somewhere." Wes's eyebrows tug together slightly. It can barely be considered an expression, but still, I'm not used to seeing it on his face. When I picture Wes, his eyes are distant and brooding, and there's a wry twist to his smile that says you didn't get the joke. Concern looks strange on him.

A shiver goes through me. Nothing's the way it should be tonight.

He glances at me. "If you need to go to the gym, that's cool. But I'm coming with you." A pickup truck cuts him off and he steps too hard on the brake, causing the car to jerk. I slam back against my seat, my breath a hard lump in my throat.

After a beat, I fumble for my seat belt, thinking about what Final Girl said. *Forty-seven percent of people killed in car accidents weren't wearing their seat belts.*

Next to me, Wes releases a low breath. "Is this about what happened to that girl in the cornfield?"

"It's not a prank," I rush to say.

Wes raises an eyebrow. "I never thought it was."

"Really? Because everyone else is convinced it's just some big Halloween joke."

"Yeah, I heard that version," Wes says, his voice low and even. "Sounds like a pretty fucked-up joke to me. You sure you don't want me to take you to the cops?"

Relief opens up inside me. At least I don't have to worry about explaining that. "No," I say, turning to Wes. "No cops. Right now, I *have* to find my sister. Just trust me on this, okay?"

Wes chews his lip. Despite the stress of the moment, it strikes me as almost funny that he's hesitating. He likes to pretend he's such an anarchist, but deep down, he's just a good boy who follows the rules like everyone else. It's the kind of thing I would tease him about if everything wasn't so messed up right now.

Eventually, he turns his gaze back to the road. "All right," he says. "Let's find your sister."

He jerks his steering wheel to the side without bothering to use his turn signal, causing the Jeep to fly across two lanes of traffic.

• • •

Claire's not at the gym. I ask a few people whether they've seen her tonight, but apparently everyone's just gotten here, so no one knows anything about anything. Perfect.

"Where now?" Wes examines a fresh-looking scab on his arm as we make our way back to his car.

"I don't know." I hug my arms around myself, feeling sick. Claire could be anywhere. She could already be dead.

Why did I let her out of my sight? How could I have been so stupid?

"Hey." Wes puts a hand on my shoulder. I expect him to offer me some comforting platitude, to tell me he's sure my sister's okay, that this is all going to work out just fine, wait and see. Instead, he just squeezes once and lets his hand fall.

I say, my voice wavering, "Two other girls are already dead. How can you be so calm?"

"I've had a lot of practice," Wes says. He spits something on the pavement, then adds, "Do you know her Apple log-in?"

"What? Why?"

"Find My iPhone."

I close my eyes, thinking, *Duh*. Claire doesn't know I know the password she uses for everything. It's her initials plus her school ID. I found it written on the wall in the back of her closet about a week after her funeral and went through a super-morbid phase of logging on to all her social media accounts and reading through her old DMs and texts and saved posts. I'm the creepiest human alive.

Now I type it into my phone and hit enter, anxiously watching the twitching compass as I wait for the website to load.

Please work, I think.

Please. *Please*.

A map appears on the screen, like magic. My heart soars—

And then, just as quickly, it sinks. I recognize those street names, those curving, twisting roads. I should. I was just there.

"She's driving back to Erin's house," I say, numb.

Wes drags a hand over the scruff on his chin. "That's . . . not good."

My mouth feels dry. Of course she's on her way back to Erin's house. How could I be so stupid? She *told* me she was going to pick me up after she checked out the gym. It even makes sense that she isn't answering any of my texts. The service in Erin's neighborhood is total garbage. She's probably not even getting them.

I picture Claire's dusty Jetta pulling up to the security gate. She cuts the engine and climbs out, all alone. Rain mists her hair as she approaches the gate and peers into the woods where I last saw the killer. Maybe she even calls my name.

And then—

I snap my eyes shut before my mind can go there. "We have to go back," I say, already climbing into Wes's car. "We have to get her before the killer does."

Every Family Has a Few Skeletons

"Alice, wait." Wes grabs my arm. He's not gentle, but I don't think he means to hurt me. Just *stop* me. "You *just* told me the guy who killed your friend is back at that house."

"Exactly," I spit.

"So, going there ourselves makes a ton of sense," he deadpans.

"Good, you get it." I tug my arm away from him and pull my door closed, cutting him off. He swears and slaps the top of the Jeep, rattling the car around me, then strides over to the driver's side and rips the door open.

"No . . . Alice, that was *sarcasm*."

"Your sarcastic voice sounds exactly like your regular voice, so you can see why I might be confused."

"Yeah, I've heard that before." Wes frowns, his face all harsh lines in the darkness. Something sparks in his eyes. It reminds me of the look he got right before punching that reporter in the face, that wild-dog look. I bet it kills him that he has to be the voice of reason, the one advocating *against* running toward danger.

"Here's what we're going to do," he says evenly. "I'll drop you off . . . wherever. Home, if you want, or a gas station; I don't give a shit. And then I'll go back to this chick's house—"

"Alone?" My voice cracks in half. "It's my *sister*."

I'm trying to appeal to some emotion here, but it occurs to me that I don't know anything about Wes's family, if he has a brother or a sister, if they're close. Maybe he hates his whole family. Maybe he can't figure out why I'd bother.

He studies me for another second. I brace myself, waiting for him to keep arguing. But he just swears and starts the Jeep's engine.

I exhale, relieved. "Thank you."

"Start calling her." He keeps his eyes on his rearview mirror as he backs out of his parking space. "Not just texting. The service in this neighborhood sucks, but sometimes I can get a call to go through if I keep trying."

I nod and hit the call button on my phone screen, trying to ignore the tightening in my chest as I listen to the phone ring and ring and ring.

No answer.

Raindrops start tapping the roof of the Jeep, the sound low and hollow. Wes pulls onto the highway. A loud song comes on the radio, drowning out the sound of ringing.

"Well?" He glances at me.

I shake my head and hang up. Dial again. Wes's face looks tense in the dim light coming off his dashboard. The sound of the Jeep's engine grows louder as he speeds up, speedometer climbing past seventy-five miles per hour, then eighty . . .

She's still not answering.

I hang up. My fingers tremble as I go to dial again.

This time, my phone lights up before I touch the screen: an unknown number calling me.

I hit answer. "Claire?"

"Allie? Can . . . you . . . ?" The service is terrible, Claire's voice coming in perfectly clear one second, then cutting out entirely the next. "Can't . . . where are you?"

I sit up straighter. "Claire? Can you hear me?"

I can catch only half of what she's saying. ". . . borrowed . . . but . . . still don't have my . . ."

"Claire, you need to meet me back home, okay?" I shout through the static.

"What . . . don't need me to . . . Allie? Allie, are you there?"

"Claire? Did you hear me? Meet me at home." I'm practically shouting into the phone now. "Can you hear me? You have to get out of there. The killer—"

The line goes dead before I finish. I close my eyes, hissing, "Shit!"

"She heard you." Wes's voice is so low that I barely catch what he says over the hum of his car radio. I nod and look out the window, not trusting myself to speak. My stomach suddenly feels very tight. God, I hope he's right.

Wes must've gotten off the highway while I was talking to Claire because we're on a neighborhood street now, trees and houses flying past us as we drive.

"Where are we going?" I ask, frowning.

"Your place, from the sound of it?" Wes glances at me expectantly, like he's waiting for further instructions.

"Fifty-Ninth and Underwood," I tell him, nodding at the window. "It's the other direction."

Wes pulls a U-turn in the middle of the road.

• • •

Fifteen minutes later, Wes turns down my familiar tree-lined street and pulls up next to the curb in front of my family's old house.

At some point along the drive, he cranked the stereo up again, filling the Jeep with a sound like two chain saws fighting. People seem to be singing. Or maybe screaming is a more accurate description because I can't make out what they're saying. And it might actually be Russian.

"You have interesting taste in music," I say.

"Yeah, well, I like to be able to feel it, not just hear it." Wes glances at me, then back at the road. "You see your sister's car?"

"Sometimes she parks in the back," I explain. Our house is on the corner lot, our front door facing one street, back door facing the other. Claire doesn't like parking out front because of all the trees; birds perch in them and shit on her car.

"Should I drive around?" Wes asks.

"It'll be faster if I just go inside."

"I'll keep the car running."

I'm not sure what danger he expects me to find here, at my own house, but I appreciate the gesture. I shiver and move to push the door open. It's really coming down outside. Rain beats against the sidewalk and the Jeep's windows, so thick that I can barely see the front door of my house.

"Wait," Wes says. "Take this."

He shrugs off his navy blue peacoat and tosses it on my lap. For a second I just stare down at it, my hand resting on the door.

"It's so that your leather jacket doesn't get wet, Sherlock."

"Oh." I pick up the coat and slide it over my jacket. It's heavier than it looks and crazy soft. Cashmere, probably. The collar smells like him, like some sort of musky, woody cologne. My stomach turns over. "Thanks."

"I'll wait out here for you."

I nudge his car door closed with my hip. The sky is black and starless above me, the air so cold it hurts to breathe.

I feel my heart beating a little faster as I dash up the driveway.

She's okay, I tell myself. She probably didn't even get out of the car back at Erin's place. She heard me tell her to meet me at home on the phone.

She's okay. Everything's going to be okay.

But I can't shake the feeling that I messed up. I never should've let her go off on her own. I should've thrown myself in front of her car, done anything to stop her. If anyone's doomed tonight, it's Claire.

I can't let her out of my sight again.

The pavement is so slick with rain that I have to focus on where I place my feet to keep from slipping. Wes's headlights cast dusty yellow streaks across my yard, illuminating my house.

I take the steps to the porch two at a time, like always, but hesitate when I reach the door. Our front door is a deep eggplant purple. We painted it as a family when I was six and Claire was seven. I wanted a blue door and Claire wanted a red one, so we'd compromised on purple. It's the only house I've ever seen with a purple front door.

I feel a pang, remembering. Claire and I had lived in this house since we were born. I could walk down the stairs and around the corner to the kitchen with my eyes closed. I know every scuff on every wall by heart.

Or I did. My mom and I moved out right after the divorce was finalized. For the last six months, we've been living in a two-bedroom apartment downtown. The new apartment always smells like bologna because of the sandwich shop next door, and the only outdoor space is this tiny balcony off the kitchen. I lost so many things over the last year that I never really gave myself permission to mourn losing the house on top of all the rest, but now, standing here, I can feel tears prick my eyes.

Wes's Jeep gives one of those engine-burps, making me flinch.

Get a grip, I tell myself. It's just a house. I force myself to blink and start digging through my bag for my keys, all too aware of Wes sitting in the car behind me, watching everything.

My fingers feel thick, clumsy. Rain pricks the back of my neck and plasters my hair to my forehead. I know it's only a few seconds before I find my keys, but it feels like longer.

The sound of shattering glass erupts from just inside, startling me so much that I flinch, keys slipping to the ground with a wet splash.

"The hell," I murmur. Fear prickles through me. I quickly kneel to scoop the keys up.

I hear voices now. Loud, arguing voices. I frown and lean a little closer to the door, trying to make out what they're saying. The voices have the cadence of a fight, the sharp rise of my mother followed by the lower, more patient sound of my dad, but the wood muffles their actual words.

I hesitate, not sure what to do. I've never heard my parents fight before. Never, not even in the lead-up to the divorce, when my dad's drinking was so out of control that his eyes always looked out of focus and I'd sometimes smell whiskey in his coffee. My mom only ever responded with steely silence and a tight jaw, a request that I keep my voice down because my father wasn't feeling well. I didn't even think they knew how to fight.

The argument grows louder. There's no way my parents are going to hear the door open, but I'm still careful as I slip my key into the lock. I hold the doorknob until I'm sure the latch won't click, and I don't dare breathe, easing the door open without a sound.

"Enough," my mom is shouting. "I'm so sick of the lies, David. Just tell me the *truth*!"

"Please, just calm down—"

"Calm down? Calm *down*? Can you even hear yourself right now? I think I deserve a goddamn explanation! I think you owe me that!"

Something shatters, and a glass shard skates across the floor, inches from the toe of my sneaker. I leap backward, startled, and throw my hands over my mouth to keep from making a noise.

My parents don't even pause in their screaming.

"How many have there been?" my mom is saying. "Two? Three? God, don't tell me it was more than that."

"Laura—"

I glance down, realizing that I recognize the flower-and-ivy pattern along the edge of the shard of glass. It's from our dinner plates.

Mom's throwing our dinner plates.

I reach behind me, fingers wrapping around the doorknob. It was a mistake to come inside. It's clear to me that Claire isn't here, and I don't want to hear any of this. I have to get out of here.

"Tell me their names," my mom is saying, as I ease the door open and slip back outside. "They were important enough to you that you were willing to destroy our family for them. I should at least know their names!"

I close the door before my dad has a chance to answer. For a moment, I just stand there in the cold and the rain, my entire body numb with shock.

All this time, I thought my parents split because of Claire's murder, my father's drinking. But the way my mom was talking just now makes it clear that something else was going on.

How many have there been?

My dad was cheating on her. Really cheating.

Tears prick my eyes. Why didn't Mom ever tell me? Why did she just let me assume all their problems were because of what happened to Claire?

Wes has climbed out of his Jeep and now he's frowning up at me, his face hazy in the rain. His angry chain saw music spills out of the car.

He cups his hands around his mouth, shouting something that sounds like "She there?"

I shake my head. I don't trust myself to speak right now. I can still hear the rise and fall of my parents' arguing voices echoing from the house behind me.

Tell me their names, my mom said. Is that what my dad's doing? Is he saying the names of the women he slept with? The thought makes my stomach churn. Suddenly, the only thing I want is to put as much distance between myself and that argument as humanly possible. I race down the driveway and back to Wes's Jeep, hoping he'll think the tears running down my face are just rain.

Once I'm inside the car, I sit for a moment without saying a word, letting the angry music turn my thoughts to static. Maybe that's why Wes listens to this. It's so loud, you can't hear yourself freak out.

The windshield is slick with water, and when Wes hits the wipers, a wave crests over the side of the car and crashes to the sidewalk. It feels like being underwater. I blink, imagining water bursting in through the windows, seeping in from the cracks around the doors. It feels like I haven't taken a breath in hours.

After a very long moment, Wes turns the music down and looks at me, eyes narrowed. For a moment, he seems to forget about trying to look cool and he just *looks* at me. Like he gets it. I wonder how much of that argument he heard before turning the music up, and suddenly I feel heavy, like there's something tied to my feet, tugging me down. If we were underwater, this is when I'd drown.

My throat gets tight, and my eyes start to burn. "Can you just take me somewhere?"

"That I can do," Wes says without hesitation.

Carb Up! You're Gonna Need It...

We go to O-Town Dough, a doughnut shop that sits so perfectly in the stretch of no-man's-land between my high school and Mercer College that neither school can officially claim it as their own. It's packed when we walk in, students from both schools piled into the thrift-store chairs and cracked vinyl booths, wearing Halloween masks and face paint, "Monster Mash" blasting from at least three different phones. Orange-and-black streamers dangle from the ceiling, and everything smells like brewing coffee and fried dough and cool rain blowing in from outside.

Wes goes up to the counter to order us some coffee, while I slide into a booth near the back, phone in hand.

Claire just texted me. Home now. Why aren't you here?

Change of plans, I write back. Meet at O-Town instead.

I tap my fingers against the table, anxious, as I try to work out how long it'll take her to get here from home. Ten minutes. Less if she doesn't hit the lights.

I check my phone again, but Claire hasn't responded. My stomach feels like a clenched fist. I don't think I'll be able to relax until I see her walk through the door. In fact, I want to rewind the whole night and do everything differently.

Ironic, since that's already what I'm doing. Maybe the lesson here is that it doesn't matter how many times you rewind, there's always something you're going to regret.

Wes returns to the table, carrying our coffees and a tray of at least a dozen brightly frosted, Halloween-themed doughnuts.

"Sugar's here to save the day," he murmurs, sliding the tray between us.

"Thanks," I say. A girl screams on the other side of the café, and I flinch even as the scream dissolves into laughter. Wes cocks an eyebrow at me, so I try to pretend I was just reaching for a doughnut.

"Does that mean you don't want to talk?" he asks as I shove half the doughnut into my mouth.

I shrug, studying the remains of my doughnut so I don't have to look at his face. It was frosted to look like a jack-o'-lantern, but now only one of its tiny triangle eyes and half its jagged smile is left.

"It's cool; you don't have to tell me what's going on if you don't want to." He fists and unfists his hand and then picks up a doughnut frosted like a ghost and bites off its head.

For a few minutes, there's only the sound of chewing and muffled voices, rain hitting the window behind us. Across the room, someone puts on "Monster Mash" again.

"One time, I went a whole month without seeing either of my parents," Wes says out of nowhere. "My dad had these back-to-back business trips, which is whatever, happens all the time, but then my mom didn't come home for weeks and weeks, either. It was so weird; I was all alone in this big house, you know, like *Home Alone*? I didn't even go to school, just watched TV and fucked around online, ate grilled cheese for every meal. It was cool until the bread ran out." He pauses to throw back some coffee. "Found out later that my mom went to Belgium with this friend of hers, a director, I think?" He shrugs. "She swears she left a note."

He says this all so matter-of-factly, like *Don't you hate when that happens?* My parents freak out if I'm ten minutes late for dinner.

"How old were you?" I ask.

"Fifteen."

"You don't have any siblings? A brother or . . . ?"

"Yeah, but he's older. College."

"Oh." I'm quiet for a moment, considering what I know about Wes. Or what I've heard about him, all those rumors. There have been lots of stories about fighting and drugs and parties, stories that make his life seem big and exciting and full of adventure. This story is the opposite. It makes his life seem small, lonely. "Why did you tell me that?"

"In case you want to talk about what happened but are too embarrassed." Wes is smiling, but he doesn't seem happy. A muscle stands out on his neck. "And if you don't want to talk, I can do this all night. Want to hear about the time my dad forgot my name? Just completely forgot it. He kept calling me Bradford, which is *his* dad's name, and apparently what they were supposed to name me except my mom hates my dad's dad. Or I could tell you about how my dad threatened to stop paying my older brother's tuition because he wanted to vote Democrat."

"So, I take it you didn't move out here to escape the Irish Mafia?" Wes raises his eyebrows.

"It's one of the many things people say about you," I explain.

"Ah. No, no Mafia." Wes shakes his head a little and looks down at his hands. He's quiet for a long moment, so long that I'm worried he's going to switch back over to the quiet, brooding Wes again.

Instead, he sucks in his lips, then releases them. "I know there are a lot of rumors about me."

"Understatement of the year."

"When I first got here, I didn't want to tell anyone what was going on with me. It's not some big dramatic secret or anything; it's just my grandpa . . . he's sick. Alzheimer's. The kind where sometimes he leaves the house without any pants on."

I blink twice. "Wes . . . I'm so sorry."

"It's just not something I wanted to spread around. He can't take care of himself as easily as he used to, and he's the only person in my family that I actually like, so I came out here to stay with him, look after him." Wes let his hands fall open. "And that's it, the whole story."

"You must be really close."

Wes glances down at his hands. "He's a cool dude. He was at Berkshire Hathaway for years, used to work directly under Warren Buffett. That's why he lives all the way out here when the rest of my family's on the East Coast." Wes looks up at me, smiling a little. "You'd like him, I think. He's teaching me the value of hard work and a McDonald's two-dollar breakfast. But he goes to bed at, like, eight, which is why I needed all the horror-movie recs. There's not a lot to do here after dark."

Wes lets the full weight of his dark eyes fall on me, like a challenge. I take a moment to consider how different this version of him is from the one most people see, the brooding, bored rich kid who spends too much time on the free weight bench at the Mercer gym.

I blurt, before I can stop myself, "You're a lot different from what I thought you'd be like."

Wes sort of smiles and says, "I guess that's the problem with those horror movies you're always watching. They make you think everyone's really simple. You know, the pretty girl, the bad boy, the geeky sidekick. But real people are never just one thing. Life's a lot more complicated than that."

I stare at my hands for a moment, trying to figure out what I'm supposed to say next. This is the most Wes has ever told anyone here about his life. It might be the most he's ever said at one time *period*. To me, at least. I feel like I owe him something in return.

"I sort of heard my parents fighting," I admit.

Wes doesn't say anything for a moment, but his eyebrows go up just a little. "Bad?"

I shrug and stare down at my half-eaten pumpkin doughnut. It would be easiest to tell him everything's fine, that I just felt awkward and had to get out of there.

But then I think about the day my mom told me she and my dad were getting divorced. It was about two months after Claire died, that weird time between Christmas and New Year's, only it felt doubly weird because no one had wanted to celebrate Christmas after what happened; we hadn't even gotten a tree.

My mom came up to my room and told me to throw a coat on over the pajamas I hadn't changed out of in three days, and she'd taken me here, to O-Town, to get hot chocolates like I was five. Neither of us had really wanted to be out in public, so we drank our hot chocolates in the car with the heater blasting. When she told me Dad was going to move out, I hadn't even been sad. I'd just felt numb. Everything in my life had already gone to shit. It seemed sort of right that my parents would implode, too.

The doughnut tastes suddenly wrong in my mouth, thick and tacky, like Play-Doh. All this time, I thought I knew what had destroyed my family. But it had been something else all along. Something that had been festering.

I force myself to swallow the hunk of doughnut. I can't talk about this with Claire, I realize. She worships our dad. If she knew he did something like this, it would destroy her. But I can't keep it all to myself, either. I feel like I'm going to explode.

I look up at Wes. "Actually I, uh, heard something I really didn't want to hear," I say hesitantly. "It kind of messed me up."

Wes takes a careful sip of his coffee. He seems to take a second to really think about his words before asking, "Was it something about you? Or something about them?"

"Them," I say. And then, before I can talk myself out of it, I blurt, "It, um, sort of sounded like my dad was cheating on my mom."

"Fuck." Wes puts his coffee back down on the table.

I nod. "Yup."

"And you didn't know?"

"No, I didn't know." I shove the rest of the doughnut into my mouth, regretting having said anything. Wes knows who my dad is because of the gym. And more than that, he knows other people who know my dad, people he could tell about this.

Suddenly I have the sensation of trying to hold water in my cupped hands only to watch it stream out through my fingers. Secrets are like that. It's impossible to keep them from getting out. My cheeks blaze. Why did I open my mouth in the first place?

"Hey." Wes reaches across the table to touch my arm. "I really am sorry."

"Thank you," I say, staring at his hand. The place where he's touching me seems to burn. Trying to backtrack, I add, "Anyway. I probably misunderstood. It's been a weird night."

Wes levels me with a steady look, and for a moment, I feel like he can see right through my skin, down to my bones. I cross my arms over my chest, feeling suddenly naked.

"My dad cheated on my mom, too," he admits after a long moment. "When I was little."

I hadn't been expecting this. I open and close my mouth a few times, not sure how to respond.

"Really?" I say finally. Like an idiot.

Wes just nods, seeming not to notice my incredible awkwardness. His eyes are far away. "My mom moved out for a few days when she found out. I didn't know what to do. I was pissed at him, and I didn't want to live at home without my mom, so I ran away, went to live in this old tree house in the woods. Stayed there for what felt like days, until my brother came out to find me. Wasn't even ten o'clock that same night."

"Are they still together? Your parents? Or did they . . ."

Wes's expression tightens. "Twenty-five years now. They just celebrated their anniversary. Sometimes divorce is the best thing that can happen to a family; believe me."

He takes his hand back and shoves the rest of his doughnut into his mouth, and I understand that he won't be saying anything more about his family tonight. I swallow, no longer worried he's going to blab my drama to everyone he knows. If anything, Wes has proved that he knows how to keep a secret. And the story about his parents feels like an offering, his way of leveling the playing field.

"Thank you," I say. "For telling me that."

Wes lifts his shoulder in a half shrug by way of reply. Silence settles between us. A minute passes and then another. And then—

"So . . . this isn't the right moment for this, but . . ."

Wes rises halfway out of his side of the booth and leans across the table, reaching for my face.

Oh my God. He's going to kiss me. Why else would he be moving like this, reaching for me like this?

I've been kissed only once before, my terrible kiss with X freshman year. I've never been really kissed by a guy I actually want to kiss me.

My entire body goes board-stiff, and for a second, I'm seriously concerned about the possibility that I might pee my pants. Is that a thing? Do people pee their pants a little bit when someone kisses them? Horror-movie sex scenes have not prepared me for this.

Wes's hand grazes my face—

And then falls away. I manage to pull myself out of my *I'm about to be kissed by a cute boy* coma for long enough to notice that there's an orange sprinkle stuck to the tip of his index finger.

"This was on your cheek," he explains.

"Oh." My voice is all breath. I didn't really allow myself to miss Wes over the last year, but I did. I missed this version of Wes, not the angry, bitter rich boy he becomes.

I stare at the orange sprinkle on his finger, thinking about the little orange leaf he plucked off my coat this morning. Or was it a year ago? It's getting harder for me to keep track. The place where he touched my face is on fire.

The next part happens fast. I don't make a decision. I don't actually think much at all. For maybe the first time in my whole life, I just act.

I lean across the table and take Wes's face between my hands. His cheeks are rough with stubble, his breath still sweet from the doughnut he was just eating.

He stares at my mouth for a moment. "Alice," he says, and his voice is deeper, throatier than it usually is. "What are you—"

"Just hold still."

I'm not a brave person. I'm whatever the opposite of brave is. But how many chances am I going to get to right a wrong? I do the bravest thing I can imagine doing and press my lips to his lips.

Kissing him is every single fantasy I've ever had while falling asleep in study hall come to life. It's my heart shuddering during the scariest part of the horror movie. It's warm and wet and it tastes like frosting. I feel it all the way through my body. All the way down in my toes.

And I'm not the only one kissing. I can feel Wes's mouth moving against mine, his tongue touching mine.

I'm feeling the kiss other places now. *New* places. I wonder if anyone's ever had sex on a table in here. I wonder how long I can keep doing this before the staff asks us to leave.

When I finally pull away, Wes's expression is unreadable. He seems to be frowning slightly.

Oh no. Oh *God*. Am I that bad at kissing?

"Huh," he says. And then he licks his lips, like he wants to keep tasting me. "I've been wondering what that would be like."

My heart explodes. I'm surprised it doesn't burst out of my chest and slide across the table. *I've been wondering.* Meaning he's thought about me. Specifically, the *lips* part of me. My brain has been reduced to mushy half thoughts. *How . . . ? When . . . ? Huh . . . ?* I can't form words. I can't think at all.

So, of course, I say the stupidest possible thing a human person can say. "The third."

Wesley blinks, twice, like he's just come out of a trance. "What?"

"Your name. Wesley James Hanson the Third. If you're not named after your dad's dad—?"

"Grandpa Wesley's my mom's dad. My uncle was the second, but he never had kids."

"Ah."

Wes eyes me a moment, then exhales. "Look . . . I don't want to press my luck, but should we talk about what you saw? Not your parents, the other thing. The . . . girl."

He says *girl* in a low voice, his mouth curling protectively around the word. I want to go back to the part where we're kissing, but the booth I'm sitting in seems to shift dangerously beneath me, and I have to press a hand flat against the tabletop to keep myself steady—

Erin, the golf club, the killer looking through the sliding door, those dark holes in his werewolf mask where his eyes should've been. The way he stared right through the glass, right at my face.

My phone vibrates, making me flinch. I snap it up and see a new text from Claire.

outside now just looking for parking

I exhale, relieved. Claire's here. She's safe.

"You told me you were going to explain why you didn't want to wait around to talk to the cops, remember?" Wes leans forward, like the two of us are sharing a secret. "Isn't that what you're supposed to do when you see someone get killed?"

"Yeah, well, I did that already, back at the cornfield." A lump swells up in my throat when I say the word *cornfield*, so I keep talking, hoping that will stop new memories from rising in my head. "I . . . sort of know where the killer's going to go next, but when I tried to tell the cops, they didn't believe me. They wanted to drag me down to the station instead of looking for him."

Wes blinks at me. "Is that why you were at Erin's place? Because you knew he was going to be there?"

The golf club connecting with Erin's head. Her blood spraying the glass—

I clench my eyes shut, worried I'm going to throw up Halloween-themed doughnut all over the table. My stomach roils uncomfortably. "I wanted to warn her. But I was too late. He found her first."

"He." Wes shakes his head. "Alice . . . shit, you're lucky he didn't kill you, too. Look, I still don't really understand what's happening, but I'm sure the cops will—"

A new voice cuts through the din of the doughnut shop. "Allie?"

I hadn't noticed anyone approaching our table, and I jerk around too fast. "Claire? Thank God!" Relief crashes over me, and I leap out of the booth and throw both arms around her neck, hugging her much, much too tight. Her hair and sweater are damp from the rain, and I can feel the wet seep through my own shirt, but I don't care. I just hold her tighter.

"Okay, okay, easy on the PDA." Claire unwinds my arms from her shoulders, but she gives me an extra squeeze, her smile wobbly. She's clearly been just as worried about me as I've been about her.

"Sorry," I say. "I was just worried when you weren't answering your texts."

"I didn't have my phone, remember? I just went home to pick it up." A crease appears between her eyebrows as she asks, "Why? Everything go okay at Erin's?"

"Not really." There's no way around this; I just have to tell her. "Erin's dead."

Claire's skin seems to lose all its color. "What?"

"It happened like an hour ago, back at her house. I was there . . .
I . . ." I close my mouth, unable to continue. I feel weird all of a sudden, shaky and cold.

"Allie? I think you need to sit down." Claire eases me back into
the booth, her hand on my elbow. "You're in shock."

She's right. I know from experience that you can't see something
like this without getting hit with some pretty serious post-traumatic
stress. I spent months in the shrink's office after watching Claire get
killed. My parents spent more on therapy than most people spend
on college.

But I can't afford to lose it right now, so I take a deep breath and
say, "It's okay; I'm fine, really."

"Right." Claire doesn't sound like she believes me, but she doesn't
push it. She glances at Wes, her eyes flashing. "Oh. Um, hi?"

Wes jerks his chin at her. "Hey."

For some reason Claire's nose wrinkles, like Wes is a bad smell
she's just managed to place. "What are you doing here?"

Wes looks at me, eyebrow raised.

"Stand down, Claire." I frown at my sister, surprised by her tone.
It's not the first time Claire's gone all mama bear on me, but she
likes Wes. Usually she's rude only to creepy guys who stand too
close to her at parties. "I ran into Wes after what happened to Erin.
He gave me a ride here."

"Did he?" Claire's voice has a hard clip to it, her smile sharp. I feel
my frown deepening. What's going on? This afternoon she was all
over Wes.

Wes must pick up on Claire's weird vibe, too, because he slides out
of the booth. "I'm going outside for a cigarette. You two should . . .
talk."

His eyes linger on me for a beat, and I give a microscopic shrug. I don't know what her deal is, either.

"Hurry back," Claire mutters as Wes shoulders his way through the crowd. The second he's out of earshot, she turns back to me. "Jesus, Allie, what in the actual hell?"

I blink at her. "That was going to be my question. What's your problem?"

"My problem?" Claire's eyebrows go up. "You're the one hanging out with Wesley James Hanson the Third."

Nerves claw through me. It's the way she says his full name, not like we usually say it, like he's a rock star, but kind of spitting it, like it's a bad taste she can't get out of her mouth. Like he's notorious.

It's exactly the same way I've always said Owen Trevor Maddox.

"Why?" I ask, my voice barely a breath. "What's wrong with Wes?"

Something in Claire's face softens, the way it always does when she's about to deliver some seriously bad news. "Look, you think that Owen guy killed Chloe and Erin, right?" She glances across the room, like she's worried Wes is going to sneak up on us, then slides her elbows onto the table, leaning closer to me. "So why are you still hanging out with his best friend?"

Don't You Love a Good Midpoint Twist?

The noise in the doughnut shop seems far away all of a sudden, like I'm separated from it by thick glass. The air smells like sugar and burned coffee and something else—dead leaves soaked in rain, something rotten seeping in from outside.

I say, as steadily as I can manage, "Wes is Owen's friend?"

"His best friend. Maybe even his only friend," Claire says, frowning. "I see them together all the time."

"See them together where?" But even as the words leave my mouth, I know. Owen's a janitor at Mercer. Why didn't it ever occur to me that he could've met Wes there? That Wes also knew Chloe and Erin and Sierra.

"But . . . but that doesn't mean anything," I say. "So they know each other, so what? It's not like—" All of a sudden my chest constricts, making it hard to breathe.

I'm in the woods again. It's moments after Erin was murdered, and I'm running through the trees, sure the murderer is right behind me. And then a cold hand wraps around my ankle, pulls me down, and when I look up, Wes is looming over me.

Wes was in Erin's neighborhood seconds after she was brutally murdered, and I didn't even question it, not for a second.

"He told me he lived there," I say, almost to myself. I stare at the coffee rings on the table as slow waves of nausea roll through me.

"What are you talking about?" Claire's frown has deepened. "Allie? Wes told you he lived somewhere?"

"In Erin's neighborhood." My voice sounds flat. "I— I saw him there right after she was killed."

Claire's eyes widen in horror. "Get your stuff," she says, standing. "We need to leave before he comes back."

I slide out of the booth, still feeling numb. I think of the feral, wild-dog look Wes got this morning, seconds before he slammed his fist into that reporter's face, and for a moment, I can't breathe.

How could I have been so stupid? So trusting?

I lean over the table to grab my phone when my eyes zero in on something across the room.

It's Final Girl. She's standing at the O-Town counter, scanning the brightly colored pastries lined up in the display case. The second my eyes land on her, she lifts her head, like she can feel the weight of my gaze on the back of her neck, and turns, jerking her chin at me by way of hello. "Hold on for a second, Claire," I murmur.

Claire stares at me. "Allie, this is the moment in the horror movie where the audience is screaming at the heroes to run."

"I know . . . just give me two seconds, okay? Wait for me here." I don't need Claire running into Wes in the parking lot. I want her inside, surrounded by people, where she'll be safe.

Final Girl straightens as I approach her. "Hey—"

"Was it Wes?" I choke out, interrupting her.

"Whoa. Slow down." She checks her reflection in a stainless steel napkin holder, pausing a moment to pick a single bright purple doughnut sprinkle out of her teeth.

I feel my jaw clench together, thinking about the weight of Wes's jacket on my shoulders, the smell of his cologne still clinging to the collar. And, oh God, our *kiss* . . .

I feel like I'm going to be sick.

I need to know the truth. Whatever it is.

"Wes," I say. "Are he and Owen in on this together? Is that what you sent me back here to learn? That the guy I like is a murderer?"

Final Girl does shocked, her hands pressed to her cheeks, mouth open, all wide-eyed. "A murderer?" she says, like she's a horrified little old lady. She fans her face with one hand. "Oh my."

For some reason this is what gets to me, the fact that she's acting like what's going on is *funny*. All the fear and frustration I've been feeling roar up inside me, and I find myself snapping, "I don't understand why you're being like this. Back in the van, it seemed like you wanted to *help*."

"This isn't a Disney movie, princess. I'm not your fairy god-mother. I can tell you the rules, but I can't give you the answers. That's all you."

"But . . . this isn't a *movie*! People are dying."

Final Girl gives a little chirp of a laugh. "She said people are dying. Do you honestly think I don't know that?"

"You're acting like you don't care."

"Little girl, I care more than you can possibly know. But *you* were the one who wanted your sister back. Did it not occur to you that, for that to happen, a lot of other girls were going to have to die?" She says this in a flat voice that sends guilt worming through me. Like what happened to Erin and Chloe is my fault.

But I'm not the one who picked up the chain saw or the golf club. I'm not the one who killed them. I tried to stop it.

I force myself to meet her gaze and say, as steadily as I can manage, "It's not my sister's fault that those girls are dead."

Final Girl's eyebrows go up an infinitesimal amount, like maybe she's surprised I'm arguing with her.

The door to the doughnut shop swings open behind me, and I feel my whole body go tense—if it's Wes, then I've already lost my chance to sneak away without a confrontation. I spin around, searching—

But it's just a group of teenagers in costumes. I turn back around, but I can't get my body to relax. Wes could come back any second. I have to get out of here.

"Please," I say to Final Girl. "You told me you sent me back here to figure it out. Is this what I'm supposed to figure out? That Owen wasn't working alone?"

Final Girl stares at me for a moment and then rolls her eyes extravagantly. "You know I can't just *tell* you that, right?"

Irritation prickles through me. "Then why are you even here?"

"To give you a clue, little miss ungrateful. Observe." And with a pointed look at me, she turns and stares out the doughnut-shop windows. At the street.

The *empty* street.

As in no Wes.

I feel something cold zip down my spine. Usually there are a couple of smokers standing around the ashtray in the parking lot, but there's no one there right now.

"I— I have to go." I take a single, clumsy step back. "I—"

"Shush!" Final Girl grabs my arm, holding me in place. "Manners. Didn't your mother ever tell you not to talk during the show?"

Show?

This time, when I glance out the doughnut shop's window, a police cruiser is pulling up next to the curb. Two officers sit in the front seats, but I'm not looking at them. I'm looking at the shadowy figure huddled in the back, his head ducked, hair hiding his face like a curtain.

Oh my God.

Suddenly, I can't hear anything over the sound of blood pumping in my ears. I open my mouth, but all that comes out is air.

I recognize that greasy hair, those sloping shoulders. I would know them anywhere.

I wet my lips and say, "Is that—"

"The vile, wicked Owen Trevor Maddox!" Final Girl cuts me off. "Amazing, right? I should take this show on the road."

It strikes me harder than it ever has before, seeing him in the back of the police cruiser. Over the next year, they'll take his picture dozens and dozens of times, and in each one, he looks more hardened, more like a criminal.

But tonight, he just looks like a kid. He looks scared.

I swallow and give my head a soft shake. *He killed Claire*, I remind myself. He deserves to be in the back of that car.

But the skin on the back of my neck has started to crawl, and I know that, once again, I'm missing something. This doesn't quite line up.

What is it?

I start to feel light-headed and realize it's because I've been holding my breath. I force myself to exhale, to concentrate on breathing in and out, in and out.

That's when it occurs to me: the timeline doesn't work. If the police had believed me about Owen, they would've picked him up after they left the cornfield. But that was hours ago, when Erin was still alive.

If Owen was in police custody when Erin was murdered, then he couldn't have killed her.

But Wes could've.

Just Under Two Hours Until Midnight

"Normally I don't do hints," Final Girl says, "but we need to speed this along, so if you're wondering whether he was in police custody when Erin was murdered . . . well, let's just say you're on the right track."

My stomach folds in on itself, horror spreading through me like nausea. "He didn't kill Erin?"

Final Girl looks almost sympathetic. "No, girl. He didn't."

The police cruiser's headlights switch off, making it even harder to see inside than it was before. But I can still make out the shape of Owen's shoulders and the greasy slant of his hair.

The cop car suddenly seems like a very bad omen, like a black cat darting across my path or a mirror shattering at my feet.

Things aren't going to work out the way I'd hoped they would tonight. Things are about to get much, much worse.

The slam of a car door snaps through me, breaking whatever spell I'd been under. A cop has just climbed out of the cop car, and now he's making his way to the doughnut-shop door.

It's Officer Howie, I realize, my throat closing. If he looks up, he'll see me standing on the other side of the glass. And then . . .

Shit, shit, shit.

Behind me, Final Girl starts humming the *Jaws* theme. "Duhnuh-nuhnuh . . . duhnuhnuhnuh . . ."

I scowl at her. "You aren't helping."

"Wasn't trying to," she says, sounding practically gleeful.

Officer Howie's just outside now. Any second the doughnut-shop door is going to fly open, and he'll step inside and see me here like a complete idiot. I brace myself—

And then, miraculously, he trips. I hear him swear on the other side of the window as he stumbles.

"Okay, now, *that* was me trying to help," Final Girl says, grinning at me. She waves. "Off with you."

Officer Howie's fall has probably bought me only an extra ten seconds, but I'll take whatever I can get at this point.

"Thanks," I say, and rush back over to the booth that Claire's still hovering around. "Hey, so we need to go. Like, immediately." I jerk my head toward the doughnut-shop window. Officer Howie has straightened up again, and now he's reaching for the door. A blast of icy air sweeps into the stuffy, overheated café as he pulls it open.

"Is that Nat's brother?" Claire cranes her neck to see past my shoulder.

"Yes, otherwise known as the cop who wants to take me down to the station for questioning, remember? So—" I grab her arm and start to pull her toward the back of the doughnut shop. "Let's go."

"Okay, okay." Claire quickly slides out of the booth, and I shove her toward a door at the back of the café that reads EMPLOYEES ONLY. Customers aren't supposed to come back here unless they need to use the bathroom, but none of the kids working behind the front counter look up as I yank the door open and push Claire through.

The narrow, dimly lit hall opens into a storage area filled with boxes of soda and doughnut racks. I slip through the door, leaving it open just a crack so I can see Officer Howie approach the counter.

"A cop who likes doughnuts," Claire mutters from behind me. "He's really embracing the cliché, isn't he?"

I elbow her and shoot her a look that says to shut up.

"Sorry," she murmurs.

I turn back around, holding my breath as I bring my face back to the crack between the door and the frame. I was hoping Officer Howie would just get a doughnut and go, but instead, he kneels and gazes into the doughnut case like he's gearing up for a big order.

"Crap." I pull the door closed carefully, praying it doesn't draw Officer Howie's attention. Turning to Claire, I ask, "Did you see Wes come back into the shop?"

"No," she says, frowning. "Why?"

"He wasn't out front with the other smokers."

Claire chews her lip. "Maybe he went around to the side of the building so he could stand beneath the awning? People do that sometimes when it's raining."

"Maybe." Or maybe he got into his car and took off to find Sierra.

I turn around, my pulse picking up. I must've walked through this storage room a million times to use the bathroom, but I've never really looked around before. It's dark, cluttered with stainless steel rolling racks that had been filled with doughnuts at some point earlier in the day but are empty now, except for sheets of grease-stained parchment paper and scattered black-and-orange sprinkles. A clock shaped like a cat hangs from the wall above the door, wide white eyes staring down at me, long black tail twitching back and forth, counting down the seconds.

I stare at that clock for a moment. The short hand points at the ten, the long hand just past the twelve: it's after ten. I have less than two hours before midnight. Each twitch of that tail is another second Wes has to find Sierra before I do. Another second of my gift wasted.

Figure it out.

"Where would Sierra be tonight?" I say, thinking out loud. Unlike Erin, Sierra didn't run around telling the story of how she spent the night that could've been her last. I have no idea where to start looking for her.

But Claire only blinks at me. "How would I know? She's your friend."

"She's Eli's friend," I correct her. Sierra used to hang out at our table before school and at lunch, but I never really got to know her that well. I would wave when I saw her at the gym, and I guess we'd talk sometimes, but it was mostly dumb stuff. *What'd you get up to over the weekend?* Things like that. Once, she mentioned that Chloe Bree had fat thighs, and I remember thinking it was an incredibly rude thing to say. Who gave a shit what Chloe's thighs look like?

Sierra has a secret boyfriend, I think, out of nowhere. Nerves prickle up my arms as I recall the conversation I had with Millie and X this morning.

She told me she met him at the gym.

My breath seems much too loud all of a sudden. Millie had been talking about Wes, of course. This morning I hadn't been able to think past my own jealousy, but now the conversation seems bigger than that, another clue I'd overlooked.

Wes was friends with Owen. He was outside Erin's house minutes after she was brutally murdered. In another version of the next year, he starts dating one of Owen's victims. *Why?*

My breath stops in my throat.

To get close to her? To finish the job when Owen couldn't?

"Hey, are you okay?" Claire asks, and I realize I've been frozen in place, staring at the brick wall for God knows how long.

"Yeah, um, just thinking," I murmur. I pull out my phone and shoot Eli a text.

do you have Sierra's number?

Claire doesn't seem to hear me. She's looking past me now, her eyes focusing on something just beyond my shoulder. "Hey, uh, you don't think Wes could've come back here, do you? Like, to use the bathroom, maybe?"

Sweat breaks out on my palms. I jerk around.

The bathroom door hangs open, watery yellow light trickling into the otherwise dark storage room. I stare, trying to ignore the dry rasp of breath in my throat. *Fuck.* Was the door like that when we came in? I blink two times, fast, trying to remember. But I honestly don't know. I don't even think I looked at the bathroom after I shoved Claire back here.

"No," I say, glancing back at Claire. "We would have seen him come in through the doughnut shop."

"I think there's a door to the parking lot back here," Claire says. "The employees use it when they're taking out the trash."

Dread builds in my chest. I know the door she's talking about. X smoked for a little while last year, because a guy he liked smoked, and I'd sometimes hang outside with him to keep him company. The back door is usually propped open with a brick. I can clearly remember him slipping inside to use the bathroom, coming back out with a doughnut he stole from one of the baking trays.

Which means that yes, Wes could've gotten back here without us seeing him; he could be back here right now.

I think of the door in Erin's house inching open, Wes creeping up behind her, golf club held high above his head, and for a moment I can't breathe.

"Let's get out of here," Claire murmurs, crowding in behind me. I nod and together we inch toward the bathroom. The cracked-open door splits the storage room in half. Wes could be on the other side right now. Waiting for us.

If we were in a horror movie, this is the moment the audience would be screaming at the screen, telling the dumbass girls to turn around and go back through the shop, where it's light and crowded and safe.

But Officer Howie's back there, geniuses. If he sees me, he's going to drag me down to the police station and Sierra dies. Which means that Claire dies.

So we're braving the storage room. Deal with it.

The light above us flickers. Claire and I both look up as it flashes off and on, a bug-zapper lamp killing moths. It goes dark for the final time, and I hold my breath, waiting for it to turn back on. But it doesn't. Of course it doesn't.

"Bulb must've gone out," I whisper.

"Good place for a jump scare," Claire says. I know she's trying to calm me down by appealing to my well-documented love of genre conventions, but her voice sounds too high in the darkness, edging on hysteria.

She isn't wrong, though. I can picture the movie version of this moment as clearly as if I were sitting at home watching it on my computer right now. How the camera might push in on our faces, close enough to see the way Claire's lower lip trembles, the tension threading through my jaw. How the sound in the room would drop out, leaving only our ragged breathing, the way our shoes shuffle over concrete.

Behind us, the cat clock ticks steadily.

It's not just the darkness that's so freaky. It's the details you can't capture in a horror movie: like the sickly sweet smell of sugar hanging in the air, so thick that it's starting to give me a headache, and the way the stainless steel baking equipment looks oddly sinister in the darkness, the gleaming metal making me think of knives. Everywhere I turn, there's another shadowy nook, a corner bathed in darkness. A million and one places for Wes to hide.

The bathroom door is three feet away from us.

Now two.

If this were a movie, Wes would be hiding behind that door, with a knife.

No, wait: he'd be holding one of the metal strainers the bakers use to dig doughnuts out of the frying grease, and he'd fling grease at us as we came around the corner. Horror writers love a unique kill.

I can hear a dripping faucet and the water-churning-through-pipes sound that means a toilet's just been flushed. I feel a sudden stab of pain in my temples and remind myself to unclench my jaw.

He's not there. I'm just being paranoid. He's still outside . . .

I reach forward, fingers curling around the edge of the door. My heart crashes against my chest as I swing it open—

The bathroom is small and square, dirty white penny tiles on the floor, a toilet with the lid closed. To the left, a cracked mirror, reflecting my face back at me.

I stare at my double for a moment, breathing hard.

"He must still be outside," Claire says from behind me.

I watch my reflection nod, but my brain is spinning. I was wrong. In the movie version of this moment, the bathroom would've been a misdirect, a chance for the audience to relax, thinking the danger has passed before—wham. Big kill. My skin crawls.

"Let's just find the exit," I murmur, pushing the bathroom door closed.

Claire nods and hurries past me. I hug my arms to my chest, shivering as I follow her.

We round the corner at the back of the room, and a door appears between the storage shelves and folding chairs, the neon exit sign clearly visible in the near dark. An exhale bursts through my lips, my heart stuttering with relief.

"Go," I say. My phone buzzes in my hand, and I glance at the screen automatically.

Eli.

Joke's getting old, Allie. Where are you?? You're missing everything!

My stomach clenches. The thought that anyone is still celebrating tonight is so horrible I have to close my eyes for a moment.

Bad idea. With my eyes shut I see Chloe sprawled across the ground, her dress hitched over her thigh. I see Erin walking across her kitchen, unaware of the figure creeping up behind her.

I have to tell him, I think. But I know I won't. The story will be all over the internet tomorrow morning, and Eli and everyone else will find out what really happened then. I can't stand to be the one to break it to them early.

My phone vibrates again, making me flinch, my eyes snapping back open.

Anyway Sierra's here, Eli texts. Everyone's here.

Here? I text.

Little gray dots, and another text pops up as I'm reading. We're all at Millie's. Her parents are out of town so the party's migrated over here. You coming???

"Who's texting you?" Claire asks.

"Eli," I murmur. "Apparently there's a party at Millie's. He says Sierra's there."

Claire leans over my shoulder, the orange-blossom smell of her skin wafting over me as she reads his text. "Millie lives out in West O, right? It's gonna take forever to get out there."

I groan and throw the back door open. "Yeah, but at least—"

Wes steps in front of us, and I take a blundering step backward, my stomach slamming into my throat—

"Found you," he says, his voice a low rumble.

Wear a Seat Belt

Frosty air sweeps over me, and the rain has turned to a light mist, minuscule icy droplets that immediately attach to my nose and hair as I stand in the doorway, frozen with shock. I can feel Claire hovering behind me, her hot breath on the back of my neck. I want to swat her away, but I don't dare move.

Wes's eyes move back and forth between the two of us, suspicious. In the dim light of the moon, his face looks fragile, like something made of glass. "You guys disappeared on me."

"Sorry," I say automatically, trying to steady the violent thrum of my heart. Claire's Jetta sits at the far edge of the parking lot, waiting for us. I want to push past Wes and make a run for it, but I can't let on that I know what he is, what he's done. Not when we're alone with him back here.

In the dark. Where absolutely anything could happen.

The muscles in my shoulders clench tighter.

Claire pushes me forward, the tiniest nudge, and I step outside. A razor-thin layer of frost covers the asphalt, snapping like bone beneath my sneaker.

"We, um . . ." I blink, searching for something to say, some excuse. The Jetta winks from the corner of my eye. Safety. Claire's hand finds my wrist, gives it a squeeze, and I wonder if she's thinking the same thing.

That we should just make a run for it. That we might be faster than Wes, if we catch him off guard.

Wes narrows his eyes. "Alice," he says, carefully. "What's—"

A door slams open, making us all jump, and then there are shadows moving through the storage room, barely visible past the rows of baking equipment.

A voice. "Alice Lawrence? I saw you come back here, so there's no use hiding."

Officer Howie. My shoulders crawl up toward my ears.

"Car." Claire shoves me the rest of the way outside, the door loudly clanging shut behind her. My legs turn liquid. I trip over my own feet, trying to remember how to get my body to move—

And then Wes catches me by the wrist. He's so close that I can feel the heat from his body. I can smell his sweaty cowboy smell.

"Alice," he says, searching my face. "What's going on?"

I jerk away from him, bile rising in my throat.

Wes's expression sharpens.

He knows, I think.

Claire's hand snakes under my elbow, pulling me into a run. She's the one who inherited our dad's athleticism, all those weekend squash games, the two of them going for morning runs while Mom and I hung back at the house, barely able to work up the energy to switch on the coffeepot.

Her Jetta's not even a hundred feet away, but I'm just over five feet and Claire's nearly as tall as our dad. Thirty seconds of trying to keep up with her long-legged strides, and my lungs are already screaming.

How am I supposed to be a Final Girl when I can't even *run*?

The sound of a door slamming open. I glance over my shoulder and see Officer Howie stumble outside.

"Hey!" he shouts, tearing after us.

Claire digs her car keys out of her pocket midstride and jabs her thumb at the door lock button. Across the parking lot, her Jetta honks, headlights blinking—

And then Wes explodes from behind us, long legs pumping. He looks bigger than he did sitting in the booth in the doughnut shop, all lean muscle and adrenaline. Watching him run, I remember that he used to be an athlete. And not just any athlete, a rower. A six-foot-three *jacked* rower.

I flinch, thinking he's going to grab me. But he runs past me to the Jetta and yanks the back door open, lunging inside.

"Shit," Claire mutters. I shoot her a look. *What the hell are we supposed to do now?* You don't have to be a horror-movie expert to know that you absolutely do not get into a car with a murderer.

But Officer Howie's faster than I expected him to be. He's already halfway across the parking lot, gaining speed. His face is bright red from the exertion, the raspy sound of his breathing echoing between us. Half a second more and he's going to be close enough to grab me.

Claire drops my arm and races ahead, throwing herself into the driver's seat. The engine growls to life. My legs feel like they're about to give out, and my lungs scream.

Wes has left the back door open for me. I'm just a few feet away when he leans out, calling, "Alice! Come on."

This is why people in horror movies make such terrible decisions. Because the clock's ticking and I don't actually have time to think about all the horrible things that could happen in a small car with a vicious killer. I have a fraction of a second to decide what to do.

If I don't get into the car with Wes, Officer Howie's going to drag me to the station for questioning. Sierra will die and Claire will die, and I could be the one charged with their murders.

So I get in.

Claire peels through our sleepy downtown, car trembling as she navigates over brick roads, past boutiques with darkened windows, café lights winking from the sidewalks. I close my eyes, still trying to catch my breath.

Wes takes up so much more space than I expect him to. Or maybe it's just that Claire's car is smaller than his Jeep. He has to fold his legs to get them to fit behind the driver's seat, knees practically to his chin. The tip of his head brushes the top of the car.

He moves in the seat next to me, and the soft fabric sound of his jeans brushing against the Jetta's seats fills my ears. My skin buzzes, all too aware of how close he is. His hand rests on his knee, just a few inches from mine.

I stare at that hand, imagining those fingers wrapping around a golf club, swinging it toward the back of Erin's head—

"Hey, you okay?" Wes touches my arm, and I flinch like I've been burned.

"I'm fine." My voice sounds strange, even to me. I scoot a little closer to my door.

Wes stiffens beside me, making it clear he noticed. He's quiet for a moment, and then he exhales, slow and careful. "You sure?"

I nod. "Uh-huh."

"Because you're acting weird."

Claire switches the car radio on before I can answer, the sudden blare of static making me flinch again.

Wes narrows his eyes at me. I always loved his eyes, how they're such a dark brown they look almost black.

Now I can't help thinking of the killer staring at me from behind that werewolf mask, how all I could see was the light glinting off his dark eyes.

I turn to look out my window before Wes can ask me anything else, huddling down in my coat. Which, I realize a second later, is actually *his* coat. The collar still smells like him. I hold my breath, feeling like I might be sick.

Tonight wasn't supposed to go like this. Erin's not supposed to be dead. We shouldn't be running from the cops. Owen being in police custody should've been a *good* thing, not something that twists my stomach into knots.

We drive in silence for several long minutes, nervous energy prickling through the air between us. Every time Wes shifts or exhales, I hold my breath, barely daring to move.

And then Claire slows and flips her turn signal. Her eyes meet mine in the rearview mirror, widening slightly as she pulls off the main road—onto Military Road.

I stiffen against the car seat. What is she doing? Claire knows I hate driving down this street at night. Military runs through the cornfields just outside the city, and Claire loves it because there are hardly any traffic lights, but that's just because there aren't any lights at all. You can't even see the glow of downtown in the distance, just two solid black walls of corn to either side of the two-lane road. It's the kind of road you hear about in bad urban legends. The kind of road featured in stories that end with "And they didn't find her body for weeks." If I were watching this moment happen in a horror movie, I'd be so annoyed with the characters for making such a dumb decision that I'd get up and leave.

The Jetta's headlights illuminate twin patches of asphalt just in front of us. Wind passes over the fields. I can't see the stalks shiver, but the sound is low and mournful, like waves crashing against a beach or voices echoing through a cave. I stare out the window and try not to think about the nothingness surrounding us.

Finally, Wes clears his throat. "Either of you want to tell me why we're running from the cops?"

His voice is a low rasp. My skin crawls. I dig my fingers into the leather of the car seat, thinking, *Why did you take us this way, Claire? What are you planning?*

"Allie's an evil mastermind," Claire deadpans, speeding up. We're going nearly eighty now. I brace myself against the front seat, my stomach dropping.

I can see Wes glance at me from the corner of my eye, but I can't bring myself to look back at him. "It's a long story," I murmur.

"I think we've got time," Wes says. "Where are we going, anyway?"

Claire glances at the rearview mirror again. She widens her eyes, and this time, I realize she's trying to tell me something. I frown back at her, not understanding.

She tightens her fingers around the steering wheel. "Didn't Allie tell you what we're doing tonight?"

"She told me a little," Wes says.

"There's a murderer on the loose," Claire says calmly. "And Allie's the only one who knows who he is."

Wes is still looking at me. I feel the weight of his eyes like heat. "You didn't tell me you knew who he was."

Oh God, Claire, what are you doing?

I wet my lips. "It's just a theory."

I still don't look at Wes, but I feel him watch me for a beat longer. He's still sprawled across the back seat, all casual, but it's clear from the way his hand has tightened around his knee that he's deeply, deeply bothered.

The skin on the side of my face itches.

Claire's eyes flick to the rearview mirror again, going almost comically wide this time, her frustration with me evident. I'm frowning back at her, annoyed, when my sisterly intuition finally kicks in.

Seat belt, I realize.

She's trying to tell me to put on my seat belt.

I jerk my seat belt over my lap and click it closed a second before Claire yanks the steering wheel to the left, forcing her car off the road and into the field of corn.

There's a bump as the front wheels roll off the road. Wes releases a jagged yell, and I jerk forward, my seat belt digging into my neck. Stalks of corn crack and break all around the car, smacking into the hood and windows with dull thumps as we crash through them.

The car hits another bump, and there's a sick smack before it shudders to a stop. Wes makes a groaning sound and then goes silent.

Blood pounds in my ears as I blink into the darkness. I can't see anything. Cornstalks are piled over the windshield and all the windows, their dry leaves pressed up against the glass.

I look around, trying to take calm, even breaths. I can't see anything, can't see anyone—

And then my door flies open, cold air pouring over me. "What are you doing?" Claire asks, gasping. "Run!"

Stay Out of the Fucking Cornfield!

Corn towers over us, blocking the moonlight. I can make out the jagged teeth of sky through quivering leaves, the distant glow of a moon half-covered in clouds. Otherwise, we're in complete darkness.

"Wes?" I choke out, dazed.

"He wasn't wearing his seat belt. He hit his head on the window when we crashed."

Forty-seven percent of people killed in car accidents weren't wearing their seat belts, I think as Claire tries to drag me out of the car. It's like Final Girl knew this was going to happen.

"Allie, come *on*," Claire says. I fumble with my buckle, hands shaking as I manage to release my seat belt and rip it away.

I cast one last glance into the darkness of the car. It's perfect, unbroken black. I can't see anything, not even the outline of Wes's crumpled body.

"Do you think he's dead?"

"I hope so," Claire says. Her hands are still on my arm, and now she's half pushing, half dragging at me, trying to get me to follow her.

Wind rustles through the field, whipping leaves against my face. I think of Chloe sprawled in the maze, her severed arm lying in a pool of blood. I think of Erin's blood splattering against the glass door.

Wes didn't seem at all surprised when I told him I saw a girl get murdered. I remember being a little impressed by how chill he was being, but now it just seems like another clue that he was behind this all along.

In a movie, there's no way he'd be dead, I realize, stumbling into a run. He'd wake up and follow us. He'd pop out of the corn the moment we thought we were safe.

Claire drops my arm now that I'm running and starts shoving her way through the stalks ahead of me. Heart hammering, I follow. The ground is treacherous, covered in fallen corn and rocks, seeming intentionally designed to trip us up. I have to grab at the stalks to keep my balance, the surprisingly rough texture of the leaves biting at the skin on my palms.

Claire darts through the field easily, seemingly unbothered by the uneven ground, the darkness.

"Claire, slow down," I shout after her. But I can barely hear my own voice over the moaning sound of wind, so I don't know how she's supposed to hear me, either. I push myself faster, my ankle rolling on a loose bit of dirt. "Claire—"

I hear the soft snap of a cornstalk breaking in half just below the howl of the wind and release a wild yelp. I look over my shoulder—

Nothing but dark shadows, swaying corn.

I blink a few times, eyes watering as I strain to see past all that black. Just because I can't see anything doesn't mean there's nothing there. I turn back around, legs burning as I pump them faster. *Faster.*

It's much, much too dark. Claire's only a few feet in front of me, and her black sweater and skirt bleed easily into the night. I have to focus to make out the edges of her shoulders, the swaying movement of the cornstalks as she easily pushes through them.

I follow, willing my legs to move faster. The wind is blowing harder now, the rustling sound filling my ears. But if I concentrate, I'm certain there's something else, something just below that sound.

Another snapping footstep. The sound of boots shuffling through the cornfield.

Wes must've woken up. He must not have been hurt as badly as Claire thought. He saw that we left him behind, and now—

Now he's coming for us.

I have no way of knowing whether that's true, but I can't stop myself from picturing him. He's moving through the stalks like a leopard, his long legs making it so easy for him to keep up with us, no matter how fast we run. Maybe he's right behind me now, close enough to grab my arm, only he's waiting, letting me think there's still a chance I could get away. That's what would happen if this were a movie. He'd play with us a little.

A desperate sob climbs my throat at the thought. There's a part of me that wants to give up right now, just collapse on the ground and cry.

There's another soft, crunching sound, perfectly audible this time. Wes's boots hitting the dirt? Or just my own blood pounding in my ears?

This is what it feels like to be tracked, I think, tears streaming down my cheeks. This is what it feels like to be hunted.

Then—lights flashing through the stalks.

I release a sound that's half sob, half cry of excitement as they draw closer, twin spotlights flickering through the stalks.

Claire's voice echoes in the dark. *"Headlights."*

The wind makes her sound far away, even though she's just in front of me. The two of us break into loping runs, no longer caring how badly the cornstalks smack against our arms and faces as we push through them. I see the gray slab of road through the stalks and release a relieved breath.

Finally.

Claire bursts out of the corn like a madwoman, and I stumble after her, automatically throwing my hands over my head to wave.

The headlights grow larger, closer, the car approaching fast now. It's still maybe a hundred yards away when I part my lips to call for help—

Blue and red lights flash. A siren howls to life.

I drop my arms on instinct, a brand-new fear crashing over me with the suddenness of a falling building—

Officer Howie is in that car. He must've followed us down this road.

I'm still standing at the side of the road, dumb and frozen, when Claire wraps a hand around my mouth and drags me back into the corn with her.

"Just wait," she whispers, her lips so close to my ear that her breath tickles my skin. I nod into her hand, and her grip on me loosens. Together, we watch the cop car creep, creep, creep past, its lights still flashing blue and red, its siren a low, whooping growl.

Once it's vanished over the top of the hill, Claire exhales and shuffles back onto the road. "That was close."

I hurry after her, not wanting to spend even one more second back in the corn. "What do we do now?" I ask, wrapping my arms around my chest.

There aren't any streetlamps on this stretch of road, and it's so, so dark. The moon seems farther away than usual, tinted orange in the night sky. It gives off little light and creates far too many shadows. Claire's face is all sharp edges and deep hollows, her eyes twin black orbs.

"Isn't Millie's place just a mile or so up the road?" she asks. I nod and she adds, "We can walk."

I glance back at the corn. The field is filled with small noises. Wind in the leaves, twigs snapping, something that could be a footstep, only it's impossible to tell. I release a shaky breath. "Aren't you worried Wes is going to come after us?"

"I really don't think Wes is going to be getting up anytime soon."

I roll my lip between my teeth. I still can't shake the feeling that he's hiding on the other side of the corn, waiting for the perfect moment to jump out at us, like any good slasher villain.

I swallow hard. "Let's just walk fast, okay?"

The Clock's Ticking ...

It's not raining anymore, but the asphalt is slick and damp, and it's cold enough that thin sheets of ice crack under our shoes. I shiver. I left Wes's coat back in the car, thinking it wasn't so cold now that it was no longer raining, but Nebraska is like this. Days that start out sixty and sunny quickly drop below freezing after the moon comes out, frost creeping over the city like dread.

The next streetlight is at the very top of the hill. I keep my eyes trained on the dusty circle of light, forcing myself to walk faster. A twig snaps behind us. I flinch and look over my shoulder. All I see is inky blackness.

I'll feel a whole lot safer once we get to that light.

"Aren't we breaking a rule?" Claire asks. She's not wearing a coat, either, but she doesn't seem to mind the cold. She's got her hair piled over one shoulder, and she's trying to work it into a clumsy braid. "Wandering down dark streets that cut through cornfields doesn't seem like something a Final Girl would do."

I glance at her. "And you're the expert on what a Final Girl would do now?"

"Totally," she says, knocking shoulders with me. "I learned from the best, didn't I?"

It takes me a minute to remember what she's talking about. Last summer—or just a few months ago, I guess, in this reality—Claire got it into her head that she wanted to be a movie star. She'd always wanted to be an actress, but ever since I can remember that meant Juilliard and Broadway and New York. Then she changed the plan.

"Look at me," she'd said, batting her eyelashes comically. "Wasn't my face just made for the big screen?"

I know how she can come across, how all that confidence can read as arrogance, but trust me, Claire's not really like that. The confidence was a show, her way of hiding when she felt vulnerable or when she doubted herself. The summer before she died, she applied for the Juilliard summer intensive, and she'd just found out that she hadn't been accepted. It was the third time she'd applied, the third time she'd been rejected. And she'd been getting closer to the end of high school, when she'd have to apply to Juilliard for real. I think it was starting to occur to her that she might not get in. She'd been talking about Juilliard for as long as I could remember.

But Claire would never just come out and say that she was doubting herself, so instead, she decided to pivot to movies. She found out about this super-low-budget horror movie that was shooting in Salt Lake City for some reason, and decided she had to go audition, that it was going to be her big break. And she needed to bring me because I was the one who knew about horror movies.

"You can spend the entire car ride turning me into the perfect Final Girl," she'd said.

It's one of my favorite memories. Me and Claire road-tripping to Salt Lake, quizzing each other on Final Girl stats. It occurs to me for maybe the first time that I never actually found out whether she got that part. She died before I could ask her about it.

I glance at her. "Whatever happened with that movie, anyway?"

Claire shrugs. "They probably never figured out how to pay for it. Hey, why didn't you want to go home?"

The sudden topic change throws me. "What are you talking about?"

"You told me to meet you at home, and then you changed your mind and said to go to O-Town Dough instead," Claire says. "Why?"

It's such a non sequitur that I can't come up with a good lie. I think of the fight I overheard back at the house. Mom screaming, *How many have there been? Tell me their names.* As if I needed anything else to occupy my mind tonight.

After a few tense seconds, I swallow and say, "It doesn't really matter right now."

Claire glances at me sharply. "Our house is closer to Erin's than O-Town is. You should've had time to stop there and meet me while I went back for my phone." She glances at my mud-splattered jeans, the hole in my shirt I don't remember getting. "It would've made sense for you to change, at least."

"Is that what this is about, Claire? You're annoyed that I didn't change into something cuter after I saw a girl get killed?"

"I'm just saying it would've been logical for you to throw on some clean clothes. So why didn't you?"

I hesitate, not sure what to say.

"You heard Mom and Dad fighting, didn't you?" Claire asks when I don't answer her.

I release a low exhale, my breath hovering in an icy cloud before me. This is exactly the kind of twisted logic that Claire excels at. You think she's talking about one thing, being an asshole, and then she brings it back around on you. She should work for the FBI.

She sighs and flicks her braid back over her shoulder, where, without an elastic, it starts to unwind. "Was it because Mom found out that Dad's cheating?"

I cut my eyes at her. "You *knew*?"

She shrugs and glances down at her feet. I stare at her for a moment, but I get the feeling that she's keeping her eyes averted so I won't see how upset she is. Claire always has to be the strong one.

"I found a phone in his things," she says after a while. Her voice sounds normal enough, almost like she's trying to pretend none of this is a big deal. She picks a twig off her tights. "It was one of those disposable ones. I didn't look on it or anything, but I figured . . . I don't know. The only reason a guy buys a burner is if he's doing something seriously messed up."

My stomach clenches, thinking of Claire finding Dad's phone, dealing with all this on her own. "When was this?"

"Last year."

I stop walking, stunned. "You've known about this for a *year*?"

I can't imagine keeping something like this quiet for a year. It was hard enough not telling her about it the second I found out.

But Claire just looks up at me, unblinking. "Yeah, well, I kept waiting for Dad to ask me where his phone went, but he never did. I guess he was embarrassed."

"Wait, you *took* the phone?"

"I threw it away."

"But . . . why would you do that?"

"Because I didn't want Mom to find it." Her face gives nothing away, and I get the feeling again that she's trying to hide something from me, some emotion she's embarrassed to feel.

Either that or she's testing me. It's hard to be sure with Claire.

"Okay . . ." I start, my head still spinning, "so you didn't tell Mom?"

Claire keeps her eyes trained on me for a beat longer, and then she shakes her head, clearly exasperated. "Allie, normally I love how you think the world actually follows all those rules you learned in movies, but sometimes you can be so naive."

"Hey, that's not—"

"If I'd told Mom, she would've left Dad a year ago. This way he had some time to get his shit together." Under her breath, Claire adds, "Not that he used it."

I say nothing for a long moment. I'm thinking, randomly, of this thing that happened when we were both in junior high. I'd been looking through Mom's purse for some ChapStick and found a pack of cigarettes instead. I'd been completely shocked. Mom didn't smoke. Or at least I didn't think she smoked. She'd been lecturing us about the dangers of smoking for years, telling us how disgusting it was, how dangerous. Finding those cigarettes had felt like such a betrayal. I remember holding the pack up to Claire, letting it dangle between two fingers like it was something truly horrible, unable to speak.

But Claire hadn't seemed remotely surprised. She'd just rolled her eyes and plucked the cigarettes out of my hand, taken the pack to the bathroom. There, she'd flushed the cigarettes down the toilet, one by one.

"It's for her own good," she'd explained, when I'd asked her what the hell was going on. "Cigarettes are expensive. Eventually, she's going to get tired of buying them."

It was only then that I'd realized this must've been something she did a lot. Finding Mom's cigarettes, throwing them away. Saving her from herself. I'd been so proud of my sister in that moment. I would've put the cigarettes back, horrified, and pretended

I'd never found them, but not Claire. Claire was going to fix it.

But Dad cheating on Mom . . . it's not just a bad habit that he needs to kick. It's bigger, worse. I wet my lips, thinking of how things have been this past year. Dad's drinking, the distance between him and Mom. Him and me.

There are some things that are so broken you can't put them back together, no matter how hard you try.

Another pair of headlights loom in the distance, distracting me. I shield my eyes, my heartbeat spiking.

"Hey," I say, nudging Claire. "Put your thumb out."

Claire, following my gaze, takes a step into the road and sticks out her thumb without asking any questions.

The headlights get bigger, closer. I squint as their glow fills my eyes, so bright it's practically blinding. The car slows and relief crashes over me as I back onto the shoulder, giving it space to pull over.

It parks about a yard ahead of us, engine still grumbling as the front door creaks open. Someone sticks their head out, slowly turning to face us.

He's backlit by the car's headlights. It takes me a second to make out his face in the darkness.

No, I realize, as my eyes adjust. That's not his face. My mouth goes dry as I realize that the driver is wearing a mask.

And not just any mask. A werewolf mask.

The same mask the killer wore to bash in Erin's head.

The masked man climbs out of the car, his movements slow, patient. He's clearly in no hurry to get to us. He knows there's nowhere for us to go.

I'm so completely stunned that I don't even try to run. I want to shrink away from him, but there's only the cornfield behind me.

I manage to take a single step backward, colliding with Claire, who, annoyed, mutters, "Come on, Allie, watch where you're going."

"Claire," I whisper, tremors of fear slowly overtaking my body.

The masked man tilts his head, those black eyeholes trained on us. His car's headlights are still on, shining uselessly onto the empty road ahead, lighting him from behind so that his clothes and his head and his body—everything except for the gray skin of his mask—is all in shadow.

I grasp for Claire's arm without taking my eyes off him, my fingers shaking, clumsy. "Run," I choke out, stumbling back another step. A cornstalk's leathery leaves crunch into my back.

But Claire doesn't move. She frowns at me, confused. "Allie? What the hell?"

The masked man is only a few feet away now. I stare, thinking he's going to kill Claire and then he's going to kill me, and all of this, the whole night, will have been for nothing.

I clench my eyes shut—

"Alice?" says a familiar voice. I open my eyes again, blinking into the headlights.

"X?" I shield my eyes, squinting as X pulls the mask off and takes another step toward us. He's still mostly in darkness, but I can tell now that he's shorter than I originally thought, slighter.

"Hey, you guys okay?" he asks, frowning. "What are you doing walking alone around here?"

"We need a ride to Millie's," Claire explains, but she's still looking at me, frowning slightly. "Allie? What is it?"

I realize I'm still tightly gripping her arm. She shrugs me off, and I quickly clasp my hands together, heat blazing up my neck.

"It's nothing." I blink, forcing myself to really look at X's face. I knew he'd be wearing that mask tonight. Everyone's going to be wearing it.

Claire narrows her eyes at me. "Allie, are you sure you're okay?"

"Fine," I murmur, my eyes still on X. He's pulled the werewolf mask back on, and those dark eyeholes make me deeply uncomfortable. "Let's just get into the car, okay?"

Claire frowns, like she's still not sure whether I'm totally okay, but she shuffles up to X's car and climbs into the back seat, graciously leaving me to take shotgun. This might not seem like a particularly magnanimous gesture, but I know how much Claire hates sitting in the back. She even tells people she gets carsick so they'll insist she take the passenger seat.

"Thanks," I murmur, and pull my own door shut.

It's not until I remove my hand from the latch that I realize my fingers are still shaking.

You're Not
Out of the
Cornfield Yet

I'm still feeling shaky, panicky. It takes me two tries to get my seat belt buckled. When it finally clicks into place, I wet my lips and, turning to X, say, "I'm sorry; I didn't mean to freak out before, it's just been—"

Wham!

I jerk in my seat, stomach leaping into my throat as a body slams into my window, blood-covered hands starfished against the glass.

It's Wes. He has blood smeared over his forehead and in his hair. "Alice! Open the door! Alice!" He reaches for the car door, but I slam my hand down on the lock just in time, the hard plastic driving into my palm.

"No!" Wes groans when the door won't open. He slaps my window again. "What the fuck, Alice, you have to—"

"Jesus, X, drive!" Claire shouts, pounding on the back of X's seat with her fist.

"Oh my God, who is that?" X asks, fumbling his keys.

"Does it *matter*?" Claire asks.

"Alice!" Wes says again, his dark eyes meeting mine through the glass. He's gasping harshly and swaying on his feet.

My stomach clenches. He's in rough shape. If I'm wrong about what I think he's done, it would be monstrous to leave him here.

I stare into his eyes, searching them for some clue that he's the guy I'd thought he was all this time, that my suspicions are way off base.

But who did I even think he was? What do I know about him—*really* know about him? Just what he told me at the doughnut shop, and there's no way to verify any of that. He could've been lying. Everything he told me could have been a lie.

My cheeks flush. I feel so stupid, so gullible. All this time I thought it was so interesting that no one knew anything about Wes's past, that he wasn't on social media, that his entire identity was this giant question mark. Now I see it for what it is. Not mysterious and cool—suspicious, strange.

"X," I say, looking away from Wes. "Go!"

X hits the gas, and we peel away, leaving Wes standing in the road behind us.

I swivel around in my seat, watching him grow smaller and smaller. My body hasn't realized that the danger's passed. My heart is still going fast, and my palms are damp with sweat.

It's okay now, I tell myself, collapsing back into my seat. Wes can't catch up to a moving car. We're safe.

I check the time on my phone: 10:35. We just have to dodge Wes for the next hour and a half, and then everything will be okay.

Next to me, X says nervously, "Will someone tell me what the *hell* is going on?"

We're climbing out of the car in front of Millie's house when I finish telling X the broad strokes of what's happened tonight.

Chloe. Erin.

He doubles over in the middle of the street, hands braced against his knees, taking deep, gulping breaths, like he's about to hurl.

"Breathe, X," Claire murmurs. She pats him on the back gingerly, like she's worried he might break.

"We . . . we all thought it was just a prank." He's not looking at me but staring into the distance, his eyes glassy. "We didn't know."

"I know that," I tell him. He doesn't seem to hear me. It's a weird thing to see someone really terrified, not just scary-movie terrified. I've seen X scared so many times, but I've never seen him like this.

"We didn't know," he says again. He has his werewolf mask pushed back like a headband, ears sticking out from beneath the rubber. It still creeps me out to catch any glimpse of that gray mask, so I try to keep my eyes on X's face.

"And you've been running from the police?" he says, not looking at me. "Do you have any idea how messed up that is?"

X doesn't get mad that often but I've known him long enough to know the signs. Like how he refuses to look me in the eye, and how he keeps shaking his head and pressing his lips together.

"I know," I say. "I'm sorry, it was stupid."

"Stupid?" And now he looks at me, finally, his eyes narrowed and angry. "Alice . . . this isn't some dumb slasher we're watching down in your basement. This is real life."

I frown, a little surprised that he's so pissed. "I know that—"

"Do you? Because *you* might be able to run from the cops without worrying about getting shot, but I'm a Black teenager in Nebraska, hanging out with two white girls on the same night a couple of *other* white girls turned up dead." His eyes widen. "Get it?"

I feel a horrible twist in my gut. I didn't even think about that. All this time, I'd been so focused on saving Claire that I hadn't even considered the very real ways I was putting my friends in danger. "X ... I'm so sorry. I didn't think."

"No shit, *you* don't have to think about things like that." He scrubs a hand over his mouth and shakes his head, again, like he still can't believe this is happening. I haven't seen him this upset since we were all twelve years old and we saw a stray dog get hit by a car down by the park where we used to hang out. Me and Millie had immediately burst into tears, but X had just stared, eyes wide and shocked. We thought he was okay, shocked but fine, until he went behind a bush to throw up.

That's what he looks like right now. Like he's going to be sick.

"Everything about this is so messed up," he says under his breath.

"Maybe you should go. You can find Millie and Eli and the three of you can get somewhere safe." It suddenly seems very important to get my friends as far away from here as possible. I'm the one who dragged them into my horror story, after all. If anything happens to them, it'll be my fault.

X looks at me like I'm crazy. "Are you seriously pulling some white savior shit on me now? You're one of my best friends, I'm obviously not leaving you behind when there's a killer on the loose. And Millie's not going anywhere, either. This is her house. Where's she going to go?"

"I don't know, you can make something up, get her over to O-Town, or ..." I try to think of somewhere else they could go, somewhere safe, and come up blank. This whole city feels dangerous tonight.

"Allie, think about this; they might actually be safer here, sur-rounded by all these people," Claire points out. She weaves her arm through X's, pulls him into a stumbling walk. "Maybe we should just focus on finding Sierra."

"Why? What's up with Sierra?" X looks like he doesn't actually want to know.

"We think she's the next victim," I murmur. I expect him to ask me how I could possibly know who the next victim's going to be, but he only nods.

"Let's just get inside," he mutters. "It's really creeping me out to be standing here in the dark."

Millie's house is familiar like a security blanket, white with black shutters and no personality, the scene of countless sleepovers and movie marathons and late-night study sessions. Bad music pours from the windows, people crowding the porch and spilling into the yard. No one looks the least bit scared or sad. I walk past a group murmuring excitedly about being questioned by the police in the cornfield, hands flapping as they talk about how *real* it all felt. A sign hanging over the porch reads WELCOME TO THE HALLOWEEN MASSACRE in dripping red letters meant to look like blood.

"This is all so messed up," X says again.

"Yeah." I swallow, looking away from the sign. "I think I'm going to throw up."

Claire nods, her face pale. "It's not their fault. If we hadn't seen Chloe, we'd probably think it was a prank, too."

We have to push our way through a wall of bodies just to make it into Millie's living room, where it seems like every kid in our school is dancing and drinking, even the kids who never, ever go to parties. I spot Zareen Syed, saxophonist in the school jazz band, standing on the other side of the room. She's talking to Nick Fairchild, who usually spends his nights doing youth-group scavenger hunts and

Bible studies. But no Sierra. Nerves make the hair on my arms stand up.

Where is she?

"Can you look for Sierra?" I ask X. The music's turned up so loud I can barely hear myself think, so I have to shout. He gives me a thumbs-up that I would've made fun of in a different situation and quickly disappears into the crowd.

A girl I don't recognize darts in front of me, holding a pink plastic mask.

"Here you go!" she says, thrusting it into my hands. Before I can ask her what the hell, she's made her way to the next maskless partygoer.

And now, looking around, I notice that everyone's wearing masks. Billie Ericson, the head of our theater's costume department, is wearing an elaborate rhinestone-and-feather-encrusted cardboard number that just covers their eyes, and a few people standing around them are in full-on rubber monster heads. Someone on the opposite side of the room wears a werewolf mask, just like X's. Just like the killer's.

I keep my eyes trained on the guy in the werewolf mask for a moment longer, feeling uneasy. The mask is slightly too big, and it droops away from his face, making it impossible to see his eyes. The two holes where they should be are dark, empty. My throat closes up as I watch him coolly scanning the crowd. A predator looking for the weak gazelle.

Something about the way he moves reminds me so much of Wes. I glance down to see whether he has a jack-o'-lantern painted on his ring finger, but his hands are in his pockets.

We left Wes back in the cornfield, I remind myself, shivering.

There's no way he could've gotten here before us. And Owen's still in custody.

Claire touches my arm. "Allie?"

"We need to warn them," I say, looking away from werewolf guy. "I could find a way to turn off the music and . . . I don't know, climb on the couch and shout at them or something."

Claire raises her eyebrows at me. "Do you really think that'll help?"

"They should know what's going on."

"If we tell them what's going on, they're all just going freak out. And that's if they even believe us. How are we going to find Sierra if everyone loses their shit?" She lifts the mask she's holding—a plastic one identical to mine except that it's orange—and pulls it over her eyes. "Put yours on, too. We need to blend."

I glance at her and then back at the guy in the werewolf mask, feeling suddenly light-headed. She's right. I know she's right. It doesn't matter whether they all know the truth about what's going on right now. What matters is finding Sierra.

I check my phone: 10:47. There's a little over an hour left until midnight.

Claire knocks shoulders with me. "Why don't you look around for her down here? I'll check the second floor."

She winks at me and begins fighting her way through the crowd.

"Claire, wait," I call, stumbling after her. "I really think we should stick—"

Hands clamp down on my eyes, freaking me out so much that I actually scream.

"Whoa, crazy girl, it's just *me*." Eli spins me around. "Have you been drinking too much of the spiked punch? Should we find you a sandwich?"

"I'm not drunk," I say, but I'm talking too loud, too fast, all the fear of the last few hours bubbling up inside me at once. I twist around, but Claire's already gone, swallowed by the party. *Shit*.

I turn back around. I know I just told Claire I wouldn't do this, but I can't help myself. Eli's my best friend. He deserves to know the truth. "Look, Eli," I say, trying to make my voice as serious as possible. "The guy who killed Chloe is going to be coming after Sierra next. He might even be on his way here now."

Silence, probably just a few seconds but it seems to last forever. Then the corner of Eli's mouth twitches. "Come on, Alice, give it up."

I blink at him. "What?"

"Everyone's over the Chloe thing now. I mean, it was great, she totally got us and your performance was"—he gives a chef's kiss— "perfection, really."

Millie comes up behind Eli and drapes an arm over his shoulder. "What are we talking about?"

"Alice is still in character. She wants to break up the party before the *murderer* gets here." Eli says *murderer* in a low, spooky voice, and Millie releases a burp of a laugh.

"Alice, seriously, tell Chloe to come out from wherever she's hiding already. She's going to miss the whole party."

I open my mouth to respond, but my head feels suddenly crowded, so many thoughts and words tumbling through my skull that it's impossible to focus on just one. I want to yell at them that Chloe's not hiding, that this is real. I want to grab them by the shoulders and scream.

But all I can manage is "You don't understand, it's not . . . that's not . . ."

Someone bumps into me, and I stumble into a girl wearing

another werewolf mask. My eyes skate over the mask's gray skin and long, sharp teeth, and my stomach flips.

"S-sorry," I mutter, quickly moving away from her. I'm suddenly way too aware of my body, how small it is, how fragile. Why didn't I spend the last sixteen years getting really into Krav Maga or judo?

I vow to sign up for some serious self-defense classes if I manage to make it through this night.

"Where's Sierra?" I ask, turning back to Eli and Millie. I have to shout it.

Eli frowns. "She was just over on the steps with Mark Evans a minute ago."

Mark is our school's version of a generic hot guy. He's Johnny Depp in *A Nightmare on Elm Street*.

"Mark? Really?" Millie exhales a slow breath and says conspiratorially, "She should be careful, or her secret boyfriend's going to get jealous."

I'm still thinking about Freddy Krueger, and it takes me a second to process what she's just said. "Wait . . . what?"

Next to me, Eli smiles and, in a perfect echo of this morning, he says, "Sierra has a boyfriend?"

"Secret boyfriend," Millie says, looking scandalized. "Key word being *secret*."

I stare at her for a long moment, thinking, *What in the actual hell?* We've already had this conversation.

Or, no, that's not quite right. We have this conversation a year from now, when I stop by the cafeteria table on the morning of Owen's trial. But how can we be having it now if it's not supposed to happen for another year?

The only way that makes any sense is if—

And now I go still, understanding crashing over me. The only way that makes sense is if Sierra and her secret boyfriend have been together for a year.

Which means that she and Wes were together tonight. When he was supposed to be with me.

I say, my voice oddly wooden, "Does he go here?"

"No, Sierra said he's older," Millie says, same as this morning. "She met him at the gym. Hey, maybe you know him? You and Claire basically live at the gym."

Eli glances at me, a frown wrinkling his forehead. I know he's thinking the same thing I am.

He says, uneasily, "Guys, maybe we should talk about something—"

"Is it Wesley?" I interrupt. "Wesley Hanson?"

There's a pause of about twelve seconds that feels more like twelve hours. I go breathless, my shoulders climbing toward my ears as I wait for Millie to respond. *Oh my God, yes . . . how did you know?*

But she just wrinkles her nose. "That guy everyone thinks is, like, in the Irish mob?" She laughs, actually *laughs.* "Um, no?"

I'm so surprised by her answer that a sound of complete disbelief hiccups out of me. Eli puts a hand on my shoulder, murmuring, "Alice? Honey, are you sure you're doing okay?"

I shrug him off, but I can't bring myself to speak. It feels like the party has ground to a halt around me, like someone's pressed pause and now everyone's staring, waiting for whatever comes next. "You're—are you sure?"

"I mean, Sierra didn't actually tell me his name, but, yeah, I'm completely sure." Millie leans in a little closer, lowering her voice. "I thought he was a student, too, at first, but Sierra and I were just talking, and she made it sound like her guy is *older* older. Like *married* older. She said he's going to get into some serious trouble if anyone finds out he's with a high school girl."

Something skitters across the surface of my mind. *How many have there been . . . Tell me their names.* It snatches the breath from my lungs.

No. That's not possible.

"Alice?" Millie asks, frowning. "Are you sure you're okay? You look really pale."

"Fine," I say, numb. But my brain is still working, slotting this new information together with things I'd overheard, things I thought I knew. My heart is beating slow and loud, a drum, a warning.

My father wasn't . . . not with a high school girl . . . there's no way.

But then I remember standing by the side of the road with Claire, her picking a stick off her tights, not looking at me.

The only reason a guy buys a burner is if he's doing something seriously messed up.

I feel like the bottom has fallen out of my stomach. She's right. If you're just having an affair, you put a fake contact in your phone, delete the messages after you've read them, double-check that no one knows your password. But Dad bought a burner phone.

How many have there been?

My phone beeps. I feel myself reach for it and pull it out of my pocket, my eyes shifting down without consulting my brain first.

Every muscle in my body seizes up.

It's Wes.

We need to talk, the message reads.

I'm still staring at the screen when another comes in, also from Wes.

I'm outside.

Of Course He's Outside

Fear clamps down on me like a vise. Suddenly, everything seems so much louder, so much closer. If tonight is a horror movie, the sound has been turned up to blaring, and I'm all too aware of the number of people pressed around me, their overlapping voices making it impossible to focus on the thoughts bouncing around inside my own head.

Wes's message stares up at me.

I'm outside.

Outside. He's outside. Right now. He found us.

"Shit." I stuff my cell phone back into my pocket, hands shaking so badly I nearly drop it.

Eli touches my arm and I flinch, bumping into Nat Howard, who's standing directly behind me. Nat's a shoo-in for best dressed, and here I've gone and spilled her drink all over her throwback Britney Spears costume. Awesome. She scowls at me and mutters a nasty word before trying to wring out her Catholic-schoolgirl skirt.

Eli looks scandalized. "*What* is going on? Seriously, Alice, you're acting crazy tonight."

"Sorry," I say. "I'm sorry, I—"

Luckily, Claire appears then, saving me the trouble of trying to figure out how I'm supposed to finish that sentence.

"Hey," she says, one hand already on my arm, gently easing me toward a hall at the back of the room that leads into the kitchen.

I want to ask her about Dad and Sierra; I want to know if it's true, if she *knows* and she never told me, but Eli trails after us, so I keep my mouth shut. I love Eli, but I can't share this with him. Not yet. Not ever.

In a low voice, Claire says, "Okay, so don't freak out, but that officer guy just pulled up."

"What?" I swivel around, a feeling of utter hopelessness washing over me. One more thing I can't deal with right now. I rise to my tiptoes to see over the tide of bobbing heads.

"He hasn't come inside yet," Claire explains. "He got swarmed as soon as he climbed out of his cruiser; apparently a lot of people think that, because he's Nat's brother, this is all part of Chloe's big prank."

Claire casts another look over her shoulder, making sure Officer Howie's still outside. "I think he's breaking the news about what's really going on now. Once people realize that what's happening is real and that he's here as, like, a cop and not part of some prank, things are going to get seriously chaotic. You should think about slipping out the back."

"Wait, there's a *cop* here?" Eli interrupts, his eyes monstrous behind his glasses. "Shouldn't we, like, bail?"

"That's not all," Claire says. "This part is actually kind of bad. I went outside to see what he was saying, and it sounds like they let Owen out of custody."

My heart jackknifes. "They let him go? *When?*"

Claire shakes her head. "I dunno. All I overheard was Davey—

I mean Officer Howard—saying something about how they'd brought someone in for questioning but they didn't have enough to hold him." Claire grabs the mask I'm still clutching and holds it up to my face. "He's going to come inside soon. Blend in. I'll . . . try to distract him."

I grab her arm before she can disappear again. "How are you going to do that?"

"Only way I know how." She says this in her sexy voice and wrinkles her nose at me, just in case I didn't pick up on the innuendo. My sister, queen of the single entendre.

"Claire, this isn't the bouncer at some club you're too young to get into. He's a freaking *cop*. You can't just flirt with him and expect it to get you anywhere."

But she just shrugs. "It'll be easy. Nat's brother's always had a thing for me." And then she's weaving through the crowd again, a little extra swivel in her hips.

Groaning, I yank the mask down over my face and head toward the hall. I've seen Claire get like this often enough to know there's no arguing with her, and if I'm being perfectly honest, I have too much on my mind right now to worry about whether she's about to make a fool out of herself in front of a cop.

My phone feels hot inside my jeans pocket, Wes's last text practically burning through the fabric, scalding my leg. I shove my way past freshmen sticky with alcohol and girls who look way too young to be in high school, ignoring the dirty looks they toss my way like grenades. Claire's right; once people start realizing there's a cop out front, the whole night's going to devolve into chaos.

Eli's right on my heels. "Alice? Alice, slow down, please. Tell me what's going on."

He tries to get me to look at him, but I drop my eyes because I don't have an explanation for him right now, not with my head still so full of my dad and Sierra. And Owen released from police custody and Wes, just outside, wanting to *talk*. And all my friends who are caught up in my mess, who might be in real danger.

I feel like I'm dissolving, little bits of me coming off and floating away.

Wes is a murderer. He and Owen are in on this whole thing together. It doesn't actually matter that my dad was sleeping with Sierra. *Wes* killed Erin. He was outside her house right after she was murdered while my dad was all the way . . .

I stop walking, horror slamming into me like a fist. Where was my dad when Erin was being murdered? Not home. I know that because of the phone call, Claire and me in her Jetta, heads close as we listened to Dad's voice booming from my phone's speaker.

I'm in the car now; I can bring your phone to you.

He was in his car, and then, maybe twenty minutes later, when I tried to find Claire's cell on Find My iPhone, that little dot was hovering around Erin's neighborhood. I'd thought Claire had gone back there to pick me up—but she didn't have her phone.

My dad did.

Which means Wes wasn't the only one outside Erin's house after her murder.

The phone in my pocket doesn't feel hot anymore. It feels heavy. Out of nowhere, I think of walking into a pool of water with my pockets full of stones, letting them drag me down and down until my lungs fill and I start to choke. That's what this feels like, like drowning. My dad was in Erin's neighborhood right around the time she was getting brutally murdered. Why would he be there? What possible explanation could he have for that?

"Alice?" Eli touches my arm hesitantly. The expression on his face is half worried, half cautious. He says, carefully, like he's afraid of the answer, "Alice, please, tell me what's going on."

My father was sleeping with one of Owen's potential victims. He was outside of the other one's house seconds after her murder.

No no no no no.

"I . . ." I trail off, noticing that an uneasy whispering has swept through the crowd gathered in the hall. I hear the word *cop* and have to dart out of the way as a couple of kids push past me to dump their drinks in the sink.

Phone screens flash, and a muffled news announcer voice echoes from at least three different speakers at the same time: *"Police are saying the body of a young girl was found . . ."*

Someone lets out an ugly sob. A bottle crashes to the floor.

"Alice?" Eli's voice is a squeak. "We should leave, right? Before the cop comes back here?"

"Eli, you have to listen to me—" I've just grabbed his arm and pulled him into the kitchen when something on the other side of the room catches my eye.

It's Final Girl. She's calmly drinking a beer as everyone around is dumping their SOLO cups and searching for an exit. My heartbeat kicks.

Oh thank God.

"I need you to find Sierra and meet me outside," I tell Eli. "Can you do that?"

"Sierra?" Eli frowns. "What does she have to do with anything—"

"She just does." I glance back at Final Girl. She's looking at me now, and she jerks her chin by way of greeting, like she'd been waiting for me to find her. I turn back to Eli. "Please, just do this for me? You know I wouldn't ask if it wasn't really important."

Eli looks like he still wants to argue, but we've been friends for a long time, and I guess that earns me a little trust. He sighs heavily, but he says, "Yeah, okay."

"If we get through this alive, I'm filling your car with Sprite Zero. Cases and cases of it."

"I'm going to hold you to that," he says, and rounds the corner.

"Cool shindig," Final Girl says, wrinkling her nose. "You enjoying yourself?"

"My dad," I choke out, ignoring her. "Was he sleeping with Sierra?" It twists my gut to say the words out loud.

"Whoa, girl, last time we talked you were all worked up about your little boyfriend." Final Girl takes a long drink of her beer and wipes the foam from her upper lip with the back of her hand.

A freshman I don't recognize bumps into her and says under his breath, "What are you doing? Dump that shit; the cops are here," but she just nods at him, unconcerned.

"Where is the boyfriend, by the way?" she asks me. "He was cute."

I glance over my shoulder, getting nervous that Officer Howie might find me. "You have to tell me what you know about my dad," I beg her. "Please. I— I have to know."

"Do you?" Final Girl considers me for a moment, seemingly unmoved by my pain. "You know, there's a moment in the transcendent Adam Sandler film *Click* when national treasure Christopher Walken tells Sandler that all the things he thinks he wants, all the money and power and fancy vacations and expensive toys, they're all just cornflakes."

I'm so thrown by this sudden change in topic that, for a moment,

I just stare at her. She gazes back at me, eyes slightly narrowed, like the two of us are sharing something deeply profound. When I don't immediately respond, she makes an explosion sound, fingers wiggling next to her head like her mind's just been blown. "Deep, right?"

"Why are you talking about that stupid movie again?" I snap. "What does it have to do with anything?"

Her gaze hardens. "Do you think we go around sending privileged little girls like you back in time for our own amusement? We do it because we're hoping you'll learn something. When Adam Sandler found a magical remote control that could fast-forward time in the criminally underrated movie *Click*, he used it to get money and power, and by the end of the movie, he learned that was wrong. Get it?" She blinks at me, waiting for me to catch up. When I say nothing, she rolls her eyes. "Well? What lesson do you suppose you're here to learn?"

Lesson?

I stare back at her, at a loss for words. For some reason, the only thing that comes to mind is this thought experiment I heard about on a TV show, the trolley problem. It's this famous philosophical puzzle about ethics and morality. It goes like this: You're standing in a train yard, next to a lever, when you notice a runaway trolley barreling down the tracks toward five people who are tied up and unable to move. You can pull the lever and make the trolley switch tracks, but there's another person down that track.

So you have two choices: If you do nothing, the trolley will kill five people. But if you pull the lever, the trolley will kill only one.

I feel like I'm living some version of the trolley problem right now. By coming back here, I've screwed everything up. I've discovered things about my family that I never wanted to know. I've probably doomed three girls to die.

But maybe it'll mean my sister gets to live.

Maybe that's what she means by "lesson." Maybe I was supposed to learn that going back in time and messing with things isn't a good idea. Maybe I was supposed to learn to appreciate what I had.

I swallow and look down at my feet. "I— I don't know what you expect me to learn from this," I say, because I don't want to admit that I didn't learn that, not even close. I would do this all over again in a heartbeat. I would choose Claire every time. Even if it means knowing something about my father that makes me sick. Even if it means my family's going to implode. Even if other people die. I always choose Claire.

"I can't tell you what your dad was up to," Final Girl says, her voice flat. "Like I said before, you have to figure it out on your own. But I *can* tell you that the rest of your night's gonna be a little rough."

I gape after her. "Rough *how*? What are you—"

The *Halloween* theme starts to play from inside my pocket.

"You're going to want to get that," Final Girl says.

I know who's texting me before I even pull it out of my pocket, but I still feel a little shiver go through me when I see Wes's name on the screen, followed by just one word.

Please.

Nerves creep over my skin. My head pounds, and my palms feel damp with sweat. This is obviously a bad idea. If this were a horror movie, the Final Girl wouldn't even answer the text because it's *so obviously a bad idea*. There's no way the audience would stand for it. People would cheer for the death of someone stupid enough to meet the obvious killer outside, in the dark, alone.

Especially after she's just found out that the *other* obvious killer has just been released from police custody.

But...

Figure it out.

I want answers. No, I *need* them. If Final Girl isn't going to give me any, this is the only way I can think to get them.

I start typing, not giving myself any more time to doubt what I'm about to do, and then I press send, holding my breath as my text appears on the screen.

Meet me out back

You Think You Can Handle the Truth?

Millie's backyard is black. The stars and moon are tucked beneath heavy storm clouds for the night, but the rain seems to have stopped for good, and everything that was damp has frozen over, the trees and grass glittering like they're made of glass.

I take a breath and hold the cold in my lungs, bouncing in place for warmth. The back door opens and a group of people swarm around me, waving as they cut across Millie's backyard to a gate that leads out to an alley. I hear the gate screech open and closed and then they're gone, and I'm out here alone. In the dark.

Waiting for a murderer.

I hug my arms to my chest. *There are still a lot of people right inside,* I tell myself. *If this doesn't go my way, I'll just scream.*

To prove this to myself, I glance through the window on Millie's back door. But most people have already left. There are a few stragglers hunting around for coats and bags, someone throwing up in the sink. Eli is gone, and Final Girl is gone, and I have no idea where Claire went with Officer Howie. Something squirms through me. I don't think I want to know.

I turn back around, shivering. Maybe it's the darkness, but all my other senses seem more intense. I smell the smoke from a neighbor's chimney, and I hear the distant sound of frightened voices, the slam of car doors. They're hollow sounds, sad sounds. The people at the party finally figuring out what's going on tonight, leaving as quickly as they can.

I've just about convinced myself that Wes decided not to meet me after all when his voice reaches out from the other side of Millie's yard. "Was that your way of telling me you aren't interested?"

I freeze, my entire body humming as Wes steps out from beneath the deep shadow of a tree, one hand holding something balled up to his forehead. His eyes fix on my face. "Because next time you can just stop answering my texts."

"Wes," I breathe.

He stays hovering at the edge of the shadow. "I figured it would be better if they didn't see me," he says, nodding at the people who just cut across Millie's backyard. "Or, hell, maybe I shouldn't have worried. They'd probably just think I was in costume."

I let my eyes travel down, taking him in. I left his coat back in the car, and all he's wearing is a white V-neck undershirt that's too tight around the muscles in his arms, jeans ripped open at the knees. The glimpse of leg I can see looks shredded. Everything is stained with blood.

"Are . . . are you okay?" I gasp.

"Is that all you have to say to me?" Wes swallows and looks away, a muscle working in his jaw. "Seriously?"

My voice sticks in my throat, a piece of food I can't quite choke up. "What do you want me to say?"

He says, bitter, "How about 'Wes, I'm so sorry I left you to die in a cornfield'? Something like that."

"I didn't want you to die."

"You still left." He takes a step toward me, and I flinch backward. Some emotion flickers through his eyes—hurt, maybe—but he blinks, and it's gone so fast I have a hard time convincing myself I saw it at all. "Why are you scared of me?"

My face burns. I glance over my shoulder again, hoping for the comfort of knowing there are people close enough to come running if I scream.

But the kitchen has emptied out, except for the dude vomiting into the sink, and I doubt he's sober enough to help me. Wes could do whatever he wanted to me and then climb into Claire's car and drive away, and no one would even know he'd been here.

A fresh wave of fear crashes over me. I should run. I should be running right now. But my head is a jumble of thoughts:

Chloe's arm in the cornfield and Erin's blood on the glass door and Owen stabbing my sister with her own knife. My dad and Sierra, the blinking dot showing me that he was in Erin's neighborhood seconds after her murder. The thoughts weigh me down, making it impossible to move.

I have to know.

"How do you know Sierra Clayton?" I ask carefully.

Wes's forehead creases; he wasn't expecting this. "Who?"

"Sierra Clayton," I repeat, saying the name slower this time. Wes blinks, and I feel a surge of anger roar up inside of me. "Come on, Wes, I know you're not stupid. She's got dark hair, my height, gorgeous. She's on the varsity softball team, so she's at the gym all the time. You must've seen her around."

"Yeah, girls like that tend to hang around." Wes shrugs. *So?*

"You've never spoken to her?"

Wes's expression stills for a moment before shifting into annoyance. He smiles the way people do when they don't think something is funny. "Is this, like, a jealousy thing?"

My cheeks warm despite the frigid air. "Don't do that."

"Because you're not my girlfriend, you know." His voice is crueler than it was a second ago. "We've never even been on a date."

The logical part of my brain knows that, of all the things I should care about right now, whether or not Wes thinks I'm the type of girl who gets annoyed about something this stupid shouldn't remotely register. But the emotional part snaps, "I could seriously give a shit who you talk to, Wes."

"Is that right?" He lowers the hand he'd been holding to his forehead and looks across the yard in silence. The only sign that he's bothered by what I've just said is the anxious way he keeps tapping his open palm against his leg. I don't think he realizes he's doing it.

After a long moment, he says, "Girls like Sierra . . . I've never really been into that. Maybe you don't give a shit, but this"—he ticks a finger between the two of us—"you and me, whatever we are, were, it actually meant something to me. For whatever that's worth."

A muscle shivers near my spine. I say, before I can figure out whether it's smart, "It meant something to me, too."

Wes stops tapping his leg and looks at me. He's standing closer than I realized and staring so intensely that I can see the gold flecks in his brown eyes. There's blood dried along his hairline, the gash already closing up.

"Sierra," he says, after a long moment. "I've seen her around the gym. We never really talked or anything but—" He stops abruptly, his eyes flicking up to my face and then away again. It's a small enough moment that I might've missed it if I hadn't been looking for it. My heartbeat stills.

He knows something he doesn't want to tell me.

"What is it?" I ask.

Wes shakes his head. "Nothing."

"Then say it."

"It's a bullshit rumor."

"Then *say it.*"

"Fine." Wes looks at me, his gaze sharpening. "I never bought any of this shit, but some of the people around the gym, they say it's kind of funny how some of the . . . better-looking high school girls seem to, like, hang around a lot. With some of the coaches." He lets his hands fall open. *Happy?*

It's like a nightmare, like waking up to find that the sky is on fire and the ground is lava and nothing, *nothing* is what you thought it was.

This can't be real. Someone tell me this isn't real.

"You mean they hang around my dad," I say, numb.

Wes says nothing, which is the same thing as agreeing. After a moment, he exhales, mumbling, "Like I said, I never bought it."

"These girls," I say slowly. "We're talking about Chloe Bree, Erin Cleary, and Sierra Clayton, right?"

Wes swallows. "No one ever named names. Like I said, it was just rumors. But if I had to guess . . . yeah, those three make sense."

My eyes fill with tears, but I blink fast so they don't fall. And there it is. The truth. My father wasn't just cheating on my mom. He was taking advantage of young girls, girls who trusted him. It doesn't matter that none of them were technically under the age of consent at the time. He was their coach. He had power over them.

He's a monster.

It doesn't mean he's a killer, I tell myself, as increased panic sets in. My father's girlfriends—his victims—might have been the same girls who got murdered, but that could still be a coincidence.

"You think he has something to do with what's going on tonight." Wes looks at me, unblinking, as if challenging me to disagree with him. When I look away, he releases a low laugh. "And me too, right? That's why you left me in the field. That's why you flinch whenever I come close to you." He shakes his head. "That's fucking dark."

"Two girls are dead," I murmur.

"I didn't kill anybody," Wes says. I'm staring at the ground now, but I can feel him looking at me.

"It makes sense, though, doesn't it? You asked me out today, out of nowhere, almost like you needed me for something." I keep talking, the theory coming to me as the words are leaving my mouth. "Say, for instance, you were helping someone do something bad and . . . it would make sense for you to ask me to watch a movie with you later that night, give you an alibi. Maybe you even thought I would lie to the police for you, if you really made me think you liked me."

"You really think I'd do something like that?" Wes's voice is calm enough, but his hand is clenched in a fist.

I don't say anything. My heart is beating very loudly in my ears. Wes worked out at the same gym where my dad met those girls, and he clearly knew what was going on. Maybe he was jealous, or maybe he wanted to punish them or—or—

"Alice . . . I asked you out because I legitimately *like* you. Why is that so hard for you to believe?"

Something inside me twists. "I'm awkward and—and I'm not hot, not like Claire or Sierra, and I say weird things and—"

"And you're really funny and authentic. The world isn't divided into hot people and nerds. Maybe if you spent a little more time living instead of watching movies, you'd get that." Wes takes another step toward me, and now he's close enough to touch. "I need you to believe me, Alice."

I want to. But then I think of *Scream*, of how it was looking pretty bad for Sidney's dad until—surprise—it was sexy boyfriend Billy all along.

I stop breathing as Wes reaches out to tuck a stray hair behind my ears. I don't know how to trust him. I don't know how to trust anyone anymore.

In a horror movie, there would still be some final twist. I have to be careful.

"But you don't believe me," Wes says. "Do you?"

Out of the corner of my eye I can see through the window into Millie's kitchen. It's completely empty now. No more sink guy. No one to come running if I scream. No one to come save me. Fear makes it impossible for me to move, to speak.

If I tell him I believe him, isn't it the same thing as saying I think my dad's a killer?

How am I supposed to live with that?

Wes stays in front of me for a long moment, waiting for me to look back up at him, to tell him I trust him. When I don't, he sighs and heads back across the yard, disappearing under the shadow of the tree. I flinch when I hear the gate slam shut, telling me he's gone.

It's not until I exhale that I realize how close I am to tears.

I go inside and head back over to the stairs where Sierra was supposedly sitting with Mark. There are a few more people over here, not many. Two sophomores, Imani Cheatham and Josephine Varela, rush past me, hands entwined, giggling. Sierra's nowhere. I stayed outside for too long.

I start up the steps, swearing under my breath.

X is coming down the staircase as I'm making my way up. His eyes light up when he sees me. "Allie! I thought you left," he shouts, grabbing both my arms. "I can't find Sierra, and I'm getting seriously freaked out."

I glance past him to the second floor. "She isn't upstairs?"

"No one's up there," X says, frowning. "Everyone's already gone."

"What about my sister? Or Eli?"

X makes a face. "Um, no, but I heard Claire was with Nat's brother earlier, so she's probably still around here some—" Some guy I don't recognize stumbles into X's back, causing him to lurch forward. "Seriously?" he shouts, scowling over his shoulder. "There are, like, two people here; you can't watch where you're going?"

"I'm going to go look for her," I say, heading up the stairs. "But you should leave."

"I'll wait for you outside," X calls after me.

"X, just find Millie and get out of here. *Please.*"

I don't stick around to argue with him. The upstairs hall is empty. Someone's forgotten purse lies crumpled in the corner. Cups roll along the floor, leaking trails of sticky mystery liquid. I throw open doors, checking bathrooms, bedrooms, closets.

No Sierra or Eli or Claire.

Before I know it, I'm at the end of the hall, only one door left. I swing it open and poke my head inside. "Hello?"

My voice seems to echo now. I run my hand over the wall until I find the light switch, flick it on.

A single bulb dangles from the ceiling above me, swaying slightly.

It's just a laundry room. A stacked washer and dryer stand to one side, a folded ironing board leaning against them, bottles of detergent and bleach arranged on the shelves above.

I stare for a moment, my nerves pricking. Something's off about this room, something I can't quite put my finger on. I look around before deciding that it's the bottles, how they're so carefully placed, all lined up in a neat row with their labels facing out. Like this is a store.

"Weird," I murmur, stifling a shudder as I start to pull the door closed. The heel of my sneaker feels tacky, I notice. I lift it and examine the sole, the light bulb still swinging over my head. The circle of pale light moves across the floor in slow arcs, illuminating a pool of something. I stare down at it for a moment, unnerved. The tile's dark, and I can't tell what color it is.

Detergent, I think, frowning. For a second I'm so sure that's what it is that I look back up at the shelves, scanning for the broken bottle. The light sways overhead, illuminating the bottles, then casting them in shadow.

Light, shadow, light—

Dread rolls through me like nausea. My eyes flick back up as I realize what was bothering me.

The light bulb.

Why is it moving?

The hair on the back of my neck stands straight up. I pull my phone out of my pocket, thumbs fumbling, and somehow manage to get the flashlight on, illuminating the tile floor.

Something's in here. Or someone is. Otherwise, why would the light bulb be moving like that?

My stomach goes oily. I look past the washer and dryer, to

the far side of the room. The light doesn't reach back there.

I wet my lips. "Who's back there?" I move the light back and over, stopping when it hits the edge of another pool of dark liquid. In the light from my phone I can see that it's a deep, dark red.

"Oh God." Something rises in my chest—this feeling like I've missed the last step on a staircase, like I'm about to fall. I shuffle forward another step, legs trembling. My hands are so slick with sweat, I can barely keep hold of my phone.

There's a shoe on the floor. A pink Converse high-top with Sharpie polka dots, the laces unraveled. I take a step closer, and now the light hits a leg, blue veins stark against pale white skin.

I press my free hand to my mouth, shuddering hard. *No. No no no no no no.*

The girl lying on the floor doesn't move. I stare at her for a long moment, my body already shifting into panic mode. I feel a vein throbbing at my temple, my breath going cold in my lungs.

It's Millie. Her eyes are open, gazing up at the ceiling without seeing anything.

Less Than an Hour Left

The inside of my mouth tastes rich and bitter, like black licorice. For a surreal moment, that's the only thing I can focus on, that taste. When was the last time I ate black licorice? Have I ever eaten black licorice?

Panic, I think. The second the word enters my brain, I realize that's exactly what's happening. I'm panicking. I remember learning about this in my anatomy class. Adrenaline is flooding my system and my brain is shutting down, focusing on something mundane to protect me from how horrified I am that one of my best friends is lying on the floor in front of me. Dead.

Millie stares up at the ceiling without blinking. Her eyes don't look like human eyes anymore. They look like glass, like a doll's eyes.

I force myself to inhale. I should be doing something right now, but I can't figure out what it is. Screaming, maybe, or running away. Instead, I take a step closer to Millie's body without making the conscious decision to do so. My hands shake as I crouch next to her, but I still don't feel anything. Not horror or sadness. There's a buzzing sound in my ears, though. Like when I can't find a station on the car radio.

Millie's lips are slightly parted, a thin trickle of blood spilling down the side of her chin. Staring at her chin, I notice an angry red pimple.

That pimple's never going to heal, I think to myself nonsensically. She's going to have it forever. For some reason, that's the thought that breaks through all the numb. I feel a sharp twist in my gut, a pain I've felt only once before, after Claire. The ground seems to tilt beneath me.

"Millie?" I croak. Millie's been stabbed. I can tell she's dead just by looking at her, but I can't make myself believe it. I bring a hand to her cheek, slapping lightly, like I'm trying to wake her up—

I recoil, gasping, and my cell phone drops to the floor. Her skin is still warm. It's impossible to believe she's not about to sit up and tell me this is all a joke. Millie, who used to come to my house for sleepovers every Friday, and who tried to copy my homework on Mondays when she forgot to do it over the weekend and was always down to watch horror movies with me, even though she had to watch them through the gaps in her fingers.

Wes didn't know Millie. And he was downstairs with me when this happened to her. Which means someone else did this.

My dad used to make us popcorn when Millie stayed the night. He was always recommending new horror movies, obscure things we'd never seen. Once, he made Millie laugh with a joke about a depressed horse.

I picture him grabbing her, *stabbing* her.

I can't breathe. It feels like someone has reached into my chest and squeezed my lungs between their fists. Millie's life wasn't supposed to end like this. Millie was supposed to wear overalls and Doc Martens and try to save the world one cause at a time. She shouldn't be lying on the ground, dead.

I touch Millie's shoulder, jostling her slightly. Tears clog up my throat, turning my voice thick and soggy. "Millie? Millie, please—"

Downstairs, someone screams.

The sound lasts forever, or it seems to. Adrenaline kicks to life inside of me. I jerk to my feet and throw myself out the door.

"Claire?" I shout. My dad would never hurt my sister, but that didn't keep her safe last time.

That night in the corn maze plays out in my head like a movie. I see Claire kneeling on the ground, crying, blood matted in her hair. And Owen standing over her, the mask balled up in one hand, his other hand groping his bleeding stomach, Claire's little pocketknife sticking out of him.

They must've seen my father hurt Chloe. Owen grabbed my father's mask, revealing his face. And when my father ran, Owen must've tried to call the cops, to help Chloe.

But Claire . . .

I press a fist to my lips, shaking hard. Claire would do anything to protect our family. I think of how she flushed my mom's cigarettes to stop her from smoking, how she hid Dad's burner phone because she thought that would keep him from cheating.

She would've assumed our father had some reason to do what he did, even if she didn't understand what it was. She would've defended him, no matter what.

So she stabbed Owen. To stop him from calling the cops and turning our father in. When he stabbed her back, it wasn't to kill her. It was self-defense.

My heart is beating very fast. I could still be wrong. There's still Owen's manifesto to consider. But Final Girl was right; anyone could've written that.

I'm shaking so badly I can hardly breathe. The only thing I can think about is finding my sister, making sure she's okay. I shout again, louder, "Claire!"

Now that I'm out of the laundry room, I realize Millie's body had a smell to it, the smell of blood and dead things. It clings to the insides of my nostrils, crawls down the back of my throat like an insect. I double over on the far side of the hall and heave, but the only thing I cough up is stringy, foul-tasting spit.

With effort, I stumble down the hall, down the stairs. My thoughts are desperate.

Not my sister. Not again.

"Claire!" I scream. I take the last few stairs at a run, my eyes traveling over the small living room, nothing left but plastic cups and smooshed candy wrappers, forgotten Halloween masks. Cold seeps into my bones. I have that feeling like I'm a little kid again and I'm standing somewhere dark and everything, everything is hiding something dangerous.

Like there, the door to the bathroom. It's open a crack, and I can see the tile floor on the other side, the edge of a toilet. My skin buzzes. My father could be ducked down behind that door and I wouldn't know until I was too close, close enough for him to jump out at me. I feel suddenly light-headed, unable to catch my breath.

My father wouldn't hurt me, I tell myself. But three girls are already dead. Can I really be sure that I'm safe? Do I really know what my father would or wouldn't do?

I need a weapon, I decide. Just in case. There are probably knives in the kitchen. And maybe something in the hall closet, an old set of golf clubs or a baseball bat.

I hold my breath as I inch across Millie's living room, one step, two, my eyes swinging wide, trying to take in the entire room at once. And then I yank the closet open—quick—before I lose my nerve.

Empty.

I release a sudden, sharp exhale that's halfway to a sob. A set of golf clubs leans against the back wall. I remove the largest and hold it with two hands, propped over one shoulder. My hands are trembling, sweating. I squeeze tighter, trying to fight down the nerves.

I glance down the galley kitchen as I walk past, see that there's no one there. I spot the knife block on the counter and start to reach for the butcher knife—

But the butcher knife is already gone. The slot where it should be is empty.

My pulse ticks up. I feel an eerie, creeping sensation on the back of my neck. There's only one room on the main floor that I haven't searched yet. The den. The door is on the other side of the kitchen, slightly open. There's a light on in the other room, watery gold spilling onto the kitchen linoleum.

I glance at the empty knife block. Then back at the door. Steeling myself, I reach out and shove the door open, my heart hammering in my chest.

For a moment I stare at the scene in the den without being able to process what I'm seeing. It's as though the horror has caused my brain to short-circuit. I lose my grip on the golf club and it falls sideways, slamming into the wall before rattling to the floor, the sound echoing through the now-empty house. I lift my hands to my mouth, numb.

Eli sits propped in a leather club chair on the far side of the room. Someone has built a fire in the fireplace beside him, and the leaping flames paint the otherwise darkened room in soft golds and oranges. The light makes Eli's skin glow. He looks like he's about to reach for a leather-bound book and a brandy, read me a story.

Except that he's dead. The thick wooden handle of the butcher knife that should've been in the kitchen juts out of his body, six inches of steel buried into his chest.

Figure It Out

For the past year, I've thought of myself as more aware than other people. More awake. Most people think of death as something distant and mythical, something that happens to other people, other families—not them. I used to be one of those people, but then I watched my sister die and I changed. I know now how sudden death is, how final. I'm intimately familiar with the way it can rip through your life like a tornado, destroying everything it touches.

I understand death. Or I thought I did.

But this . . .

I so wasn't prepared for this.

My body responds before my brain does. I begin to shake, and then I can feel the hair along my arms and the back of my neck stand straight up, the skin below prickling in horror. I take a quick step backward, colliding with the sharp edge of the door.

"Oh my God," I croak.

First Millie and now Eli. *My* Eli, my best friend in the world, is gone.

I squeeze my eyes shut, thinking, *No, no, no, no.*

But when I open my eyes again, he's still there, staring back at me. He has his ankle crossed over his leg and he's leaning back against the chair, exactly like he always sits. In death, that pose looks strange. Unnatural. Like someone arranged him that way on purpose.

"Eli?" My eyes are blurry, and I can't seem to make my voice work like it's supposed to. "Eli? No, you're okay; this is a bad joke, right? Like, a Halloween joke?" My brain clings to this idea. It has to be a joke. Eli can't really be dead. I drop in front of him and shake his shoulders, snot and tears running down my face. He'll start moving again when he sees how upset this is making me. "You're okay, right? Eli?"

Eli and I have been best friends since kindergarten, when we both reached for the same crayon and, instead of fighting over it, Eli broke it in two so that we could each have a piece. He stayed over at my house the night before our first day of high school, and we spent the whole night talking about everything we were afraid of, everything we were excited about. He cared more about health than anyone I've ever met. He wanted to go to Princeton and study medicine and volunteer for Doctors Without Borders.

He can't just be *gone*.

But there's so much blood. It oozes out around the wound in his chest, ruining the silk vest he'd been so happy to find at the Goodwill out west. I stare at the vest, realizing that Eli would never ruin it on purpose. Eli loved clothes and bargains.

Which means . . .

I start crying now, really crying, the sobs bubbling up from deep in my chest. Everything I thought I understood about death rearranges itself inside my head.

This shouldn't have happened. This was never supposed to happen.

• • •

Somehow, I manage to stand and stumble to the living room, out the front door, onto the porch. The cold outside hits me like a slap. My teeth start to chatter. There are still a few people milling about on the sidewalk, waiting for rides. I search their faces for Final Girl, but she's not here.

I blink, not quite believing my eyes. Final Girl's supposed to explain what this means. She's supposed to tell me what to do now. If she's not here, I'm lost.

Hours ago, she said tonight was a gift. But I don't understand how *this* can be a gift. Eli's dead and he's not supposed to be.

And not just him. Millie's dead, too. And Chloe, and Erin.

I start crying again, hot tears slipping faster and faster down my cheeks. Is this the lesson I was supposed to learn? That one person's life isn't worth all this death?

Final Girl said that if I "figure it out" by midnight, I get to keep whatever changes I make tonight. Claire would get to live. But Chloe and Erin and Millie and Eli would all stay dead.

And if I don't figure it out? If I just let the clock run out? What happens then?

There's a thick grove of trees near the edge of Millie's property, casting black shadows over her grass and porch. It would probably be beautiful in the daylight, like a little patch of woods. Now it looks sinister.

My eyes linger there for a moment, looking for movement. The murderer—my father—is still here somewhere. My skin crawls as I picture him weaving through the trees. Hunting us.

Figure it out, Final Girl said. If this were a horror movie, the only thing left is the big speech, the murderer explaining why he did it. I don't know if I can stand to listen to my father try to justify the things he's done.

But Claire . . .

Freshman year of high school I didn't have a date for homecoming. Claire did, this really hot junior she'd been obsessing over for months, but when she found out I was skipping, she told him she couldn't go, either. She took me bowling instead. While everyone else dressed up and got their hair done and rode around in limos, Claire and I ate greasy burgers and pushed bowling balls through our legs.

Later, when I asked her why she didn't go to the dance, why she spent the night hanging with me instead, she'd just shrugged and said, "No sister left behind." Simple as that. It became our mantra. No sister left behind. If you jump, I jump, too. Tonight was supposed to be about saving her.

Someone places a hand on my shoulder. My stomach drops, and I have to bite back a scream as I whirl around—

"Whoa," X says, both hands flying up in front of his chest, like he's trying to ward me off. "I'm sorry; don't freak out."

"X." I exhale, my breath leaving my chest in a sudden whoosh, like air out of a balloon. "You scared the shit out of me."

"Yeah, I think there's a lot of that going around."

"I thought you left. What are you still doing here?"

X drops his hands, his gaze shifting back to Millie's house. "I can't find Millie. Did you see her while you were inside? I'm getting really freaked out."

"Millie," I murmur, my gut twisting. I can still picture her lying in that pool of blood on the laundry-room floor, her eyes like glass, her mouth hanging open. The smell of blood fills my nose.

If I tell X what happened to Millie, there's no way in hell he'll leave me here alone. I have to protect at least one of my friends tonight.

So I just shake my head, working to keep my expression calm. "Do you know where that cop went? Officer Howard?"

X frowns. "Why?"

"My sister was with him."

X hugs his arms close to his chest. "The last time I saw them, they were heading into Millie's little brother's room."

He doesn't have to say the rest. There's only one reason people seek out empty bedrooms at parties.

Despite everything, I feel a pang of annoyance. Seriously, Claire? With Officer Howie? *Ew.*

I look back at Millie's house. The windows are dark. "Did you see them come out?"

X shakes his head.

Which means they could still be in there. And Claire didn't see the dead bodies, so she doesn't know the murderer's found us. At least she's making out with someone who carries a gun.

I keep staring at the windows, my chest clenching like a fist. This time, I think I see a flicker of movement behind the glass.

Do I go back inside? Or do I stay out here?

It's the trolley problem all over again.

Do I save my sister? Or do I save everyone else?

"Do you know what time it is?" I ask X.

X frowns at me, then pulls his phone out of his pocket. "Looks like eleven twelve."

Forty-eight minutes left.

"I have to find Claire," I say, already moving toward the house. I can't let my sister die again, no matter what. I have to save her. "Will you please get someplace safe?"

X glares at me. "And just leave you here? Are we seriously having this argument again?"

"Come on, X, if you don't make it through tonight, who's going to write the movie version of all this?" I ask. It's an awful attempt at a joke, but I'm desperate to get him to leave.

X gives me a long, measured look. "I'll compromise with you, okay? I'm going to wait out here with the car running. Don't bother arguing with me," he says, when I open my mouth to do just that. "Just come back as soon as you find Claire, got it?"

I can tell he's made up his mind, so I nod. "Fine, okay."

"If I'm going to write the movie version of this night, the least I can do is make sure a Black man lives to the end, right?"

I can tell he's trying to make things lighter, so I attempt a smile and say, "I thought it was a myth that the Black character always dies first in horror movies?"

"Yeah, you white girls die way more frequently, but that's only because they don't usually think to include Black characters." X goes to unlock his car, then turns back around, adding, "And, uh, stay out of the basement. Nothing good ever happens in a basement."

Careful You Don't Trip

Millie's house is still, quiet. The living room looks a lot smaller with none of the lights on. I glance at the windows on the far wall and away, skin prickling. I don't like the way the darkness outside turns them into a fourth, black wall. I can picture someone hovering on the other side of the glass right now, watching me.

My father, hiding behind a werewolf mask. Getting ready to deliver his monologue, to make his final kill.

Find Claire, I tell myself. That's all I have to do. Just find my sister and get the hell out of here. If Claire lives, all of this will be worth it.

I swallow and grope along the wall for a light switch—

Flick, and the overheads switch on, illuminating the room. I glance at the windows again, my heart thumping loudly in my chest. Now I feel like I have a spotlight trained on me, announcing my location to anyone in the yard. I consider switching the light off again, but the idea of wandering around this space in the dark is just too awful. I'll have to risk it.

I go into the kitchen and pull a knife from the block on the counter. It's just a steak knife, much smaller than the one lodged in Eli's chest. But it's sharp. I imagine stabbing my father with it and feel a shudder of horror. Even now, knowing everything he's done, I don't think I could do it. One step at a time.

"Claire?" I call, my voice barely a whisper. My mouth feels dry, and my shoulders are clenched near my ears, the muscles unable to relax. "Claire, are you still in here?"

There's a sound like a twig breaking outside. I jerk around, knife coming up—

But all I see is my own reflection staring back at me from that wall of windows.

Still holding the knife before me, I cross the room and fumble along the wall for the switch to turn on the back-porch lights. It's a moment before I find the right switch, flip it—

The outside lights blink on, flooding the grounds in an eerie blue glow. Snowflakes have begun to fall, the mushy, wet kind that are almost rain and melt the second they hit the ground. I press my face right up next to the glass, my breath leaving little clouds of condensation as I watch for movement.

The snow has almost covered the yard, dusting the top of a grill and a little kid's swing set. I can see the back fence, the neighbor's roof. But no people.

I exhale, shakily. I feel weirdly giddy all of a sudden, like I might burst out laughing. The feeling is so strong that I press my fist to my mouth and force myself to breathe through my nose until it passes.

It's the adrenaline. My fight-or-flight response kicking in. My body knows that it's in danger, and it's preparing itself, trying to keep me alive.

Use it, I tell myself. *Find Claire.*

Don't die.

• • •

I check every room downstairs, but Claire isn't in any of them. My palm grows slick against the handle of my knife, my heartbeat ticking louder.

"Claire?" My voice is a low rasp. "Where are you?"

No answer. I find myself holding my breath each time I turn a corner, worried that every twitching shadow is the killer, that he's been waiting for me all this time. But there's no one, always no one.

I hobble back through the living room, over to the staircase. "Claire?" I call, a little louder this time. "Are you up there?"

I take the stairs slowly, wincing a little each time the wood creaks beneath my feet. She's in here somewhere. She has to be.

I try the door at the top of the staircase and find a little boy's room. My eyes move over scattered toys, unmade bunk beds, a dresser spilling clothes onto the floor. Millie's little brother's room. The room X said he saw Claire and Officer Howie go into together.

I put my foot down on something small and jagged as soon as I step through the door. My leg twists out from beneath me and I go flying, pinwheeling my arms for balance, my heart leaping up my throat—

I grab for the door frame, fingers digging into the wood, shoulder slamming into the wall.

"Shit," I murmur, wincing. I try to straighten up again, and pain blisters through my ankle. I clench my eyes shut, exhaling.

Of course I twisted my ankle. The Final Girl always hurts her damn ankle.

"Okay," I whisper to myself. "Come on, you can do this." I try to put a little weight on my leg and my ankle lights up—but it holds. I ease forward another step, and then another, cringing every time I shift onto my leg.

I can walk, barely. I'll just have to go slow.

I swallow and ball my hands into fists at my sides. I look on the other side of the bed and around the dresser, but the room looks empty. No Claire, no Officer Howie. But also no blood, no bodies, no sign of a struggle. Wherever they are, I think they might be okay.

I'm about to pull the door closed again when I hear a hard scrape on the floor, like fingernails on cardboard.

The hair on my arms stands up. I pause, still gripping the door-knob, tremors moving up my arms, making me shake.

I listen for the sound again, but my breathing is too heavy now. It fills my ears with white noise. I can't hear anything over it.

I limp into the room, studying the bed, the dresser. The bed's too low to the floor for anyone to wiggle beneath it, and there's no other heavy furniture to duck behind.

So where the hell did that sound come from?

My eyes land on a set of bifold doors on the opposite side of the room, the kind with rows of narrow slats that you can see into. And out of.

The closet.

I feel cold all of a sudden. I have doors like that on my closet back home. I can remember hiding behind dresses and winter coats while playing hide-and-seek with Claire, holding my breath as I watched her move on the other side of the door.

I tighten my grip on the knife. I don't like the way the door is ever-so-slightly open, like someone yanked it back too quickly, not taking the time to make sure it closed all the way. And I don't like the feeling I get looking at it. Like I can see something pulsing.

I cross the room and fling the door all the way open before I lose my nerve.

A shadow jerks inside the closet, two hands coming up to cover a face, hair sliding forward.

I blink. "Sierra?"

Sierra is tucked into the corner, curled in a ball. At the sound of my voice, she lifts her head, and I see that her eyes are wide and rimmed with red. But she doesn't seem to be injured.

I'm hit with a flash of naked, animal relief—*oh thank God*—gone a second later. My sister isn't with her.

Where the fuck are you, Claire?

I don't have time to think about that now. I kneel in front of Sierra and say, in the calmest voice I can muster, "We have to get out of here."

Sierra's eyes flick to my knife. She wets her lips. "Please . . . please don't . . ."

I glance at my knife, confused. It's a moment before I realize that she's scared of me.

"Sierra, it's okay; I'm not going to hurt you." I place the knife on the floor and hold my hands up, fingers spread wide, the universal gesture of *You can trust me.* "I promise, I'm not going to hurt you," I say again. "But we have to leave now, okay?"

Sierra's still staring at the knife, her eyes wide with fear. It's like she thinks the weapon's going to leap off the floor and stab her all on its own.

I try again. "Sierra? You know there's someone in the house with us, right? Someone dangerous?"

A pause. And then Sierra's eyes flick from the knife back to my face. Slowly, she nods.

"Okay," I say on an exhale. At least we're getting somewhere. "Okay, so we need to leave before he comes back. We need to go outside, where there are other people. Then we'll be safe. Can you do that?"

I hold out my hand. Sierra stares at it for a moment. Her shoulders slump. She nods again and reaches forward, her hand finding mine—

Then a noise in the hall, the soft fall of a footstep. Someone trying to walk closer without making a sound.

Sierra's lips move, mouthing the words without speaking.

It's him.

You're Never Gonna Make It

Out in the hall, the sound grows louder. It's a low, shuffling rustle. Footsteps muffled by carpet.

There's a pause. And then the creak of door hinges.

Oh God, I think, my eyes falling closed. I know what he's doing because I just did the same thing.

He's checking each room, looking for Sierra.

I'm practically frozen in terror, my legs locked, my hand glued to the closet door. I can't make myself move. I can't even make myself turn to look over my shoulder, to make sure that my father's not already at the door, that he hasn't already seen me.

He won't hurt me, I tell myself again.

Right?

There's the sound of wood brushing wood: a door closing. With a high moan, Sierra rises to her knees and grabs my wrist. She yanks me down into the closet with her, fumbling to get the door closed again. Clothes rustle above our heads as the door slides shut.

I crouch beside her, balling my hands into fists to keep them from trembling. I can see the bedroom through the slats in the closet door. The unmade bed, the kids' toys and clothes.

And just inches from the closed closet door, my knife lying on the carpet.

I stare at the knife for a long moment, horror rising inside me. I put it on the floor when I found Sierra, but I forgot to pick it up again. I left it out there.

Oh God oh God oh God.

I glance at the bedroom door. The hall just outside is still empty. Maybe I have enough time to ease the closet door open again, just an inch, to reach out and grab the knife before my father arrives?

I exhale and lean forward.

Sierra seems to guess what I'm thinking. She catches my eye in the darkness and shakes her head, urgent. *Don't you dare.* But if I leave the knife on the floor outside the closet, he's going to see it. He'll know we're in here. And we'll have no way to defend ourselves.

I pull myself out of Sierra's grip and reach for the closet door, not even daring to breathe. I start to slide it open—

A shadow falls across the bedroom.

I'm so surprised that I flinch, knocking my elbow against the back of the wall. The sound is just a dull thump, muffled by the clothes, but Sierra still grabs me, her fingernails digging into my skin. We both freeze, staring at the bedroom door.

Did he hear it?

The shadow moves into the room. One step. Two. I can see now that the shuffling sound of his footsteps is because he doesn't lift them all the way off the floor, but drags them along the carpet.

My pulse picks up. I think of how Mom used to make fun of him for walking like that, like he was too lazy to pick his feet all the way off the ground. How, whenever Claire or I caught the other walking like that, we'd say we were "Dad-walking" and laugh. My throat closes up. I lift my eyes, trying to make out the lines of his face in the darkness.

Suddenly a bright white burst of light shines into the closet—

I cringe and cower backward, Sierra still tightly gripping my arm. Clothes swing above us, threatening to fall.

It's a cell phone flashlight. As I watch, the light tilts, sending a beam of white up, illuminating the gray skin and comically large teeth of the werewolf mask.

It's like my father wants us to see him. Like he knows we're in here watching.

He crosses the room. He stops next to the bed and lifts the thin sheet in an exaggerated gesture, like he's teasing, like this is all just a game of hide-and-seek. A sour taste fills my throat. I've never known my father to be like this. Cruel, taunting.

He cocks his head as he shines the flashlight beneath the sheets, then shrugs, the gesture made awkward by the bulky werewolf costume. *No one there!*

Sierra stiffens beside me, but I don't dare look at her. I can't remember the last time I blinked, the last time I inhaled. What he's doing, playing with us like this, it's *sick*.

He stops near the dresser now. Slowly, slowly, he inches a drawer open, and peeks inside. He pretends to scratch his head.

I can still taste blood in my mouth, and my tongue stings from where I bit into it. I look past him, letting my eyes settle on the bedroom's open door. I can see the corner of the staircase banister in the hall just outside. It's three feet away. Maybe four.

I swallow, the taste of blood making me cringe. If I run as fast as I can, could I make it down those stairs? Call 911?

Or will he catch me first?

My father wouldn't hurt me, I tell myself again.

I'm almost entirely sure.

I shift forward to my knees. My ankle still hurts. I can feel blood pulsing through where I twisted it, making it swell, and I grit my teeth together, thinking of how badly it's going to hurt when I start to run, how it's going to take all my willpower to ignore the pain slamming through it and keep going.

I move slowly, testing. My legs feel trembly, unsteady, and my ankle is throbbing. I feel a sob bubble up my throat and clench my lips together, tight, to keep it from bursting out.

This is our only shot, I tell myself. Any second now he's going to look at the closet; he's going to see the knife. Maybe if he runs after me, he won't even see Sierra. I can save one person tonight. At least one person.

Sierra leans forward, frowning at me.

What are you doing? she mouths silently.

I nod at the door. *Stairs*, I mouth back.

Her eyes go wide. She shakes her head wildly, clearly hating this idea. Her anxiety is catching. Unease threads through me.

Is this stupid? Should I just hide here and hope for the best? Let him find us?

My father's kneeling on the floor now, pretending to look for us beneath a shoe. I stare at him, hating him for this. Maybe I can slam into him before I get to the stairs. Maybe if I knock him over, he'll hit his head and—

He stands suddenly, as though responding to some dog whistle cue that I didn't hear. I watch, stunned, as he turns and walks purposefully back into the hall.

A moment later, I hear shoes echoing against the steps. A door opens and closes on the main floor.

I slump against the closet wall, releasing a slow exhale that dissolves into an incredulous laugh. We didn't die. I can't believe we didn't die.

"Sierra? You okay?" I glance at her. Her skin is as pale as a sheet. I give her arm a shake. "Sierra?"

She still doesn't respond but only stares straight ahead, barely breathing. Moonlight trickles in through the slats in the closet door, striping her face.

Fear rises in the back of my throat. Her body looks broken, small. Can you die of fright? Can you be so scared that your heart just stops working?

Then a shuddering breath passes over Sierra's lips. "Yeah," she murmurs. "Yeah, I'll be okay."

I exhale, relieved. "We need a phone," I whisper. "We have to call the cops."

Sierra nods and pulls her cell phone out of her pocket. Her fingers tremble as she dials a 9 and a 1—

Before she can get the last number out, her screen lights up and a sharp ring blares through the closet.

"Shit," Sierra murmurs. She hits ignore but not fast enough. I see the number flash across the screen before she can shift the phone away from me.

"402-555-0673," I murmur, reciting it from memory. A cold feeling settles in my gut as I lift my eyes to Sierra's face.

It's my father. He's calling her.

The Basement? Seriously?

Blood rises in my neck, flooding my face. He's looking for her. That's why he called, so he could listen for her ringtone and follow it to find her. To find us.

Any lingering doubts I might've had about my father's guilt vanish. I imagine the first time Sierra gave him her number, never guessing that someday it would be used for *this*.

My father is a monster, I think again.

Sierra mistakes the look on my face for something else. "Alice," she breathes, her eyes wide. "That was, I mean, I don't—"

"Shut *up*." I grab her phone, fingers shaking as I silence it. He might not have heard it. We might still be safe.

Then door hinges creak. *Oh God.* I lift a hand to my mouth, trying to muffle the sound of my breathing. I feel Sierra tense beside me.

Rapid footsteps thud through the outer room. The closet door slams open, light spilling over us. I cringe and throw a hand over my eyes to shield the sudden glare.

My father is a black silhouette on the other side of the cell phone flashlight. Squinting, I can make out the lines of his arm and torso, the comically large werewolf costume hiding his body.

He's holding the knife I left on the floor.

My scream reverberates through the closet. He takes a sudden step backward, startled by the sheer volume of my fear, or maybe just surprised to find me here at all. It's only a fraction of a second of a pause, but it's enough. My eyes flick to the door behind him, to the staircase in the hallway, and I do the only thing I can think to do.

I leap to my feet and lunge.

I catch him by surprise and he jerks out of my way and into the closet door, which crashes open, sending him stumbling. He releases a low grunt as he falls, arms flailing.

I barely notice. I can't spare another millisecond to look his way and see whether he'll recover. Pain lights up my ankle as I slam into a run, blood pumping in my ears, breath roaring up my throat. I force myself to breathe and push through it.

The door's just three feet away.

Two.

Nausea claws up my throat, the pain in my ankle too great to ignore. I hear the ragged sound of Sierra's breath just behind me, her footsteps crashing into the floor in time with mine. It's the encouragement I need to keep going.

I grab the staircase banister and propel myself down, trying to ignore the blistering pain shooting up and down my leg, turning my stomach. I can't hear anything over the white noise sound of panic in my ears, the roar of my own blood and breath. My whole body is coated in sweat. I leap down the final two steps, and then we're around the corner and through the hallway, into the living room. The front door is just ahead. My breath leaves my body in a ragged gasp of relief.

Thank God.

I lunge for the door—

My father appears before me, gasping. His werewolf mask

hangs lopsided from his face, the eyeholes not quite matching up with his eyes.

He twitches the knife at me like a finger.

Not so fast.

I take a quick step backward, slamming into Sierra. She sobs at my shoulder. "Oh my God, oh my God . . ."

I grab her, cowering to the side of the dark hall as he closes in on us, knife raised. Sierra's arms shake so violently that I have to dig my fingers into her skin so I don't lose my grip. I'm so scared that I don't even feel scared anymore. I feel numb; I feel like stone.

Was this how Erin felt a second before the golf club slammed into her skull? Do all animals go numb before they die?

"Oh my God, oh my God . . ." Sierra's voice echoes in my ear, a song played on a loop. It jerks me back to life.

Don't die, Final Girl said. I have to find a way out of this.

I force us backward, throw open the first door I find:

Basement.

Dread turns my stomach.

Of course it is.

"Down here," I murmur, and I push Sierra down the steps before she can object. My arms and legs feel stiff, clumsy. It seems to take me forever to get them to move the way I need them to.

My father lunges, but I manage to wrestle the basement door closed, wood bulging with his sudden weight. I fumble for the little bar lock, my hands shaking—

The doorknob turns—

I flip the little lock closed a second before the door slams into it and then collapse against the wall, breathing hard.

We're safe.

The door jerks against the lock, slamming into the side of my body. I flinch, taking a quick step backward. There's already a sliver of an opening between the door and the frame. The lock won't hold for long.

"Come on," I say, grabbing Sierra. I take a single step down the stairs when my leg crumples beneath me, the sudden pain in my ankle blotting out all other thought. I grit my teeth together, trying to remember how to breathe.

Sierra grabs my arm. "Oh my God, Alice? Are you okay? Can you walk?"

The door behind us bucks again, making us both start. We can't stay here. I blink the tears from my eyes. "Y-yeah," I say, cringing as I force myself to stand. "Let's go."

The basement is dark, unfinished, rough wooden steps erupting with splinters. It's so dark that I can't actually make out the floor below, and I can't help imagining that it's endlessly twisting down into the earth, never ending. Once the image enters my head, I can't seem to push it away.

Sierra puts one hand under my elbow, helping me stand. I take one step down the stairs, two—

On the third step my ankle twists to the side. And then I'm falling, tumbling down the stairs and into the darkness below.

I hit the cement floor hard, all the air leaving my lungs in a sudden whoosh. For a long moment I just lie there, listening to the sound of my own breathing. I have a passing thought that maybe I should just let whatever's going to happen next happen. I don't know how I'm supposed to live in this new reality. I want to close my eyes and wake up on the courthouse floor and realize that none of this was real, that it was a dream brought on by watching too many horror movies, listening to too many podcasts.

Pain surrounds me in a thick black cloud, making it impossible to think about this for very long.

I groan and force my eyes back open, trying to lift my head. Everything is dark, everything except for a thin sliver of light from the door at the top of the stairs.

"Alice?" Sierra shrieks, running down the stairs. "Alice, are you okay?"

I blink a few times, groaning. Above, the basement door bucks again. I hear wood splinter. I'm not sure how I'm supposed to stand up. Everything hurts. I'm worried I broke an arm or busted some ribs in my fall down the stairs, so I move slowly, rolling over to one side and pushing myself up only when I'm sure my arm will hold my weight.

"Oh my God." Sierra drops next to me and lets out a loud, wet sob. "Alice? Oh my God, are you okay? Are you hurt?"

I finally manage sit up and lean back on my hands. "He drove us down here," I say, my voice low, trembling. "He wanted us to get trapped."

Sierra takes two shaky breaths, then glances around the basement, her shifty, frightened eyes reminding me of an animal in a cage. When those eyes dart back to me, I see that they're glazed over and red. "Are we going to die?"

Yes, I think. Probably. But I can't make myself say the words out loud. *Don't die*, Final Girl told me. I let her warning echo through my head now, like a prayer. *Don't die, don't die, don't die.*

"There has to be a way out of here," I say through a fresh moan of pain. I pull my leg toward my chest, careful not to put any pressure on my ankle. "A window or something. Look around."

Sierra blinks. "You want to climb out a window?"

Above us, the basement door shudders again. We have only a few more minutes before he breaks through it. Maybe less.

"That lock isn't going to hold. If we want to live, then yes, we're going to have to." *We'd be lucky to find a window to climb out of,* I think, but I don't say that part out loud. Sierra's freaked out enough as it is. She won't be any help to me if she's too scared to move.

Next to me, Sierra drops her face into her hands, her shoulders trembling. I grab her shoulder and shake. "Sierra, pull yourself together. Help me."

She sniffs loudly. But she looks up again and nods. Okay, we're in business. Gingerly, I push myself up to a stand. My leg still feels shaky, but it doesn't immediately collapse under my weight, which is progress, I guess. I brace a hand against the wall behind me to ease some of the pressure and take a second to catch my breath.

The basement walls are made of large gray stones, the kind you don't want to lean against because they're jagged along the edges. The staircase splits the room in half, creating little alcoves in the corners. I can see the outline of a column of cardboard boxes beneath it, words written across them in faded Sharpie: *kitchen, closet.* I groan and look away, searching the rest of the basement for a window or a door. In all my years of hanging out at Millie's, I don't think I've ever come down here. There's nothing and more nothing, until—

There, on the far side of the basement, a door leading into a narrow hallway. It's probably a storage room or something, but I can't see anywhere else to go, so I grab Sierra's arm and point.

"Come on," I say, and she helps me hobble across the room. We pause on the other side of the door and struggle to pull it closed behind us, but the hinges are rusted, and we can't get it shut all the way.

There's a shuddering sound as the basement door slams into the lock again. Sierra and I both jerk our heads up, silently watching to see whether it holds.

We don't have time to wrestle with the door. He'll be down here soon.

"Look," Sierra says. She holds her cell phone out in front of her, but her hands are shaking so badly she drops it. It clatters to the packed-dirt floor and the light flickers off. In the sudden darkness, I hear her release a dry sob.

"Sorry," she murmurs, dropping to her hands and knees. I hear her fumbling around on the ground for her phone, but I don't kneel to help her. I've just noticed something in the sudden darkness, a thin strip of light just ahead. My stomach clenches.

It's a door.

I grab Sierra's arm. "Look."

She lifts her head, a smile darting across her lips. "Do you think that goes outside?"

I don't have time to answer her. There's a sudden crash behind us, and then Sierra's face changes, her eyes growing wider, frightened. She pushes her lips together, falling silent as the stairs behind us start to creak. Every nerve in my body flares.

Those are footsteps.

"He's coming," I whisper.

Tick, Tock, Tick, Tock . . .

The cellar door is just ahead, beckoning us. My legs are shaky as I stumble into a run, and my entire body screams with pain.

All that matters is getting to that door. Getting outside, to people, to safety.

A staircase made of rotten wood lifts out of the ground. I fall onto hands and knees as I stumble up it and I reach out, releasing a strangled sob when I finally feel the door beneath my fingers. I grasp for a handle, and when I can't find one in the dark, I throw my shoulder into the wood.

The impact shudders through me. My head snaps back and dull pain blasts through my shoulders, making my eyes tear.

"Hurry," Sierra sobs from behind me.

I release a choked, desperate cry and throw my shoulder into the door, again, ignoring the feeling of my muscles seeming to separate from my bones, the fire shooting through my veins like blood.

This time the door bursts open, sending me flying, rolling onto the ice-kissed grass, legs giving out beneath me. I taste dirt in my mouth. Icy rain pricks the back of my neck, and wind howls around me, immediately reaching through my thin shirt and jeans to chill my skin.

A fraction of a second later, Sierra climbs out of the cellar behind me and collapses onto the grass, crying hard.

In that moment, exhaustion overwhelms me. I let my eyes fall closed, gasping for breath. I feel dizzy, disoriented. I want to lie here forever, let my body go numb as it falls into the sweet oblivion of sleep. The idea of pushing myself to my feet, of trying to run, feels impossible. Everything hurts. Everything.

Then I hear a noise just behind me, a scuffle, like a shoe scraping against concrete. My eyes pop open and I shove myself back up to hands and knees, my pain and exhaustion forgotten in a sudden surge of adrenaline. I jerk my head around, looking back down into the basement—

It's empty.

My breath slows even as my heart starts beating faster, confusion clouding my brain. *What the hell?*

Why isn't he there? Where did he go?

From this angle, I can see through the narrow hallway and into the large, dark room beyond. I can see the staircase and the basement door hanging open at the top of it. But my dad isn't there.

A bitter taste fills my mouth.

What does he know that I don't?

"Sierra," I murmur, grasping for her. "Where did he go?"

Sierra blinks into the darkness, looking hopeful. "Maybe he left," she says in a small voice. "Maybe he was worried he was going to get caught."

I bite my lip. I don't think that's what happened. "Come on," I say to Sierra. "Get up. We have to get out of here."

"But if he's already gone . . ."

"He isn't gone." I can't explain why, but I'm sure about this. My father's still here, hiding now, somehow one step ahead of us.

Goose bumps prickle up my arms as I look around the dark yard, at the distant outlines of bushes, the six-foot-high privacy fence casting everything in deepest shadow. The party stragglers all seem to be gone. Everyone's gone.

My eyes land on the little gate leading out front, and my throat closes.

That gate. It leads to a side entrance that you can get to by going through Millie's kitchen. If the killer backtracked when he saw us heading for the cellar door, he could be there now, waiting on the other side of that fence for us to come through.

My chest rises and falls rapidly, panic setting in. The only way out of this yard is through that gate. But I can't risk it. I have to be smart.

Don't die, I think.

What would a Final Girl do?

"We need to find somewhere to hide while we call the cops," I say, my voice barely a whisper. "Somewhere safe."

In the darkness, all I can see are the whites of Sierra's eyes. "You want to hide out in this *yard*?"

I chew my lip, glancing back at the gate. I don't want to say what I'm thinking out loud in case he's on the other side of that gate, listening to us. Once he realizes we're not going to go through that way, there will be nothing to stop him from bursting through that door, rushing us.

"Alice?" Sierra says, frowning at me. "What—"

I hold a finger to my lips, quieting her as I look around the yard. My eyes travel over a dark shed that I happen to know is filled with dangerous lawn equipment and tools, and the shallow grove of trees where Millie used to bury her hamsters when she was a kid. Nope and nope.

I glance at the neighbor's house on the other side of the fence. I could throw some rocks at their windows, try to get their attention. But the windows are all dark, and there aren't any cars in the drive. It doesn't look like anyone's home.

My eyes swivel back to the driveway.

Cars.

Of course. X said he'd be waiting with his car running. If we can get over the fence, we can make a run for his car.

Assuming he's still there.

I glance back at the gate, my heartbeat picking up. It's not a perfect plan. X said he'd be waiting almost an hour ago. Who knows if he's still there. Still, it's the best we've got, if only because I don't think the killer will expect it. I catch Sierra's eye and jerk my head toward the back fence, motioning for her to follow me. She frowns but nods.

We hurry across the yard as quickly and silently as possible. I flinch every time the icy grass crunches beneath my shoes or whenever my breath comes out in too loud an exhale, my eyes flicking back to the gate on the other side of the yard.

It stays closed.

My hands shake like crazy. Every movement burns through me; every breath aches. I have no idea how I'm getting over that fence. Now that we're close, it seems so much taller than when we were all the way across the yard. Insanely, impossibly tall.

"Alice." Sierra touches my shoulder, and I flinch, nearly smacking her in the face with my elbow as I jerk around.

Her eyes are wide with fear, her lower lip trembling.

"What is it?" I hiss, and she lifts a hand to point to the other side of Millie's yard.

I stare for a moment, my heart beating in double time.

The gate's open.

"Go," I say, grabbing Sierra's arm. Her skin is like ice beneath my fingers, cold and wet. "Go, hurry." I turn back around, yanking her toward the fence—

Wham!

I slam into something solid, something *human*. Arms come down around me, hands grabbing my shoulders to hold me in place. I try to jerk away, but the hands hold tight. Someone strong.

"Alice? Hey, it's okay, it's me." Wes's voice.

I blink until I can make out the lines of his face in the darkness. The stubble covering his jaw, the curls falling over his forehead. There's blood dried around the gash on his head, flecked across his cheeks. His eyes look monstrous in the dark.

"I— I thought you went home," I choke out.

Wes's eyebrows draw together. "I did, but I came back. I couldn't just leave you here with a killer on the loose."

"Oh." My nerves feel jittery, live wires, hot to the touch. Something about this is all wrong. Wes shouldn't be here. And it's strange that I'm seeing him again only now, after the murderer's disappeared into the darkness.

It's just like last time. Erin died, the murderer chased me, the murderer disappeared, and suddenly, there was Wes.

My body stiffens. I take a quick step back, colliding with Sierra.

Wes's expression darkens. "You still think it's me, don't you?"

"I— I don't know," I say. I really don't. My father called Sierra. He knew all the victims. I'm so sure it's him. But now Wes is here, and it's such a big coincidence. Too big.

If this were a movie, I'd be shouting at the screen. *Are you crazy? Don't trust him. Run, run!*

I can't think straight. I can't think at all.

Sierra huddles in close behind me, her breath hot on my neck. I curl my hands around her wrists, too scared to move.

"Alice," Wes says, pleading. His jaw is set, anger or frustration making him tense, and he has that look in his eye again. The same one he got when he punched the reporter this morning.

He reaches for me. "You have to—"

Sierra gasps, and I catch a whirl of movement from the corner of my eye, something bright and flashing.

Wes goes still, his eyes wide with shock. He's not looking at me anymore but staring at something just beyond my shoulder, lips parted like he's about to tell me a secret.

"Wes?" I gasp.

"Alice . . ." He lurches forward, the full weight of his body dropping onto me, making my legs buckle.

With effort, he lifts his head. Blood appears at the corner of his mouth and drips down his chin in a thin stream.

I'm shrieking now, screaming without thinking about what I'm saying. "Oh my God, Wes! Wes!"

He gropes for his stomach. I look down and see a blade jutting out of his gut, slicked with blood.

I recoil. Behind me, Sierra is screaming, grabbing for me, trying to pull me away from Wes. I stare, frozen, too horrified to move.

The blade sucks out. Wes's body crumples to the ground.

I look up.

The werewolf mask seems to be hovering in midair, the darkness swallowing the killer's body.

"It's more fun if you're running," says a low, rasping voice.

It doesn't sound like my father. It doesn't sound human at all.

My heart jump-starts inside my chest. There's no time to spare

Wes even one more parting glance. I just run, tearing after Sierra across the pitch-black yard, my breath screaming inside my throat. My shoes slip on the grass, and I almost fall once, twice, and each time I'm certain I'm about to feel the sharp edge of a knife between my shoulder blades.

The killer follows. Slowly.

Playing with us.

The fence looms up ahead. It's too high, just like I knew it would be. I leap uselessly, my fingers inches from the top of the fence, nowhere near being able to grasp it. I'll need to stand on something to pull myself over.

I glance down, quickly finding a wooden slab halfway up the fence. It's narrow, and the wood looks old enough to break beneath my weight, but it'll have to do. I angle my foot above the slab and brace my hands against the fence as I climb up, my body screaming with the exertion. I grope along for the top of the fence, desperately, feeling my body begin to pitch backward, pulled by gravity, when my fingers finally wrap around splintered wood.

The fence shudders, and I catch Sierra at the corner of my eye, climbing next to me. I grasp the top of the fence and pull—

The killer seems to realize we're going to get away. He lunges—

For a moment, the only thing I'm aware of is the shock of pain exploding through my body. My vision goes black, and my breath gets caught inside my chest. I can see nothing, feel nothing. I barely notice that I've wriggled to the other side of the fence. But then the ground slams into my feet, a fresh jerk of pain shuddering through me.

I'm on the other side.

Sierra drops to the ground next to me, gasping, her eyes wide.

I'm sure the killer will cut us off if we try to make it to X's car out front, but Claire's car is angled across the alley, windshield smashed, the passenger door hanging open. Wes must've driven it here after Claire crashed it in the corn.

I practically slam into it, my fingers shaky and clumsy as I pull the door open and shove Sierra inside. I climb in after her and pull the door closed behind me. Shaking. Hard.

"Who was that guy?" Sierra asks me. Her eyes are wide, and her lips are shaking. She looks out into the darkness, her fear palpable.

"He's someone I know," I say in a small voice, still unable to make myself believe that Wes is really dead, really gone.

And not just Wes, but Eli and Erin and Chloe and Millie.

So many people. Too many.

Figure it out, I think, swallowing hard. If I solve the murder, they all stay dead. But I get my sister back. Claire gets to live.

I double-check that all the car doors are locked, and then I turn to Sierra. "Do you know what time it is?"

She frowns at me, clearly not expecting this question. But, with shaky hands, she digs her phone out of her pocket and shows me the screen.

11:56.

Only four minutes left.

Four Minutes!

I keep my gaze on the windows. The night is black on the other side of the glass, only the white frosted tips of grass visible in the darkness. The wind has stopped moving. Everything is still.

Everything except for me. My heart pounds in my ears, and I can't quite steady my breathing. It leaves little plumes of fog on the windows.

Figure it out, I think again. But I've been trying to "figure it out" for hours, and I'm no closer to understanding what's happening than I was at the beginning of the night.

The killer isn't Owen, and it isn't Wes.

And that voice, it didn't sound like my father, either. It didn't sound like anyone.

I lower my head to my hands, clenching my eyes shut.

In horror movies, this is the moment of catharsis, the moment the audience has been waiting for. The Final Girl unmasks the killer and listens to his inane reasons for slaughtering innocent people. And then she bests him. She wrestles his knife away and stabs him with it, or else she finds an abandoned gun and shoots him in the chest, or uses her wits to concoct some sort of elaborate trap.

Good overcomes evil, every time.

But real life isn't like that. It's realizing that the people you love, the people you *trusted,* they might not be who you thought they were. It's making choices that put your friends in danger, even when you don't mean to. It's running and fear and death. So much more death than I was prepared for.

If I "figure it out," all those people will stay dead.

But Claire . . .

A tear slips through the corner of my eye and carves a line down my cheek. For the past year, I've mourned my sister. I've wished she were still alive, not even thinking about what that would have meant, how many people would have had to take her place. I thought my life couldn't get any worse than it was, but I was wrong.

So, so wrong.

No person's life is worth this much death.

"I learned my lesson," I whisper, just in case Final Girl is listening. "No one's life is worth all this death. I don't want this anymore, okay? I just want to go home. Please, please just send me home."

I open my eyes, staring out the cracked windshield as I try to steady my breathing. Sierra is frowning next to me, asking me who I'm talking to, if I'm okay, but I ignore her.

"Please," I whisper again. *"Please."*

There's movement at the corner of my eye. I look at the rearview mirror as a dark shadow looms up in the seat behind me.

My chest seizes. *Oh my God.* It's him, he's found us, he got here first somehow—

"Haven't you ever seen a horror movie?" Final Girl says, leaning forward between the seats. "You always, *always* check the back seat before you get into a car."

I exhale, relieved. "You," I breathe.

"Me," Final Girl says, beaming. "It seemed like you wanted a chat."

Sierra's grabbing my arm, fingernails pinching into my skin. "Alice, who is that, what's—"

I shake her off. "I figured it out, and I don't want this anymore," I say to Final Girl. "I don't want *any* of this. Please just send me home. Please."

Final Girl wrinkles her nose, all sympathetic. "I'm afraid it's not that easy," she says.

Her voice sounds different than it used to. Deeper.

"What do you mean? I learned my lesson, okay? No one's life is more important than anyone else's. I get it now. So just"—I snap my fingers—"send me back."

"Like I said, girl, can't do that."

I stare back at her, dumbfounded. "But . . . but people are *dying*. So many more people are going to die if I stay here."

Final Girl blinks. "That's kind of the point."

Something cold moves through me. "What?"

"Do you really think I brought you here to learn a *lesson*? Do I look like your damn fairy godmother? I have a quota."

My mouth feels dry. *"Quota?"*

Final Girl smiles. It's a strange, unsettling smile. Too wide, and with far too many teeth. Staring at it, I feel a tremor move through me, a realization.

For the first time tonight, I actually understand what's going on.

God, I was stupid.

Final Girl is an angel, all right.

She's an Angel of Death.

"You wanted this to happen, didn't you?" I say. "You wanted all those people to die. That's why you sent me back."

"What did you think this was? A fairy tale?" Final Girl says. "Did you think I was going to wave a little wand and make your life what it was before?"

"You tricked me," I say, numb.

"I told you to figure it out. It's not my fault you couldn't put the clues together. But hey, you still have two minutes left." Final Girl kicks the door open and climbs out of the car. "Oh, and Alice? I know how much you love horror movies, so I have one more fun little twist for you."

I feel a drop in my stomach. I don't think I can take another twist. "What are you talking about?"

"Check out the floor underneath your seat. You'll see." And then, with a wink, she's gone, faded away in the darkness like she was never there at all.

Sierra and I are alone in the car again. Sierra looks at me, her breathing still ragged. "Alice?" she gasps. "Alice . . . what the fuck?"

I ignore her.

Check out the floor underneath your seat. I have one more fun little twist for you.

I don't want to know what it is. But I *have* to know. I lean forward and look down.

There's something peeking out from beneath the mat covering the car floor. Something white.

Fingers trembling, I dig it out.

It's a small white card with Owen Trevor Maddox's photograph on the front. His library card. The same library card he used to upload his manifesto—supposed "proof" of his guilt—to that incel website.

I hear Final Girl's voice in my head. *How do you know Owen wrote that manifesto? The cops traced it to a computer in a public library.*

Someone logged on to that computer using Owen's username and ID. But they couldn't prove it was him.

"No," I whisper. When Final Girl first told me this, I thought it was ridiculous. Did she really think someone stole Owen's library card and used his information to log on to the library computer, to frame him? It seemed completely absurd.

But his library card is here, in this car.

I flip the card over.

Owen's username and password are scrawled on the back in Sharpie.

My hands start shaking now. I feel like I can't breathe.

A sudden click breaks the silence. I jerk and turn to look at the passenger door—

The lock just popped open.

Don't Die

Sierra's staring at the passenger-door lock, her eyes bugged, her chest rising and falling rapidly. "What's happening?" she hisses, eyes jerking back to me. "Did you unlock the door? Who—"

The question is only half out of her mouth before the door behind her flies open. The killer lunges forward, one matted-fur-covered arm looping around Sierra's neck and dragging her from the car, her legs kicking. The werewolf mask still hangs lopsided, misted with rain.

"No!" I leap after them, trying to wrestle Sierra away. But I'm too late. The steel blade of the knife flashes, piercing Sierra's neck. Her eyes find mine and widen with horror as blood gushes from the wound, spilling down her chest.

The killer drops the knife and reaches for the mask. I don't have time to look away. I barely have time to brace myself for the face I know is going to be staring back at me.

The mask falls to the ground.

The killer's cheeks are red, her forehead damp with sweat even as cold air blows in through the open door behind her. Her hair hangs over her eyes in frizzy clumps, looking more disheveled than I've ever seen it before, but when she looks at me, she smiles.

"Hey, Alley Cat."

"Claire?" I choke out.

Claire stares at me. "You're surprised? Really? You've been playing it cool all night, but I was *so* sure you saw me with Chloe in the corn maze."

I blink fast. I had a horrible feeling I knew the truth the second I saw that library card, but I still can't make myself believe it. "But . . . but how? I was right behind you in the corn maze. I would've seen something."

"I thought you did, but you must've gotten knocked out at exactly the right moment."

"But you were with me when I heard Chloe scream." Even as I say the words, I realize that it didn't matter. I remember this from last year; Chloe didn't scream while her arm was being cut off. She screamed afterward, when she looked down and discovered it missing.

Claire would've had plenty of time to run away, to find me.

"You know, it's weird, but she didn't make a peep when I came at her with the chain saw. I think she was in shock." Claire shrugs. "Guess I got lucky."

Sierra releases a wet sob, drawing my attention back down to her. She'd been pressing a hand to the wound at her neck, desperately trying to stop the flow of blood, but now that hand drops to her side, lifeless. Her eyes roll up in her skull. Then go still.

Staring at her, I feel a fresh wave of horror. My sister just killed a girl. She did it in front of me.

Somehow I manage to say, my voice barely a whisper, "Why?"

Claire doesn't answer right away. She looks down at Sierra, as though making absolutely certain that she's not still breathing. And then she takes a step back, letting Sierra's body collapse to the ground with a thud. She brushes her hair off her face with the back of her hand, leaving a trail of blood across her forehead.

"How can you ask me why?" Claire says, finally looking back at me. "You know what was going on with Dad."

"The girls," I say, numb.

"The girls," Claire repeats, her voice ugly in a way I've never heard before. She wipes the handle of the knife off on her leg—removing the prints—and drops it to the ground next to Sierra's body. "I couldn't believe it when I found out. I mean, how stupid can you get? He wasn't even *smart* about it. He left voice mails, pictures, texts." Her face becomes hard. "And he left that burner in his pocket, like it was *nothing*. I knew then that it was only a matter of time before he was going to get caught. I had to do something. Take care of the problem, just like always."

"Take care of the problem?" I can't believe what she's saying. "Is that what you think you're doing?"

"I did this for our family," Claire says, her tone conversational, like she's explaining why she needed to cheat on her math test. "To *save* us. What Dad was doing was evil. I was helping him, taking away the temptation, just like always."

I think of Claire flushing Mom's cigarettes down the toilet. Was that all these girls were to her? Things to be discarded?

"That's why you killed Chloe and Erin and Sierra." It takes all my energy to keep my voice from shaking. "But why Eli? And Millie, and—and Wes."

Claire tilts her head, studying me, her eyes slightly narrowed.

I feel a chill move through me. Those eyes . . . something about them worries me. My sister is dangerous; that much is obvious. But I never thought she could hurt me.

Then Claire blinks, and the moment passes. "I know you liked Wes, but he wasn't good enough for you."

"So you *killed* him?"

"It was better this way."

"What about Millie? Eli?" As I say the names, I realize what they all have in common. Proximity to me.

"No sister left behind, remember?" Claire says, seeming to read my mind. "I know you thought those people were your friends, but they were just going to hold you back in the long run. But *you're* special, like me. We were made for bigger, better things. Besides, I really want you by my side for this next part."

"Next part," I repeat, numb.

"You actually gave me the idea, Alley Cat. Remember this summer? How you were telling me all about Final Girls on the way to that audition? It made me have an epiphany. When I didn't get the part, I realized there was another way I could play the Final Girl." Claire's eyes flash. "And not just in some low-budget slasher. In *life*."

I let my eyes drift down, falling on Sierra's unmoving body. Something inside me twists. I think of how quickly Claire shifted from wanting to be a stage actress to wanting to be a film actress after her latest Juilliard disappointment. I'd always seen it as a good thing, her eternal optimism, her unflappable confidence. That kind of ambition was what separated the dreamers from the doers.

Maybe I was wrong. Maybe Claire was just desperate to be famous.

"Th-that's why you did this?" I choke out.

"Think about it. Everyone loves the only survivor of some horrible crime. I mean, the only *survivors*, since there are two of us."

There's a catch in her voice when she says this, something that makes me wonder. Was I even supposed to survive? Or was it just supposed to be her this whole time?

Claire's talking faster now, her voice rising in excitement. She sounds manic, unhinged. "Survivors get to go on talk shows and podcasts; they get book deals. And true crime is so hot right now. If I can't be a famous actress, this is the next best thing." She grins with just her mouth, her eyes cold and far away. "I'll be such a good survivor, Allie. The world won't be able to resist me."

"Stop it. Please, just stop talking." I close my eyes, horrified. "You're sick."

"You think so?" Claire tilts her head, her smile flickering. "I don't see it that way. And I don't think America will, either."

Red-and-blue lights flash in the trees, police sirens howling like wild animals. Claire looks down at the mask and knife at her feet, at Sierra's mutilated body. She begins peeling off her wolf suit. "We have to get our stories straight," she says calmly. "Owen came here after the police released him from custody. He attacked Sierra, and then he ran off when he saw the cop cars, okay? He left all this stuff behind, though. Sound reasonable?"

"I— I can't do that. I can't pin this on an innocent person!"

"Of course you can." Claire digs out her phone and checks her screen. "It's 11:59, almost midnight. Which means we can say he left like three minutes ago." She looks at me, eyes hard and unblinking. "You'll keep my secret, won't you?"

I stare back at my sister, shocked. This can't be how this night ends. It *can't* be. There has to be something I can do, some way I can still fix this.

I'm shaking my head, no, no, no, when I see something on the ground.

It's the knife Claire used to kill Sierra. It's just sitting there.

Don't die, Final Girl said. She said it over and over again.

But she was a liar.

Something occurs to me. It's a long shot, but maybe . . .

I fumble for the knife. The handle is cool to the touch.

Claire frowns. "What are you doing?"

I turn the knife around so that it's pointed at my own chest.

Claire's eyes go wide. "Alice, *no*—"

I inhale, deep.

And then—

Well. That's when everything goes dark again.

Halloween,
Today

X's voice is buzzing from the earbuds lying on the floor next to my head. ". . . not like it is in these movies. In real life, we all know it's way more likely for trans women to be the ones getting murdered."

Another voice—Billie Ericson's, not Millie's—adds, "Particularly trans women of color."

"So true," says X.

"I'm getting pissed just thinking about it, so maybe that's our cue to sign off for the week," Billie says, their voice echoing strangely from my headphones. "Stay safe, everyone. And remember—stay out of the cornfield."

"Stay out of the fucking cornfield—"

I bolt upright and start clawing at my chest, expecting to find the knife I was just holding, a wound, something. There's not even a scar.

Slow waves of pain crash over my head and trickle down the back of my neck, making me feel woozy and slightly sick. I blink a few times, my eyesight all darkness dotted with distant pinpricks that I think might be stars.

Then, slowly, slowly, a ceiling comes into focus. It sways above me like something I'm seeing underwater. I frown. Ceiling. Not the night sky. And beneath my head, something hard. Cringing, I look to the left.

Salmon-pink tile. A wall of sinks.

I'm back in the courthouse bathroom.

Oh thank God.

I push myself to my feet. My head spins, and I have to grab for the edge of one of the sinks and lean over until it stops. When it does, I notice that the pain in my ankle is gone. All the pain in my body is gone. Except for my head, of course. My head kills.

We're playing by Cinderella rules, Final Girl said. *You only have until midnight.*

Midnight's come and gone. My sacrifice—it must've worked.

Everything's exactly the way it was.

Tears prick my eyes as I lift a hand to the back of my head. There's a goose egg poking out from beneath my hair, the skin tender to the touch. I'm not sure whether it's from the door smacking me in the back of the head or from when I fell. The bathroom's empty, lights off, no sign of Final Girl anywhere, so it's not like I can ask her.

There's no sign of Claire, either, I realize. Relief washes over me, surprising me with how strong it is. I thought I knew my sister, but Claire was a psychopath, a killer. Her death was for the best, especially if it means that everyone else gets to live.

I make my way for the door, my heartbeat vibrating in my throat. There's still one more thing I have to do, one way to make this all right. My testimony.

Claire might be gone, but Owen's still going to go down for what she did.

Unless I do something about it.

I stumble through the now-empty courthouse halls, dazed, and push open the heavy double doors that lead to the courtroom where they're holding Owen's trial.

The moment the doors swing open, hundreds of faces swivel around in their seats, anxious to see who's walking through them.

For a long moment, everything is quiet, the only sound my own blood pounding in my ears as everyone stares.

And then the whispers start. People turn to their neighbor and mutter some version of "That's the little sister; she's testifying today" under their breath. My cheeks burn. Head ducked, I hurry down the narrow aisle to the bench at the very front of the room, where my mom's already sitting.

"Where have you been?" she murmurs as I slide into the bench next to her.

You have no idea, I think. But out loud, all I say is "Bathroom."

She presses her lips together, her mauve lipstick bleeding into the creases at the corners of her mouth.

Lipstick, I think, frowning. She wasn't wearing lipstick this morning. And her hair looks different, too. It's not pulled back, like it was, but hanging in loose waves around her face, like she got a professional blowout. Her golden-brown highlights match her eyes.

I frown, confused. She looks so different.

Why does she look so different?

She clears her throat and says, "Did you happen to see—"

I figure she's going to ask me whether I've seen Dad, but before she can get the words out, the doors on the far side of the room open, and the jury filters into the room.

I scan their faces as they take their seats, a little surprised when I find Sidney Prescott sitting in the middle of the first row. She's not wearing her Final Girl T-shirt anymore, and her hair has been pushed away from her face with a thin black headband. She looks respectable and older.

I stare, willing her to look at me. But her eyes pass right over me, like she doesn't recognize me at all.

Oh God. I feel sick.

A bald man in a brown security guard uniform stands beside the judge's bench. "All rise."

There's a thunderous sound as everyone in court stands.

"Court is now in session," he continues, "the Honorable Patricia E. Harvey presiding."

A woman in a long black robe enters through a door on the opposite side of the court and swiftly takes her seat. She's an older woman, with short graying hair and a deeply lined face. She nods at the guard.

"You may now be seated," the guard says. Judge Harvey clears her throat and folds her hands on the desk before her.

The room is silent. You could hear a pin.

"Mr. Maddox," Judge Harvey says curtly.

In the defendant's box at the front of the room, Owen and his attorneys stand. I'm staring at the back of Owen's neck so hard that I swear he must be able to feel his skin pricking. I half expect him to swat at his neck like I'm a bug he can smash with his palm. But he just stares straight ahead, so still he could be made of stone.

"Are you ready to enter your plea?" Judge Harvey asks.

Owen leans forward, speaking into a mic on the table in front of him. His voice is deep and clear. "Yes, ma'am."

I curl my fingers around the back of the bench in front of me. My chest is so tight I feel like I'm suffocating.

"Owen Trevor Maddox," Judge Harvey continues. "You are on trial for the first-degree murders of Millie Kido, Sierra Clayton, Erin Cleary, Chloe Bree, and Eli Cummings."

My stomach drops a little further with each new name out of Judge Harvey's mouth.

No, I think, gripping the bench so tightly that my knuckles turn white. *No no no no no.*

This can't be right. If I actually changed the past, if Millie and Sierra and Chloe and Erin and Eli and Wes are really dead, then that would mean—

There's a sudden flicker of movement at the corner of my eye. I turn, dazed, and see my sister sliding into the bench next to me. She wears a gray shift dress and a navy blue cardigan, her red hair woven into a neat little braid.

I open my mouth, but I can't make any words come out. Claire looks so perfectly like the innocent schoolgirl I always thought she was. Not like a murderer at all. She glances at me, frowning when she sees the look of complete shock on my face.

"Sorry I'm late, Alley Cat," she murmurs under her breath. "Did I miss anything good?"

ACKNOWLEDGMENTS

There's a myth among authors that some books just come to you. That they appear in your head, fully plotted, as though by magic. I've heard of such things happening to other writers but never dared hope it might happen to me. But, reader, it did! This is that book, and I truly hope you had even half as much fun reading it as I had writing it.

Even the books that come easy require a lot of hard work from a lot of people, and this one is no exception. My agent, Hillary Jacobson, sold this book in the middle of a global pandemic and read it more times than any other person alive, maybe even including me. Hillary, thank you for your faith and your guidance, from the moment you "gasped out loud" while reading a one-paragraph pitch, all the way to that final line edit. Thank you for fielding dozens (hundreds?) of panicky emails, for the hours of brainstorming to land on the perfect title, and for talking me down and building me up. Also, a huge thanks to everyone over at ICM, to my foreign rights team for helping this book abroad, and to Josie Freedman and Randie Adler, for the work you've done to try and bring this story to the big screen. I'm very grateful to be surrounded by so many talented people.

I'm so lucky to get to work with the incredibly talented team of book lovers over at Razorbill. They've been supporters of my work for ten years now (!) which . . . wow. Every writer talks about wanting to find a publisher to grow with over their career, a publisher that will support their work as it changes and evolves and believe in them enough to take big chances. I can't quite believe that I actually got that. From the bottom of my heart, thank you.

Thank you to my wonderful editors, Casey McIntyre and Simone Roberts-Payne, for loving this book and seeing its potential in a fifty-page sample. It's because of them that Wes wears a Hello Kitty barrette and that we get some of my favorite scenes between him and Alice at the beginning of the book, not to mention the many, many other improvements they encouraged me to make. Of course, it takes many, many people to make sure that every line in a book is perfect, so thank you to my proofreaders, Sola Akinlana and Vivian Kirklin, and to my copyeditors, Marinda Valenti and Sarah Chasse, for helping me seem . . . How should I put this? More smarter. I was also lucky enough to work with Alaysia Jordan on a sensitivity read and I can't thank her enough for her thoughtful review of my work and for helping me to see just a few of my many blind spots. This book is better because of her. Thanks, also, to my publicity, marketing, and sales team, and specifically to Vanessa DeJesús and Felicity Vallence, for helping this book find readers. You know how people say you shouldn't judge a book by its cover? Ignore that. PLEASE judge this book by its cover. Theresa Evangelista went through many drafts to come up with the one you're holding now, and it is just so absolutely perfect and beautiful. Thank you thank you thank you!

I didn't have crit readers for this book, but my author friends were still there to listen to me complain about tricky plot beats and gush about cool bits of dialogue, often over wine, sometimes over Zoom. As always, thank you for listening and always knowing the perfect thing to say to make me feel like I'm not alone in even my strangest of complaints.

And, of course, thank you to my beautiful family. Ron, thank you for reading this and loving it and always being my biggest fan.

Harry, you at times seemed to be actively plotting against me finishing this book, but thank you for the cuddles and the color breaks and for reminding me that sometimes it really is very important that we stop and pick up that crunchy-looking leaf. Sawyer, thank you for the free babysitting. As per our agreement, your name will be in the next one. Mom and Steve, you also provided free babysitting, but you didn't barter so you will not get to be made into slasher victims. Next time, negotiate!

Ripley and Jones did nothing to help the writing of this book, but they did purr softly from the chair in my office, which was lovely. Thank you, both.

And finally, thank you, the person holding this book. Some of you have read all my books. Some of you know that I also publish under the names Danielle Rollins and Danielle Vega, that I've written about exorcisms and ghosts and time travel. Some of you have talked about me on social media, have let me sign your arms, have created art based on characters I invented, and have tweeted asking me for updates on the movies (I don't have any!). Some of you have written reviews and reread your copies until they fell apart and stood in line and met me in person. You truly have no idea. Okay I'm crying now. Thank you.

TURN THE PAGE FOR BONUS CONTENT:

A BONUS CHAPTER OF

How to Survive Your Murder

HALLOWEEN,
MINUTES LATER

The world seems to tilt beneath me. I lean forward, grabbing the back of the next bench, half-convinced I'm going to fall onto the ceiling. The guy sitting in front of me turns, shoots me a dirty look.

"Alice?" Claire asks, frowning at me. "You okay?"

Cassie is alive. *Alive.*

I close my eyes, blocking her out.

A split second and the world steadies again. I'm not going to fall, but I can't stay sitting, either. I don't know how long a trial lasts, but I can't imagine spending even one whole minute of that time sitting next to my sister.

I have to do something, go somewhere.

I stand and shove my way into the aisle, ignoring the backward glances, only vaguely aware of the whispers breaking out around me, the sound of a gavel banging, the judge shouting, "Order!"

Everything's going too fast. I haven't had any time to think. *If Owen's on trial, does that mean I agreed to lie for my sister after all? Did I cover for her? Did I help her frame an innocent person for murder?*

The taste of acid hits the back of my throat. I really am going to be sick. I practically slam into the double doors at the back of the courthouse, expecting someone to grab me, dart in front of me, stop me. No one does.

The door shuts behind me, cutting the noise from the courtroom in half. I squeeze my eyes closed, and count to ten, quickly first, then again, slow. *One.* Pause. *Two.* Pause. Ms. Martin, the counselor I went to for exactly one session after my sister died, was a big fan of counting to ten. I tap my fingers against my palms and repeat the numbers over and over in my head. *Onetwothree. One. Two. Three.*

I thought it would be easier to think without anyone else around, but it's the opposite. The silence is deafening, oppressive. The sun outside is steady and bright and its heat seeps in through the floor-to-ceiling windows, leaving the hall sauna-hot. It's like trying to breathe in an oven.

My brain keeps circling one thought: *My sister's alive. Which means other people are dead.*

Chloe, I think, horror rising in my chest. *Erica.*

Millie. Eli. Sierra.

Wes.

A sob chokes out of me, echoing down the hall. I press my knuckles to lips. I did that. It doesn't matter who was holding the knife. *I killed those people.* If it weren't for me, if I hadn't done what I'd done, they'd all still be alive. If it weren't for me, the real killer would be six feet underground.

"Something wrong?" asks a voice and—in an instant—every part of my body, every cell and nerve, every ounce of blood goes still.

My throat restricts, as if someone's squeezing it. For a moment, the silence as he waits for me to answer is absolute. I can hear it pulsing.

Then I look up.

"Wes," I breathe.

Wesley James Hanson III stands in front of me. Alive. Alive, but looking terrible. His face is covered in stubble and his cheekbones are too sharp, his eyes all pupil. In the last year he must've lost almost ten pounds and, God, it's like he's forgotten how to hold still. He's tapping a finger on his leg, scratching the back of his neck, looking over his shoulder. His eyes jerk away a second after they settle on my face, like looking at me is painful.

"In the flesh," he says. His voice has a raw, scraped quality to it, like it's been through too much pain for one lifetime. And yet there's still something so lovely about him. With the sun streaming in behind him, his eyes look dark blue, like the middle of the ocean.

I swallow. I just saw him. It *feels* like I just saw him. We were *just* standing together in Millie's backyard. He was wearing that white T-shirt, his hair stiff with dried blood, and he was so disappointed that I didn't believe him when he said he wasn't a murderer. And then my sister killed him.

Except she didn't kill him, did she? She couldn't have because he's standing in front of me now, all sharp edges and quick, shallow breaths and strange energy. I want to touch his face, to make sure he's real.

I start to say something, then stop. I can't just apologize, not after everything. Instead, I say, "I thought you were—"

"Dead?" Wes finishes, raising an eyebrow. I feel something zip down my spine.

"Yeah," I manage to choke out. "That."

He stares at me a moment longer, a new intensity in his eyes. I watch his jaw working beneath all that stubble, his lips curving into a smile that doesn't seem remotely genuine.

"Well, that shouldn't surprise me," he says. "You leaving me for dead is kind of our thing."

A Q&A WITH THE AUTHOR

A Q&A with author Danielle Valentine

1. What inspired you to write this book? How did you come up with the idea?

I've always loved the movie *Scream*. I was in middle school when it came out, and I remember thinking it was about the coolest thing that ever existed. My best friend and I wrote down all the lines of that first iconic scene in this notebook I had, and we used to perform it together, over and over (as you can see, we were very cool). I grew up watching *Halloween* and other iconic slashers of the '80s, and my love of *Scream* led me to more cheesy '90s slashers, like *I Know What You Did Last Summer* and the Final Destination franchise. All in all, you could just say I was a big fan of the genre as a whole. So, when my editor at Razorbill mentioned that she wanted a book that felt a little like *Scream* I was instantly interested.

But the thing about *Scream* is that it wasn't just a slasher. It was a commentary on the slasher genre as a whole. I knew that if I were going to write a slasher, it couldn't just be a story about a serial killer—how boring! I wanted to write something that took a closer look at the state of horror in the 2020s. And, of course, you can't look at horror in the 2020s without looking at the rise of True Crime and podcasts, so I knew instantly that this would be part of it.

The last piece that fell into place was the idea for the Flash Sideways. I'd recently seen *Happy Death Day*, and I loved the way the writer took this familiar trope—the *Groundhog Day* infinite time loop—and made it feel fresh by making it a thriller. I figured there had to be other tropes you could do this trick with, so I delved deep into the world of TV and movie tropes until I came across the Flash Sideways. This was used most popularly in *It's a Wonderful Life*, but it's been utilized again and again in movies like *Family Man* and *Click*. Basically, the idea is that you get to see an alternate version of what your life would look like if you'd made different choices. It lends itself perfectly to a slasher! Once I had that element, I instantly knew what story I wanted to tell: the story of a girl whose sister died, who wanted to know what her life would be like if she'd managed to save her.

2. Why did you want to write in this genre? What about the genre do you particularly respond to?

I grew up with horror! It's a genre my mom loved and, as children, my younger brother and I couldn't get enough. We begged for scary stories every night and my mom (probably too drained from her day job to come up with anything original!) would retell stories she'd read in Stephen King books. *It*, especially, was responsible for a lot of the bedtime stories I remember as a child.

3. Do you have a favorite horror movie or movie franchise?

Impossible to pick just one! Obviously, I love Halloween and Scream, but I'm also a HUGE fan of Alien.

4. Who is your favorite final girl?

I've got to go with Sidney Prescott! As I mentioned above, *Scream* has a special place in my heart, and I always loved how Sidney fought back against Ghostface.

I also have to give a shout-out to Laurie Strode, the final girl in the Halloween franchise. Laurie was my mom's favorite. I remember her making me watch the second Halloween movie, and there's a moment where Laurie's hurt her ankle, and she's sort of limping away. This is a total trope, the injured final girl trying to get away as the killer sneaks up on her. But then Laurie looks over her shoulder and sees that Michael Myers is coming up behind her. She completely ignores the pain in her foot and just starts running. My mom loved that! And it's stuck with me as a writer, as this great example of a small twist that completely subverts viewers' expectations.

5. What was your favorite part of writing this book?

Wes! I'm not traditionally very talented at writing love stories. I'd say it's probably my weakest skill. But I wanted there to be a good romance in this book, so I challenged myself to write just the hottest possible guy for Alice to fall for. But in early versions he was coming off as a kind of generic bad-boy type, just not unique or special in any way. And I'm in my 30s now, so I was wondering if maybe I didn't have a good understanding of the types of guys that younger girls are falling for. In my day it was Logan Echolls and Spike and Billy Loomis! So, I did some research, and of course you instantly find K-pop stars and Harry Styles and Timothée Chalamet.

The thing about all these guys is this really cool subversion of traditional gender roles.

Anyway! This is a long, drawn-out way of saying that it was just so fun to come up with Wes's personality, to make him feel fresh. And once I figured out that he was the kind of guy who wore pearls and Hello Kitty barrettes to the gym, it just became easier to see why Alice was into him. I felt like I was able to write their chemistry so much more believably once he had a personality all his own.

WRITING-RELATED QUESTIONS

6. If someone wants to write a book, how should they get started?

I think the most important thing to do when you're getting started is to develop a routine. Writing is a practice more than anything. Rather than focusing on one book or series that you want to write, focus on building a writing practice into your everyday life. The old advice was to try to write every day, but I don't think that's a realistic suggestion in modern times. There are just too many other constraints on people's time—school and work and family. That said, I think the gem of that advice is still good—even if you can't write every day, write regularly. Look at your schedule, figure out when you can carve out time for a regular writing practice and start incorporating it into your life. This might mean that you're waking up an hour before work to get some pages in before you start your day (which is what I did when I first started taking my writing seriously) but it could also mean that you're finding five or ten or fifteen minutes twice a week while you're on your lunch break. Whatever works and is reasonable for you is good enough!

7. Do you have any advice for writing thrillers or genre books?

The first thing you need to do when writing in a specific genre is to learn the conventions of that genre. All genres have rules. When I first started trying to write thrillers, I emailed my agent and asked her to recommend all the best ones she could think of. I then spent the next year reading voraciously. I read the most popular ones, and I read the niche ones and I basically tried to get through everything people recommended. I also took a lot of notes. I noticed, for instance, that most thrillers have a very big twist right in the middle of the book, and this "midpoint twist" often separates the best thrillers from the mediocre ones.

This advice has two sides. Yes, it's important to learn the rules of your genre, but it's equally important to learn which rules you can bend or even break. I was able to land a particularly unexpected twist in *How to Survive Your Murder* because I'd read so widely in this genre, and I knew exactly what readers were expecting at the end. I made it seem like I was going to give it to them and then, at the last minute, I pulled the rug out.

8. It can be very difficult to finish writing an entire novel. Do you have any advice for how to complete a book?

I'm a big advocate of outlines. I know there are people out there who honestly can't write if they're trying to adhere to an outline but, for me, they're the most important part of the process. Before I write a word, I work through the story, trying to figure out what happens when, where to put my best twists, who the killer is, who's going to die, and what the primary theme of the story is. Often these outlines end up being twenty or thirty pages long—they're almost a first draft of the book themselves!

Once I have a full outline, I start on the "trash draft." A trash draft is, essentially, an incredibly rough first draft of a book. No one reads this but me, and it's a draft I use to work out all the kinks that you wouldn't necessarily see in an outline. I'll set a timer for half an hour and write as fast as I can. The timer is important because it reminds me not to try to edit or go back and make lines too perfect. When I'm drafting, I usually aim for around 2,000 words a day, which means I have a draft within around a month.

Having a full draft of something (even if it isn't that good!) is incredible motivation to keep working on it. And if you have a solid outline, then you know that your plot points are good, even if the actual writing is a little sloppy.

9. Once you have a finished manuscript, how do you edit it?

This is the most difficult part of writing, hands down. I could probably write an entire book about how to edit your work!

The first and most important piece of advice I have is to take some time away from your work. After rushing through a trash draft, it can be tempting to go back and start editing right away, but you're not doing yourself any favors by rushing it. Try to take at least a week away from it and come back fresh.

Next, you're going to want to look at the big things. To me, the biggest pieces of any story are structure, character, and theme. For structure, are your plot points happening in the right places? Does your story start right before the action? Is there a catalyst that propels your main character into the second act, or "upside-down world" where the story takes place? Does something big and devastating happen at the midpoint, and around 75 percent of the way through the plot? Do bigger, more devastating things begin happening around the second half of your book, propelling your character to the end of the story?

For character, is your main character changing from the first page to the last? Do they go after one thing (their want) only to realize that they need something else? Theme is part of this. Your main character should be telling themself a lie about how the world works based on some past event that's haunting them. Throughout the course of the story, they should learn that this lie is holding them back, that they can be happier if they let it go.

Work on all this before you start worrying about whether or not specific lines are pretty! You never know which lines might get cut while you're moving around the larger pieces of your story!